HARMONIC
FEEDBACK

HARMONIC FEEDBACK

TARA KELLY

HENRY HOLT AND COMPANY

NEW YORK

Henry Holt and Company, LLC
Publishers since 1866
175 Fifth Avenue
New York, New York 10010
www.HenryHoltKids.com

Henry Holt® is a registered trademark of Henry Holt and Company, LLC.
Copyright © 2010 by Tara Kelly
Distributed in Canada by H. B. Fenn and Company Ltd.

Library of Congress Cataloging-in-Publication Data
Kelly, Tara.
Harmonic feedback / Tara Kelly.—1st ed.
p.   cm.
Summary: When Drea and her mother move in with her grandmother in
Bellingham, Washington, the sixteen-year-old finds that she can have
real friends, in spite of her Asperger's, and that even when you love
someone it does not make life perfect.
ISBN 978-0-8050-9010-9
[1. Interpersonal relations—Fiction.   2. Emotional problems—Fiction.   3. Self-perception—
Fiction.   4. Asperger's syndrome—Fiction.   5. Drug abuse—Fiction.   6. Rock music—
Fiction.   7. Bellingham (Wash.)—Fiction.]   I. Title.
PZ7.K2984Har 2010
[Fic]—dc22
2009024150

First Edition—2010
Printed in the United States of America

1 3 5 7 9 10 8 6 4 2

HARMONIC
FEEDBACK

1

ONE IN THIRTY-EIGHT. Bet on a single number in roulette, and those are the odds of winning. Getting struck by lightning is a little more difficult—one in seven hundred thousand. Winning the lottery? Forget it.

But the odds of me ending up homeless were pretty good. Moving in with Grandma Horvath was Mom's worst idea yet.

"It's beautiful here, don't you think?" Mom asked, cutting the engine.

I shrugged and looked out the passenger window at Grandma's house, a turn-of-the-century shack the color of pea soup. My initial impression of Washington was simple—they had trees here. And as far as I could see, that was about it.

I pushed open the squeaky door of Mom's Toyota Corolla. It was late August, and we'd just driven the 896 miles from San Francisco to Bellingham with a broken air conditioner. Even my toes were sweaty.

"It's past six," Grandma Horvath called out to Mom as she scurried out the front door. "You said you'd be here before five." I hadn't seen her for five years, but she looked exactly the same—frizzy gray hair, sharp eyes, and a pointy mouth smeared with her favorite pink lipstick.

"I'm sorry. We got caught in rush-hour traffic." Mom gave her a quick embrace.

"And you couldn't use that mobile phone you waste your money on?" Grandma pulled back, taking in Mom's outfit. "You're too old to be wearing such revealing shirts."

Mom ducked away and opened the back of the trailer we'd towed. "My battery died back in Portland."

"Andrea, give me a kiss." Grandma's wedding ring scratched my arm as she pecked my cheek, and I cringed because she smelled like perfume in a public bathroom.

"My name is Drea."

"That's not what your birth certificate says." She reached for my blue lunch box. "What does someone your age need a lunch box for?"

I shoved it behind my back. "It's my purse. Don't touch it."

Grandma made a clucking sound with her tongue and joined Mom at the back of the trailer. "My neighbor recommended a good doctor for Andrea's behavior problems."

"What about *your* behavior problems, Grandma?"

"Drea, please." Mom rubbed her temples, which meant another migraine was coming on.

Grandma's lips formed a thin line. "You spoiled her, Juliana." She turned on her heel and walked away. Her shoulders were nearly up to her ears by the time she got to the porch.

I'd promised Mom I'd be good. *Ignore her,* she said. *It will make our stay a lot more peaceful, and we've got nowhere else to go right now.* Did we ever? We always found somewhere, though; Mom either moved in with a guy or managed to stay at a job longer than six months. Even living with her last boyfriend was a step up from Grandma Horvath. He stole my razors to shave his chest and obsessed over his twenty-nine-inch waist, but Mom dated all kinds of guys. The one thing they had in common was they went away—whether they left her or we left them.

"Did you take your meds?" I knew Mom's eyes were narrow behind her shades. She did this squinty thing when she asked a question I didn't like.

"Nope. I don't feel like being a zombie today."

"Yeah, well." Mom set my acoustic guitar case on the ground. "You'd feel a lot better if you took them every day like you're supposed to."

I opened my lunch box and grabbed one of three orange bottles. "This is speed in a bottle."

"It gets you to think before you speak. I call that a miracle in a bottle." She tied her wavy blond hair into a ponytail, but strands stuck to her neck.

"You can't fix everything with pills."

Mom held her hand up, fingers spread wide. Her stop sign. "I'm not getting into this right now, Drea."

"You never want to get into it."

Mom sighed and put her hand on my cheek. "I know you're mad, baby. But we're stuck until I find a job." She nodded toward Grandma's house. "And Grandma is helping us out a lot. Medi-Cal won't cover us up here. She's offered to pay for your doctor visits and meds for now. So, please, *please* don't antagonize her, okay?"

"She talks to you like you're five."

Mom rubbed her temples. "She's difficult—yes—but she means well."

"Living out of your old pickup truck was better than this."

Mom smirked and handed me a box of effect pedals for my guitar. "Oh, yeah? Do you miss Cheetos that much?"

My stomach turned at just the thought. Mom decided to go to some campground in California once where the only sign of life was a dirty gas station. I lived on cherry cola and ninety-nine-cent bags of Cheetos because I didn't trust anything there that didn't come in a sealed bag or bottle.

"I'm going to take these in," I said, right before colliding with a strange girl standing behind me.

She looked about my age but stood a couple inches taller. Judging from the band on her T-shirt, she had horrible taste in music. "Hi, you're Andrea, right?"

"It's Drea."

Mom heaved a sigh behind me. She thought I was being rude when I didn't offer a bubbly hello and plaster a big smile on my face. Strangers made me nervous; I always ended up saying too much or too little.

The girl grinned even wider, and her blue eyes sparkled despite the dark eye shadow around them. "I'm Naomi. I live in that light blue matchbox across the street." She nodded to an aging house with an overgrown yard. "My dad sent me over to ask if you needed any help."

"Definitely. Thanks for offering." Mom smiled and held out her hand to Naomi. "I'm Juli. It's nice to meet you."

Naomi tucked a lock of tangled purple hair behind her ear, revealing a skull stud. "You too." She glanced back at me, her eyes falling on my guitar case. "Dude, you play guitar?"

"Yes." I played a mean rhythm, but processing and manipulating sound through my computer was my passion.

4

Unfortunately, most people didn't understand the concept of sound design. Mom told me not to bring it up unless someone asked.

Naomi grabbed a box and followed me into the house. I caught a whiff of something that smelled like boiled cabbage and potpourri. "Don't ask me what that smell is because I have no clue," I said over my shoulder, heading downstairs to the basement.

Naomi giggled. "It's cool. You should see it when my dad tries to make egg salad. He burns the eggs every time, and our house smells like a sewer for a week."

I yanked the lightbulb cord so we didn't trip over anything. The basement reeked of mildew, but it was roomy and dark. Just the way I liked it. "My grandma thinks liver and mustard sandwiches with boiled milk make a tasty dinner."

Naomi wrinkled her nose at me. "Boiled milk, for real?"

I set my guitar case and box of effect pedals on the floor. "Yeah, it gets this layer on top that looks like crusty skin and—"

"Stop!" She winced. "Where do I put this?"

I motioned for her to put it next to the stuff I set down and tried to imagine how the basement would look once I made it mine. Lime-green walls, purple Christmas lights strung around like ivy, and my small collection of instruments circling the bed. Sure, Grandma would have a fit—but it would be after the fact. Sometimes it paid off to be a night owl.

Naomi chewed on her thumbnail. Bits of turquoise nail polish flaked off into her mouth. "My brother left me his old drum set when he took off last year. I've been dying for someone to jam with. We should start a band or something." She pulled a strip of polish from her tongue.

"Do they have edible nail polish now?" I asked. The thought

of playing with other people terrified me. It was hard enough collaborating with other people online where we just sent files back and forth.

Naomi peered down at her frayed shoes, cramming her hands in the pockets of her gray cords. "I kinda forgot I had it on, but it's no biggie. I've ingested worse."

"Like what? Paint thinner?"

She let out a laugh and looked up at me. "You don't screw around, do you? Most girls are all fake and shady."

"People are fake in general." I headed back up the stairs and Naomi followed.

"I guess you'd know better than me. I've never lived anywhere but Bellingham. Did you grow up in San Francisco?"

I held open the front door and waved her outside. "No, we just lived there for the last two years—which is a record. We've covered every major city in California, plus Vegas, Denver, Salt Lake City, and—"

"Bellingham must be a big change." She nibbled on her ring fingernail this time.

"You have no idea."

In my sixteen years on earth, we'd never lived more than a thirty-minute drive from a big city. Urban chaos was intense stimulation for a mind that didn't have an off switch—jarring sirens, drunk people fighting with their lovers on cell phones, six-inch robo-heels chasing the bus, and the scent of piss on newspaper. Watching humans on any downtown street corner was no different than watching a group of sea lions fight over that perfect spot at SeaWorld.

Naomi stuck around and helped us with the rest of the furniture and boxes. Luckily, we had learned early on that the less

6

we kept, the easier the moves got. Mom sold her bed back in San Francisco because she knew Grandma would insist she use the bed in the guest room.

After we shoved my mattress down the stairs, Naomi leaned against a wooden beam and watched as I opened my guitar cases and put the guitars on their rightful stands.

"So you never answered my question about starting a band. . . ."

"Music is something I've always done alone. And we don't even know each other."

"What—you don't think I can play anything?"

I turned to face her. "If I thought that, I'd say that."

"You just look at me like I'm stupid or something. But it's fine. Whatever." She grinned, making it impossible to tell if she was serious or not.

What was with people and their obsession with *looks*? Sometimes I was in a bad mood. It wasn't personal.

I unpacked my didgeridoo and laid it across the mattress.

She came up behind me. "What the hell is that? It looks like a funky telescope."

"A didgeridoo. My mom brought it back for me when she went to Australia with her last boyfriend."

Naomi picked it up and stroked the tribal etchings. "How do I play it?"

"Just blow into it, but keep your lips relaxed."

She pulled it to her mouth and snickered. "This would make a great bong."

"Okay." Being a loner most of my life, I wasn't too up on the party scene. Sure, there were drugs on every campus and the girls who got stoned and popped little pills in the bathroom, but I never talked to them. The last real friend I had was a boy named

Adam in the fourth grade. We'd reenact our favorite movie, *The Terminator*, on the monkey bars every morning at recess. He wanted to be Sarah Connor, and I preferred being the Terminator, so it worked out.

"I bet you got the *good* shit in California." She blew into the mouthpiece, but the only sound was her breath.

"Pretend you're doing a raspberry."

Her second attempt was even worse. "Oh, man, I think more spit than air came out that time." She shoved the didgeridoo at me. "Show me how it's done."

"I think I'll wait till it dries first." I put it back on the mattress, taking note to clean it later. I was the messiest person on earth, but saliva, snot, and other bodily fluids made me want to bathe in sanitizer.

"Drea!" Mom called from upstairs. "Dinner's ready."

Naomi looked in the direction of Mom's voice and smiled. "Your mom is really pretty. You look a lot like her."

This was news to me. We were both about five-two, but that was where our physical likeness ended. My curly hair was the color of a penny—too orange in my opinion, and my freckles were a little too dark on my pale skin. Nothing like Mom's golden complexion. With oversized green eyes, I got called names like frog girl and leprechaun. Nobody ever called Mom that.

"Well"—I looked away—"I guess I have to eat dinner now." Grandma embarrassed me enough without an audience. I didn't want the first potential friend I'd made in years to hear all about my "behavior problems" over whatever monstrosity Grandma had cooked up. And even if Grandma didn't bring it up, Mom would. She loved to tell everyone about my *issues*.

Naomi raised her eyebrows at me, smirking. "It's cool. You

don't have to invite me. Your grandma kinda scares me any-way." She headed up the stairs. "You should come by my house one of these days. I can show you my drum kit."

"Where can I get green paint?"

Naomi stopped on the second to top step and spun around. "What?"

"I want to paint the basement this weekend. Is there any place in town that—"

"Drea," she interrupted, "we might be close, but we aren't in the North Pole. There *are* stores here, like Home Depot. Come by tomorrow and I'll take you." She waved and left.

I stared at the empty doorway, wondering why this near stranger was being so helpful. Did she really want me to drop by tomorrow? Or was it like saying *call me* without meaning it? A therapist told me that people said these things to be polite but their invitation wasn't always sincere, which made no sense. Why invite someone if you didn't want that person to show up?

Like the first day of seventh grade. I'd never forget that. These two girls asked me to eat lunch with them, and I felt this surge of excitement run through my body. I couldn't stop laughing or smiling, even after they kept asking what was funny. But I'd calmed down after a few minutes, and we had what I thought was a good conversation. I started telling them all about my favorite car, the McLaren F1—how it was the fastest in the world. And they seemed interested enough.

I sat with them every day that week, but they talked to me less and less. Finally, one girl rolled her eyes. "God, Drea, can't you take a hint?" she asked.

"What do you mean?"

She exchanged this glance with her friend, and they giggled. "Why do you keep sitting here?"

I remember my stomach tightening up in these knots. "You invited me. . . ."

"Yeah, *once*. We didn't know you'd be such a clingy freak."

My face felt hot, and my breath quickened. A response didn't come to me, not words anyway. I just wanted to stop them—their shrill laughs and wide, amused eyes. I grabbed a handful of red Jell-O off my plate and hurled it at their laughing faces. This got me cleanup duty and a note sent home for Mom to sign.

Mom didn't yell, though—her eyes looked sad. She hugged me and said it was never good to seem too anxious for friends. Neediness scared people. That an invitation wasn't always an offer for friendship, and I'd *overstayed my welcome*.

I never wanted to feel that level of embarrassment again.

Grandma eyeballed the forkful of boiled cabbage and onions I pushed around on my plate. The smell alone was setting off my gag reflex.

"You need to put on some weight," Grandma said.

As if I could help the fact that I was lucky to break a hundred pounds in winter clothing. I never got why so many people prayed for a fast metabolism. It was annoying when everyone accused me of being anorexic.

"Well, boiled vegetables aren't going to help. Got any ice cream that isn't sugar free and coffee flavored?" When Grandma was diagnosed with diabetes, her taste in food got exponentially worse.

She nodded at Mom. "Juliana was picky too. I'd find pork chops and broccoli stuffed in the crevices under the table. Sometimes she'd try to leave the kitchen with lumpy socks."

Mom scrunched up her nose. "I had to vomit on my plate before she believed the pork chops actually made me sick."

Grandma shook her head and swallowed a bite of mushy carrots. "My father would've beat me black and blue if I did that. Nobody could afford to be picky during the Depression." The only response heard was the scraping of our forks against the plates. Neither of us wanted to get Grandma started on her "When I was a little girl . . ." tangent.

Grandma twirled noodles around her fork, her eyes growing softer. "George loved pork chops." An image of Grandpa's white hair and big smile flickered through my mind. He suffered brain damage from a massive heart attack the year before I was born. Even so, he always beat me at Old Maid.

Mom patted her hand. "I know."

Grandma took care of him for twelve years—changing diapers, spoon feeding, bathing, and everything else in between. He died of pneumonia five years ago, and she still hadn't forgiven herself.

"Was that Naomi Quinn I saw here earlier?" Grandma asked, picking up a crumb that had fallen off her plate. I didn't even know how she could find it on a table painted with gold glitter. Between the Tiffany lamps, TV with bunny ears, and earthy color scheme, this house was stuck in the dinosaur age.

"Yeah, she helped us move all our stuff. Sweet girl," Mom said, poking at the cabbage with her fork.

My stomach growled for In-N-Out Burger. Their fries had the right amount of crispness on the outside.

Grandma shook her head, frowning. "Her father is never home. And every time I look out my window, she's out there smoking. With *boys*." Her hazel eyes widened at Mom.

Mom chuckled into her cup of water. "Oh, no. Boys."

Grandma got up and rinsed her plate in the sink. "You should stay clear of her, Andrea. She's trouble."

Mom rolled her eyes. "Drea is about as interested in boys as you are. I don't see her bringing one home anytime soon." She winked at me. "But it would be nice." If I'd learned anything from her, it was that boys were to be avoided. I certainly didn't want the roof over my head to be dependent on one.

"Good, she should be spending time on her schoolwork." Grandma wrung out a sponge. "Not running around with boys like you did."

"That hasn't changed," I said.

Mom nudged my shoulder before joining Grandma at the sink. "I'll take care of the dishes. Go relax."

"Just give them to me." Grandma yanked the plate from Mom's grasp and returned to scrubbing a saucepan.

I got up to put my plate in the sink, but Grandma snatched it before I could. "It's terrible the way you both waste food. Just terrible."

"Then make better food," I said.

She dropped the sponge and gaped at me openmouthed. I didn't see what the big deal was; she said blunt crap all the time.

"Drea!" Mom's dark eyes tore into mine before she turned to Grandma. "It's been a really long day, and she didn't take her medication."

"I'm so sick of you saying that to everyone. Are little blue pills the only way I can be taken seriously?"

"Calm down, baby. I'm just saying—" Mom reached for me, but I pulled away.

"I'm not a migraine you can cure with one of your pain pills." I left the kitchen before she could say anything else.

Between Mom's kaleidoscope of boyfriends and the dozens

of head doctors she forced me to see, I could write a book about psychological disorders. The doctors always threw around the term *social awareness*, basically saying I needed more of it. They pinned me with ADHD, a.k.a. Attention Deficit/ Hyperactivity Disorder, when I was in kindergarten, mostly because I preferred coloring and banging on a xylophone to story time and the stupid games the teacher made me play. As if anyone liked being forced to do something. How was that abnormal?

One time I told the doctors about Mom stomping around and cussing whenever she had a big bill to pay and asked them if she had ADHD too. Mom didn't like that much. She made me promise not to say anything like that again. I asked her why for a month straight, but she never gave me a real answer.

It wasn't until junior high, the third day of seventh grade to be exact, that one doctor suspected Asperger's syndrome. Mom wasn't convinced, so she got a second opinion—that doctor didn't agree. He said I had bipolar disorder. Mom didn't agree with that either. She made me take ridiculous tests and got seven more opinions, the last one from a doctor in San Francisco a teacher recommended. In the fall of my freshman year, that doctor also labeled me with Asperger's syndrome, but he said I displayed only mild symptoms and I'd "learned to cope well," whatever that meant.

Asperger's is an autism spectrum disorder, which makes most people think of the guy in that *Rain Man* movie. But I'm nothing like him. I don't go ballistic in airports, and I know better than to tell anyone I'm an excellent driver. After all, I've failed six driving tests.

All I know is I make sense to me—it's other people who seem complicated.

2

I WOKE UP the next morning to the sound of raised voices upstairs. It was like Mom and Grandma never left the kitchen. The sun streamed through the narrow window above my bed, telling me it was still rising and therefore too early. My body felt heavy and achy—the way it always did when I skipped a day of meds. It would be nice to go a day without needing to give in. But the withdrawal effects were unbearable, especially the little electrical zaps in my head.

I stretched and climbed the stairs, tuning in to their conversation.

"Give them to me!" Grandma hollered.

"Why are you putting them in a margarine bottle?"

"So they're all in one place and they can't get any air."

"Oh. Okay," Mom said. There was a rustle of bags.

"Not in the garbage!"

"Why are you *saving* them, Mom? It's not healthy."

"I don't want them to escape," Grandma said as I rounded the corner.

Mom stood in the kitchen with a grin and a yellow bottle in

her hand. "They're not going to escape if you flush them down the toilet. They can't."

"What's going on?" I asked, wiping the crusties from my eyes.

Mom shook her head and tossed the bottle in the garbage. "Grandma kills ants in very creative ways."

"All this yelling for ants?" I rolled my eyes. "And *I'm* the one who needs medication."

I tried to spend the day unpacking and getting started on the wah pedal I was building for my guitar. If it was good enough, I could start selling them on eBay and hopefully avoid working in retail. I got fired from the one and only job I'd ever had—one of those budget movie theaters with stale hot dogs, relish that smells like formaldehyde, and flat soda. This guy insisted I put more butter on his popcorn after ten squirts in the middle and eight on top. He threw a fit when I asked him if he'd like me to dump the entire metal container on it.

I did okay buying cheap clothes at thrift stores, dolling them up, and selling them on eBay. It was amazing what people would pay for a *unique* skirt. But it wouldn't be enough to get us out of Grandma's, and I didn't want Mom to depend on yet another guy. Some of her boyfriends were nice—one even bought me a guitar, but others thought money gave them the right to control our lives. One jerk offered to send me across the country to a "special school."

Unfortunately, Grandma made concentrating on anything difficult. Her heels clanged down the stairs just as I was in the delicate process of soldering.

"What on earth are you doing? It looks like you're running a repair shop down here," she said.

"Not exactly." I tightened my grip on the iron.

Grandma cocked her head, her thin lips stretching to form the words of whatever she was thinking. Her eyes traveled from the iron in my hand to the shells of old pedals on my desk and back to my face. "George used to fix TVs down here. I never thought I'd miss the smell." Her face softened as she scanned the walls. "Well—don't electrocute yourself."

She straightened her back and headed up the stairs, nearly running into Naomi at the top. Naomi gave her an apology, but Grandma shook her head and kept walking.

Naomi jogged down the stairs, her purple pigtails bouncing. She wore a fitted tee that read TRIX ARE FOR KIDS. "Hey, your mom let me in. I thought you were going to come over."

"I wasn't sure if you actually wanted me to."

She walked in front of me, her brow crinkling. "I invited you, didn't I?"

"Sometimes people say things they don't mean. And I don't really know you, so—"

"Well, I meant it." She reached for the board on my desk. "What's that?"

I blocked her hand. "It's the PCB for the wah pedal I'm working on. Don't touch it."

"Is that like a circuit board?"

"Obviously."

"You make your own effect pedals too?" She raised her eyebrows. "God, you're like the coolest girl I've ever met."

I shrugged. "My mom says I should've been born with a penis."

"No kidding. I'd totally jump your bones!" She laughed.

"Um, okay." I turned off the iron and set it in the holder, my cheeks feeling hot.

"So I got us a ride from this guy, Scott. I met him at the mall a few weeks ago, and he's hot, like, whoa. *And* he's bringing a friend."

My back stiffened. The last thing I wanted to do was get a ride from a couple of strange guys. "I thought it was just going to be me and you."

Her grin narrowed a bit. "Well, my dad is out of town for the weekend, and he took the car." She grabbed my arm. "Come on. Scott is leaving in a half hour, and I wanna show you my kit."

I yanked my arm out of her clutches. "I don't know—"

"Please?" She stuck her lower lip out and widened her eyes.

This was my chance to have a friend. An actual, real-life friend. A chance to be one of the girls I used to watch at school. Sometimes it looked like they were having fun, but I never really got why. I still wanted to be part of it though. To feel normal—for even a day.

"Let me grab my box," I said, but a sick feeling had settled in my stomach.

Grandma would have a heart attack if she saw the inside of Naomi's house. If they had carpeting or a kitchen counter, I couldn't find them. Papers, clothing covered in animal hair, and dirty dishes were strewn throughout the living room and kitchen. As we headed upstairs, I nearly tripped over a tuxedo cat with green eyes and a hoarse meow.

"Hi, Lizzie Wizzie!" Naomi picked up the cat like a baby and rubbed its head. She led me down a stuffy hallway to another set of stairs. "It's in the attic."

The attic was like a closet with a pointed ceiling. A black drum set made the centerpiece, and the walls were lined with various band posters. One poster was The Cure, a band I really liked, but most featured new and mainstream rock bands—the kind with autotuned vocals and overly compressed, superloud mixes. The high frequencies and distortion rattled me from the inside.

"You really need better taste in music, Naomi." I sighed. Every guy on her wall had a forced pose, shaggy hair, and a pout. Why was the world so obsessed with sameness?

"I know, right? We get shit for radio stations up here. Hopefully, you can introduce me to some cool stuff."

"I've got about eighty gigs of music in almost every genre. I'll make you some CDs."

Her mouth dropped open. "Whoa, you rock. Thanks!"

Naomi's excitement was strange. Nobody liked hearing that their music taste sucked, and just about everyone thought I was a dork—hence nobody ever got to know me at previous schools.

Naomi sat behind the drums, and Lizzie the cat made a beeline for me. She plopped on my feet and looked up, rolling on her back. I expected her to claw me or do something sinister.

"Wow, she likes you. She never pays attention to anyone but me," Naomi said. "You can pick her up, you know. She doesn't bite."

I peered down at the purring creature nudging its body into the toes of my black boots. "Um, I've never really held a cat."

"Now, that's just weird." Naomi shook her head and tested a couple of the drums with her sticks. "Ready?"

When I nodded, she started pounding out a solo. Her rhythm was a little shaky, and she went a bit overboard a couple times, but I was impressed. She had a really creative approach to the drums, often going into little tangents here and there; it made my head spin—but in a good way. Lizzie appeared to be completely detached from the whole thing. I'd think most cats would run out of the room in terror, but she stared up at me like she was floating on a cloud. I bent down to pick her up, praying I didn't hurt her in some way. She wiggled in my arms for a second before nuzzling her head under my chin, her entire body vibrating.

Naomi tossed her drumsticks on the floor and wiped her brow. "What do you think?"

"It was a little rough, but you're really good." Lizzie hopped out of my arms.

"I actually trust that coming from you. I know you won't bullshit me."

She gave Lizzie some food and water before we went out on the porch to wait for Scott. The temperature was on the warm side, but the cool breeze on my cheeks made it perfect.

Naomi plopped next to me and held out a pack of cigarettes. "Want one?" She pressed the end of her cigarette into the flame of one of those flippy-top lighters.

I shook my head. "Does your dad know you smoke?"

She shrugged, making an O shape with her lips. Ringlike bands of smoke floated around her face. "One more day until school starts—ugh. You're going to Samish, right?"

"I think that's the name Mom said." Now I had to ask her something. Small talk was like a game of Ping-Pong. People got offended if I didn't keep hitting the ball back. "What year are you?"

"Junior." She held the cigarette over her shoulder and tapped the edge. "You?"

"The same."

A breeze blew her pigtail away from her neck, revealing a couple of fading hickeys. She probably wanted me to talk about guys with her and get all giggly and excited, like the girls at school and my mom. But I'd never even kissed a boy, much less met a nice one—at least one who was nice to me. Not in person, anyway. She'd probably think that was weird too.

I stretched my lips into a smile and pointed at her neck. "Did Scott give you those?"

"Yeah. He's kind of into the rough stuff."

"Rough stuff?"

"You know—he likes to bite and stuff. But I'm a total masochist, so it's all good."

"Masochist" was the title of one of my favorite songs. I looked up the meaning once, and it baffled me. Why would someone enjoy pain? "Oh . . . I'm not."

A toothy grin erased her dim expression. "I bet you have to fight guys off with a stick. You're so pretty. Like a little pixie or something."

I shrugged, running my fingers across the rough cement beneath us. "I thought I looked like a skinny frog."

Naomi punched my shoulder. "Whatever. I could only dream of having an ass as small as yours."

"You don't have a big ass," I said. "I'd tell you if you did."

She laughed. "I know you would."

A black mustang roared up the street, and the sinking feeling in my chest told me it was Scott. Sure enough, the car skidded in front of her house, tires squealing and all. I didn't like show-offs.

Naomi squeezed my arm. "They're here!"

The driver climbed out first, a cigarette dangling from his

lips. He had shaggy blond hair and wore jeans a size too large. His friend tumbled out after him, laughing about something. He was dressed just like the driver, but was a bit shorter and had darker hair.

"What's up?" The driver nodded at us. "Who's she?" His light blue eyes fell from my face to my chest.

Naomi stood up to greet him, but I hovered behind her. "That's Drea. I told you already." She slapped his chest. "Drea, this is Scott."

"Hey." Scott nodded at me, his eyes still combing my body.

"Hi." I looked at the ground, the sick feeling in my stomach almost unbearable.

"And I'm Roger." His friend walked up to me and held out his hand. "Do you know the secret handshake?"

I backed away, keeping my eyes on the ground. "No."

"That's too bad. You can't come with us until you know the secret shake." Roger laughed.

"Don't be a putz, Roger," Scott said.

After Roger got into the car, Naomi mouthed "sorry" to me. I wanted to run back into the safety of my house.

Scott's car reeked of stale cigarettes and something like burnt coffee. The sweltering leather seat gripped the backs of my thighs. Roger spread his legs apart until his knee was touching mine, making my muscles tense. I moved away, wishing I'd worn pants instead of the white skirt I'd made with safety pins and lace.

Scott wrapped his arm behind Naomi's chair and jutted his chin at me. "So, you need to get paint or something?"

I turned away from his intense gaze. "Yeah. Home Depot is fine."

" 'Kay, I gotta make a stop first."

Scott turned up a rap song, drowning out whatever Naomi said to him. I could see her frown in the passenger-side mirror. Scott shrugged in response and stomped on the accelerator. He seemed to enjoy gunning it every time we hit a green light or rounded a corner. My head was spinning by the time we merged onto the I-5 freeway.

Roger put one end of a green metal pipe between his lips and ran a lighter over the other end. His face turned red as he inhaled the smoke and held it in his lungs. I'd never watched a person get stoned before, unless movies counted.

He caught my eye and leaned into me. "You want some?" His hot breath on my ear made my palms sweat.

I shook my head and scooted closer to the window just as Scott exited the freeway.

"Put that shit away!" Scott glared at him in the rearview mirror. "There's cops all over here."

"You're paranoid!" Roger yelled over the repetitive beat. Their shouting combined with the blaring rapper's voice made me cover my ears.

Scott shot him the middle finger and sped up. His excessive speed was going to attract the police more than anything.

"I'll be right back," Scott said when we'd finally pulled up to a destination. We were in a dolled-up neighborhood with newer houses. The house Scott went into had a fancy glass design on the door and a yard full of rosebushes.

"Is this where he lives?" I asked.

Roger laughed. "Yeah, right." He squinted at me with bloodshot eyes and a smirk. "You got a boyfriend?"

Before I could open my mouth, Naomi turned around and answered for me. "Yeah, and he's the jealous type too."

"Then why'd you tell Scott to bring a friend?"

Naomi bit her lip, and I tried to unglue my thighs from the seat. "I didn't want her to feel like a third wheel." She winked at me.

"He go to Samish?" he asked.

I nodded, not knowing what else to do.

His smile grew, showing off a crooked front tooth. "Cool, guess I get to meet him, then."

Naomi squinted at him. "I didn't know you went to Samish. I've never seen you before."

"I'm transferring from Blaine."

She wrinkled her nose. "Why?"

"My dad got booked on possession again, so I had to move in with my aunt."

"Bum deal." She shifted forward when Scott opened the driver's door and got back in. With red cheeks and a frown, he jammed the keys into the ignition and jerked the car away from the curb. Naomi kept stealing glances at him, chewing on her fingernails. Roger yanked his baseball cap over his eyes and slouched even farther into the seat. I wondered how I was going to explain my invisible boyfriend to him.

I didn't realize how tense my chest was until we pulled into the Home Depot parking lot. The breath I was holding came out in almost a cough. Naomi had tried to comfort Scott several times, but he ignored her or shrugged her off. Either way—I was contemplating walking home. The only problem was figuring out which direction to head.

I stumbled out of the back after Naomi pushed her seat forward and ran into the store. A hand grabbed my shoulder as I searched the massive aisles for the paint section. "Hey, wait up," Naomi said. "Roger is kinda gross, huh?"

I looked behind her for the guys, but they weren't anywhere in sight. "They both are."

"You don't think Scott is cute at all?"

"Not particularly," I said, keeping my eyes glued to the signs. "Guys like him are tornadoes—they shred everything in their path and then they disappear." At least that was what happened to my mom every time she dated bad-boy types.

"Day-am, you got burned pretty bad, huh?" She pinched my arm. "Man, I can't wait to hear all your crazy-boy stories."

I walked faster and kept quiet. She sounded so excited. It would probably disappoint her that I had no crazy-boy stories of my own. And I liked that she found me interesting. It made the world seem brighter somehow, a little less alien. Besides, Mom said that giving people too much information, like the fact that I didn't have any friends, would freak them out—that a little mystery would make me seem cooler, less clingy.

Mom was always giving me social advice. She used to write skits for my Barbies, and we'd spend hours pretending that plastic hunks with rubber legs were actual people. But I preferred using the dolls for other purposes, like putting them in the freezer to make *Barbie ice cubes*. It seemed like a fun idea at the time.

"There's the paint," I said, spotting the sign. "Are your friends waiting in the car?"

"I don't know. Let me go check—I'll be back."

I nodded and scanned the paint cards for the perfect lime green. It didn't take long to narrow it down to three slightly different shades. Finding the right color was a lot like getting the perfect amount of salt in a recipe. Even a little too much could overpower the meal, and the wrong shade would give me a headache or make the room drab.

Roger's wheezy laugh distracted me from my comparison. "Where'd they go?" he asked.

"They said they were getting paint," Scott said.

As their footsteps got closer, I darted into the next aisle and huddled behind a large open box.

"Don't see them," Roger said.

"You know chicks and hardware don't mix. They probably got lost." Scott chuckled. "What do you think of Drea?"

"She's all right. Kinda stuck up."

"She's pretty cute, though—nice tight body," Scott said.

"I like them thicker, like Naomi. She's hot, man."

"Yeah, but she's clingy as fuck. Calls five times a day."

Roger snorted. "Every chick calls you five times a day."

"I bet Drea still has her v-card."

I hugged my body at Scott's words, my breath quickening.

"Oh, dude, don't go there," Roger said.

Scott's laughter was like thorns on my skin.

"There you guys are," Naomi said. "Where'd Drea go?"

"Thought she was with you."

The back of my neck felt damp, and my heart pounded. I stood on shaky legs and walked into the next aisle. Naomi looked at me with wide eyes. "I need to get home," I told her.

"Jake's having a party tonight. We were gonna head over there after this," Scott said to Naomi.

"Aren't you getting paint?" she asked me.

I shook my head, eyeing the scuff-marked floor.

"Can you drop her home?" she asked Scott.

"Don't have time. Come on, it'll be fun."

"I'll just walk," I said.

"Aw, don't be like that." Roger touched my arm, but I jerked away from him.

"Don't touch me." My breakfast was creeping into my throat.

"Freak," Roger said under his breath.

The entire store seemed to be spinning around me, and Scott's laughter kept replaying in my head. I did the only thing I could do and ran for the exit. I might get lost going home, but anything seemed better than getting back in the car with those jerks.

"Hey, chica, wait up!" I tensed as Naomi caught up with me outside. "I'm coming with."

"Why?" I stopped and studied her face.

"Hos before bros." She wrinkled her nose. "Okay, that sounded cooler in my head. Anyway, I'd rather hang out with you."

Her words surprised me. I'd seen girls in the locker room swear by their friendship one day and claw each other's eyes out the next when it came to boys. "Well, you're probably better off." I told her the things I heard the boys say, but she shrugged.

"I know Scott's a player. Guess I was hoping to tame him. Lame, huh?"

"Aren't you mad?" We crossed the parking lot. The air smelled like rain and freshly mowed grass.

She nibbled on her thumbnail. "I'll get over it. It's not like I was planning on marrying the guy."

"Does he go to our school?"

"No, he's like nineteen."

I sighed in relief. At least I didn't have to deal with both of the guys on Monday. "How far away are we from home?"

"Only about a mile. I know a scenic shortcut too."

We crossed the street and headed into a greenbelt where a

narrow trail snaked through wildflowers. She lit a cigarette and twirled in circles, humming to herself.

"Do you sing?" I asked.

"Sure, in the shower." Naomi kneeled down and picked a yellow wildflower out of the grass. "Yellow is a good color on you." She stuck the stem in my hair like a barrette. It made my scalp itchy. "So, where's your dad?"

I shrugged. "Never knew the guy. Mom doesn't really talk about him. What about your mom—where's she?"

"Mommy dearest is in the OC with a new hubby and their two perfect kids." Naomi batted her eyelashes at me.

"Do you see her much?"

"Me and my brother, Greg, used to love going down there when we were little, but you can only spend so much time at Disneyland." She sighed. "It was easier for her to give us money and dump us somewhere for the day."

I picked up a stick and poked at the rocks. "Why?"

"We weren't her dream kids, I guess." Naomi pointed to the sky. "I think I felt rain."

A drop fell into my eye as I gazed at the ashen clouds above us. The trees whispered and danced with the salty breeze. As we continued to walk, the wind ceased and an eerie silence emerged.

"Why weren't you her dream kids?" I asked.

She stopped, putting her finger to her lips. "You feel that?"

I dropped the stick and hugged my lunch box to my chest. "I feel cold. Are you going to answer my question?"

"I don't want to talk about my family. It's a downer." She closed her eyes, holding her arms outward like she was waiting to catch something. "These clouds are going to open up any minute."

"That's not good." I shook my head and kept walking. A low rumble could be heard in the distance.

"Shhh. Just wait for it," she said behind me.

I turned around and studied her wide grin. Her eyelashes twitched against her cheeks as she took a deep breath. If it wasn't for the purple hair, she could be a nymph in a painting.

"There it is," she said just as a fat raindrop smacked my forehead. Within seconds, the rain hammered us like a waterfall.

"We should get home." I covered my head with my box, but she didn't budge.

"Haven't you ever danced in the rain? It's such a trip."

"No. It's cold and wet. What's the point?" Droplets leaked from my hair and slid down my back.

Naomi swayed back and forth with the trees around her. Lightning stretched across the sky, and her mouth dropped open. "Oh, my God, we almost never get storms like this here." She grabbed my hand and twirled me around. "We must rejoice!"

I pulled away, covering my head again. She continued to do her weird little rain dance, a smile igniting her doll-like features. More thunder echoed around us, making me suck in my breath and press my hands against my ears. She let out a howl and tore off her soaked top. My teeth chattered in my head with more than a chill now. Naomi had a lack of control that scared the hell out of me.

"This feels so good." Mascara ran into the corners of her mouth. "You're missing out, girl."

As if dancing topless in a thunderstorm would have a profound effect on my life. Still, I couldn't take my eyes off the graceful movement that came so naturally to her. The last time

I tried to dance, I fell on my wrist and sprained it. "I *really* think we should go!"

She wrapped her arm around my shoulder and took my free hand in hers. "I always wanted to learn swing dancing."

I nearly slipped in the mud, but she steadied me. "So, let's learn it indoors."

She rolled her eyes. "Sounds boring."

"We could get hit by lightning or a tree falling," I said, squeezing the handle of my lunch box.

"Relax. We have a better shot at winning the lottery." She grinned again, pulling me toward her.

"No, the chances of winning the lottery are one in millions. Lightning is only one in seven hundred thousand."

She crinkled her brow. "Good to know."

I couldn't help but notice her boobs. They were crammed inside a lacy white bra and nearly twice the size of mine.

"You checkin' me out?" she asked.

"Well, they're kinda hard to miss." Why couldn't I keep my mouth shut? If she didn't think I was a freak before, she certainly did now. But my thoughts always scrambled together in situations I didn't like.

"Have you ever kissed someone in the rain?"

What was the right answer? Eye contact made it too hard to think. I directed my gaze to the tops of the evergreens. Any one of them could come crashing down on us. "I-I don't know."

Her hand tightened around my arm, and it felt like she leaned closer. I tried to pull away, but her lips were on mine before I could even blink. My heart jumped in my chest, and my lips felt paralyzed. Her mouth was wet, soft, and a little sweet—like she'd been sucking on a Jolly Rancher. The warmth was nice, but I didn't see stars or get that tingly feeling people associate with their first kiss. Then again, I'd never expected it to involve a topless girl in the rain.

She pulled away, studying me. "I've never kissed a girl before. That was interesting."

I looked at the ground again. "Me neither."

She shoved my shoulder. "Yeah, I could tell when you turned into a mummy."

I moved away from her, noticing the rain had slowed. Bits of sun burned into my skin and lit up the droplets on Naomi's face.

"I didn't freak you out, did I?" she asked.

I shook my head, still unable to form words. I didn't think I felt *that* kind of attraction toward Naomi, but I'd never even felt what could be considered a crush. People were like wallpaper unless I knew them. Physical appearance was just that— an appearance. Some guitars were beautiful works of art, but I didn't want to play one unless I connected with it. The playability and sound quality mattered a lot more than the color. Although I usually only fell in love with the guitars that had the whole package. And those were few and far between.

"We should write a song," I said finally.

Her eyes widened. "I thought you'd never ask." She grabbed my hand and tugged me along.

3

THE FIRST DAY at a new school was always annoying, especially when people giggled at my sense of fashion. Clothing stores catered to the tall and twiggy, *not* the short and scrawny. I bought most of my clothes at thrift shops and sewed them to fit—usually Victorian-style skirts that I wore in layers. Today's concoction was a cream-colored slip peeking out from underneath a black velvet skirt and a matching tank top.

The lyrics Naomi wrote over the weekend spun in my head while I waited for my schedule in Samish High's administration office. Her words were catchy and rhythmic; something I always tried to accomplish but never could.

"Sweet little Jane was caught in a rut. She went too far and never paid up." I was whispering her lyrics when I noticed a guy with black hair standing near the entrance. He watched me with a smirk, drumming his hands against his jeans.

Two brunette girls and a blond guy stood in the corner, talking about a party they went to over the summer. The guy focused on how wasted he was, while one of the girls went on about her boyfriend, and the other kept talking about *that slut, Jenna.* Yet none of them missed a beat or got confused.

I'd always watched people like this, trying to figure out what they were doing right, and what I did that was so wrong. I kept thinking the more I picked up, the more I could act. Pretend. But it never seemed to be enough.

I looked at the dark-haired boy near the entrance again and he grinned. Then he walked over and plopped in the chair next to me. "You new here too?"

I nodded, pretending to be fascinated with the receptionist and the slight eye roll she gave almost every caller. Years of observing also made it easier to read people. And this guy was what I called a *common denominator*: a boring haircut (not too long or too short) and safe clothes (crispy blue jeans and a white T-shirt with a brand name across the chest). He was cute enough to be accepted, but not ripped or edgy enough to be considered salivary by the common-denominator girls he probably worshipped.

The last conversation I had with a common-denominator guy ended up on the Internet. His name was Kyle White, and he had this obnoxious, scratchy laugh. One day Kyle confessed his undying love for me behind the school library. I actually believed him until his friends came around the corner, laughing. They'd videotaped the entire thing. And Kyle wasted no time posting the video online.

"So, where'd you move from?" the guy next to me asked.

"San Francisco."

"Cool. I'm from Chicago. And my name is Justin—if you care."

I stole a glance at him. His eyes were the same color as

Mr. Fuzzy, this gray velvet blanket I used to take everywhere. "Do you like being a walking advertisement for Nike?"

Justin glanced down at his shirt and shrugged. "Haven't had a chance to unpack yet."

"Oh."

He shifted in his seat, crossing his arms over his chest. "I can dress like a Goth tomorrow, if that'll work better."

"That didn't make any sense."

"No?" He raised his eyebrows. "Well, neither did your comment."

I looked toward the receptionist's desk again, where a guy in a baseball cap was hunched over talking to her. I didn't think much of it until he turned around and I recognized his beady brown eyes. Roger, the creep from Saturday. I put my face in my hands, hoping he wouldn't recognize me.

"Hey, it's Drea, right?" The sound of Roger's raspy voice made me cringe. He'd spotted me in less than five lousy seconds.

I sat up and pulled my blue lunch box closer to my chest. "Yeah."

Roger sat in the chair on the other side of me, stretching his legs out. "Sorry about being a tool to you on Saturday." He leaned into me and lowered his voice. "That shit I smoked was really strong."

"Oh," I said, hoping for the vice principal to call my name. They sure took their sweet time here.

Roger nodded at Justin, who had busied himself with writing something in a notebook. "You must be the boyfriend."

Justin glanced up at him and raised his eyebrows at me. I rested my forehead against my lunch box, wishing I could snap my fingers and disappear.

"Roger Miller?" Saved by the balding guy with the round nose and glasses—our vice principal, I assumed.

Roger pursed his lips and leaned into my ear. "See you around."

My chest relaxed as I watched Roger follow the vice principal into the office and shut the door behind him. I still couldn't bring myself to look at Justin, but I could sense his eyes on me—waiting.

"Bad date?" he asked finally.

"My friend Naomi introduced me to him this weekend, and he was kind of a jerk. She told him I had a jealous boyfriend at school."

There was the sound of breath escaping from his mouth, a barely audible chuckle. "A school you never set foot in until today? That's impressive."

"Yeah, well, it wasn't my idea."

"Do you actually have a boyfriend?" He looked down at his hands. "Like back in Frisco or whatever."

"No. Do you?" I asked immediately. "I mean . . ." That was when my laughter escaped—these uncontrollable giggles with snorts included.

"Would it really be that funny if I had a boyfriend?"

"No." It wasn't even that gay people were new or bizarre to me. Some of my mom's friends were gay, but somehow I didn't think this guy was. At least he was nothing like her friends.

"Well," he sighed before continuing, "my boyfriend dumped me for my girlfriend. How messed up is that?"

"Why were you dating two people at the same time? It seems kind of greedy."

The corner of his mouth curved up. Then I realized that he was probably joking. I hated it when people goofed around without smiling—it reminded me of the time most of my first-grade class convinced me that our teacher was secretly Barney the purple dinosaur.

I wanted to ask him what his favorite band was or something quasi-normal, but the door swung open and Naomi breezed in.

"Hey." She knelt in front of me. "Why are your cheeks so red?"

My mouth opened, but laughter was the only thing that came out. Naomi's eyes traveled from my face to Justin's, and whatever she saw caused her to smirk.

She stood up and leaned toward my ear. "Cute," she whispered and sat in the chair Roger previously occupied.

"What can I say? She finds me hysterical," Justin said, smiling at her. "I'm Justin, by the way. And I'm betting you're Naomi." He looked back at me. "I pay attention."

"Uh, yeah. Talking smack about me already, Drea?"

"Well, Roger was here, and he thought Justin was my boyfriend because of what you said."

A high-pitched squeal came from her throat. "Oh my God, I totally forgot about that. I'm so sorry." She leaned over, grinning at Justin. "Do you mind playing boyfriend until we come up with a better plan?"

"Naomi!" I wanted to hit her.

"Can you girls keep it down?" the receptionist asked, putting her hand over the mouthpiece.

I nodded, and Naomi apologized to her. Justin bit his lip but couldn't hold back a smile.

"I wrote the lyrics to the second verse last night. Our song is going to rock so much," Naomi said just before the class bell rang. "Meet me by the quad fountain after this class, 'kay?"

She got up, tossing a thin backpack over her shoulder. "You should meet us there too, fake boyfriend." Naomi waved at him before sprinting out of the office.

"I might just have to take your friend up on that," he said.

"You really don't need to pretend to be my boyfriend. That's ridiculous." I rolled my eyes.

"I meant meeting you guys after the first class. I was hoping to meet some musicians." He brushed his fingertips against my forearm, causing every tiny blond hair to stand up. "But I don't mind helping you get rid of stoner boy."

I yanked my arm away and buried it in my lap. "That won't be necessary."

As if on cue, Roger stepped out of the vice principal's office clutching a piece of paper. "He said you could go on in, Drea."

"Okay," I said, scrambling out of the chair. Unfortunately, I'd managed to tangle the toe of my boot with the hem of my underskirt and hit the ground elbows first. Just perfect.

Roger's laughter made the pain radiating from my funny bone even worse. "Nice grannie panties," he said just as someone tugged my skirts down.

Justin knelt beside me, holding his hand out. "You okay?"

I looked away, feeling the heat in my face give way to tears. This wasn't how I wanted to start my first day here. I grabbed my lunch box and backpack off the floor and trudged into the office without looking back.

"Big change from San Francisco, huh?" the vice principal asked as he scanned the papers in his file folder. When I nodded, he held his hand out to me with a grin that made his face even wider. "I'm Vice Principal Bailey."

I barely pinched his fingertips. "Nice to meet you."

"So, I've talked with your mom, and she had a couple of your doctors fax over some information about you. . . ." His thin lips were moving, but I blocked out his words. Words I'd heard a million times before—suggestions to see the school counselor, anything they can do to accommodate my *special needs*, what good grades and test scores I had, but . . . "You got a C-minus in English. Any reason why?"

I shrugged. "Not my best subject." I knew all the big vocabulary words—in fact I loved to read the dictionary and memorize words that sounded interesting. But I failed when it came to interpreting text that someone else wrote. Characters said one thing and did another, much like real life.

Mr. Bailey jabbed the computer keyboard with one finger from each hand. He squinted at the screen, making a gurgling noise in his throat.

"Are there any open music classes?"

"Hmm." He ran a chubby finger over his lower lip and shook his head. "Nope, those tend to fill up quickly. Do you like film?"

"I like to watch movies."

He shrugged and glanced at me. "Well, it's either sixth-period film or journalism. Take your pick."

"Film."

He clicked the mouse a few times, and the printer behind him started to groan. "Class started fifteen minutes ago, so I'll write you a note. Sorry about the delay—first day back is always hectic."

"It's fine," I said, just wanting to get away from his stare. Doctors, school administrators, even my mom sometimes—they all looked at me like I was a fly under a microscope.

"Drea," he said, yanking the schedule from the printer,

"I'm going to make an appointment for you with Jackie, one of our counselors. But don't worry—all the kids love her. And I hear she gives out those mini Twix bars."

"I don't like chocolate."

"I see." He wrote "excused tardy" on my schedule. "She'll send for you in the next couple of days and help you get acclimated, okay?"

I nodded as he handed me a booklet and my schedule.

"Here's your student handbook. Make sure you go over that tonight, and let me know if you have any questions."

"Sure."

"Welcome to Samish High, Drea." He thumbed through another file folder on his desk, his wide grin fading. "Send Justin Rocca in for me, will you, please? Thanks."

I mumbled "okay," but he didn't seem to hear me. He massaged his temples and furrowed his brow at whatever was in Justin's file.

The last thing I wanted to do was face Justin again, so I kept my eyes on the ground as I walked out. "You can go in," I said, heading straight for the exit.

"Hey, wait," he called out before the door clicked shut behind me.

My first class was U.S. History, and the teacher's name was Mrs. Heinz—like the ketchup. She had blond hair, bright red lipstick, and an obsession with Abraham Lincoln. But that was all I remembered about her after the dismissal bell rang.

I glanced at the map in the student booklet as I weaved between other students in the hallway. The school was shaped like a refrigerator turned on its side—three stories tall, and getting from one end to the other took a long time.

The quad was between the main building and the gym, reminding me that I had PE after lunch. Just thinking about the shrill girly laughter in a damp locker room made me cringe.

"Cool skirt," a girl with black hair and facial piercings said as she passed me.

"Um, thanks." I didn't turn around to see if she'd heard me. Sometimes the compliments were sincere, and sometimes they weren't.

I could see Naomi's purple hair as I pushed open the double doors that led to the quad. She sat on a cement wall that encircled a rather wimpy-looking fountain; the little hump sounded like a leaky bathroom faucet.

Naomi snatched my schedule out of my hand when I approached her. "Damn, we don't have anything together." She frowned, running her finger down the crinkled piece of paper. "Wait, we've got PE."

"Maybe PE will be more tolerable, then," I said, looking around for Justin. "Why don't you show me where my next class is?"

Naomi narrowed her eyes at me. "Drea, it's room 305. Top floor. Like it's that hard to find."

"I don't want that Justin guy to see us." I lowered my voice. "You invited him, remember?"

"Aw—he was a little preppy looking, but he seemed really sweet." She nudged me. "And cute."

I glanced back at the doors of the main building. A tall guy with dark hair and a white T-shirt put his hand over his eyes and looked in our direction. "Let's get out of here." I grabbed Naomi's wrist and tried to pull her away from the fountain.

"Don't be so mean." She twisted out of my grip and nodded in his direction. "He sees us."

"I'm leaving." There was no way I could face him, not after what he saw and Roger's comment.

Naomi grabbed my shoulders and pulled me backward. "Whoa, girl. Tell me why you're freaking out."

I tried to break free, but she held on tighter, laughing. "He saw my underwear—"

"He *what?*" She punched my shoulder, her mouth hanging open. "You ho!" Her laughter sounded like it was going through a hundred-watt amplifier.

"No, not like—shut up, okay?" I glanced at the students around me. "He'll hear you."

"Relax, he's too busy talking to Kari McBitch." She nodded behind me with a sneer.

I glanced over my shoulder and saw Justin talking to one of those common-denominator girls. Blond highlights were mixed in with her brown hair, and she was dressed like a mannequin at the mall. "She's got really big boobs," I said before I could stop myself.

"Yeah, it's kind of funny how much they grew over the summer." There was an odd edge to Naomi's voice—one I'd never heard before. "So tell me, what happened with you and the new guy?" She poked me, all smiles.

I looked over my shoulder again. Justin was pointing at us. Not good. "Nothing. I fell, and my skirt flew up."

She crinkled her brow at me. "So?"

"Well, Roger was—"

"Don't tell me she's coming over here," Naomi said through her teeth, peering over my shoulder.

When I turned around, Justin was approaching us with that Kari girl in tow. He was smiling, but she definitely wasn't.

"Hey, Justin," Naomi said. "I was just about to split. But maybe I'll see you later." Naomi walked right into Kari, bumping her arm.

"Yeah, that's right. Keep walking," Kari said.

"See you at lunch, Drea!" Naomi called over her shoulder.

Justin raised his eyebrows at me, and I shrugged. Naomi really sucked for leaving me alone with him.

"Hi, I'm Kari." Her dark eyes scanned my body until they reached my feet. "You've got dirt on the bottom of your skirt."

"Oh." Part of the hem was caught under my boot.

She smiled, flashing her white teeth. "It's Drea, right?"

"Yeah." That's me. Drea with the grannie panties. I bet Justin didn't waste any time telling her either.

"What classes did you get?" Justin asked, moving closer to me. His warm breath hit my cheek as he peered down at my schedule. "We've got the next one together. And I'm in the film class too."

"Cool," Kari said. "Guess we're all going to the same place, then."

I did my best to imitate a polite smile and walked ahead of them, hoping Kari would keep Justin occupied.

"What instrument do you play?" he asked, appearing alongside me.

I tried to walk faster, but he had much longer legs than I did. "Guitar mostly. But I'm more into production and sound design."

He held the door to the main building open for Kari and me. "What do you use—Pro Tools, Logic?"

"Logic," I said, surprised that he'd heard of either recording program. A lot of people assumed I used GarageBand—which was fine for beginners. But I was beyond the days of putting a bunch of premade loops together and calling myself a musician.

"You must do electronic music mostly, huh?"

"Yeah. Do you produce?" I asked.

"Nah. I laid down some piano tracks for a producer friend of mine in Chicago."

"You play the piano?" Kari asked, moving to the other side of Justin.

He shrugged. "Yeah—started with 'Jingle Bells' when I was two and haven't stopped since."

"That's so cute!" she said.

I let them go ahead of me on the stairs. "Why is it cute?"

Kari glanced over her shoulder and wrinkled her nose at me. "It just is." She moved closer to Justin, nudging his ribs. "You should play for me sometime."

He mumbled something I couldn't hear as we reached the classroom. I nudged past them and scanned the class for an empty seat. Back row, corner desk. Perfect.

As I slid into the desk, I watched Kari pull Justin to a couple of desks on the other side of the room. He whispered something to her and she shrugged, flashing him a quick smile. My stomach did flip-flops as they headed for the two empty desks in front of me. I'd never had a guy take this much interest in me before. Part of me wondered if I was the butt of another joke.

"You're a tough girl to keep up with." Justin slid into the seat in front of me. "How am I supposed to keep Roger away?"

"I don't see him here, do you?"

He glanced around the classroom and shrugged. "Guess not." He kept his eyes on mine as if he was waiting for something.

"What?"

"Nothing." He turned around and started talking to Kari, who was eagerly awaiting his attention.

A man with a red 'fro and a Hawaiian shirt walked into the classroom and tossed a black bag on the desk. "Hey, guys!" he called out just as the bell rang. "Welcome to English Eleven! I'm Mr. Duncan—some of you had me for English Nine." Apparently Bozo was our teacher.

I looked out the window and zeroed in on a couple leaning against an evergreen tree. It took a few seconds to realize that it was Naomi and Roger, puffing on cigarettes. I wondered if they knew that people could see them from these windows, or if they even cared.

"So what I usually like to do the first day is get to know everyone. I remember faces, but I'm not so good with names." Mr. Duncan chuckled. "I want you all to find a partner to interview. I've got the questions right here." He wrestled a stack of papers out of his book bag.

Great. Two of my favorite things—partnering up with a stranger and speaking in front of a class. I'd only passed speech class because the teacher felt sorry for me.

Kari spun around and grabbed Justin's wrist. "Will you be my partner again?"

"Okay, but don't spill any iodine on me this time," he said.

I glanced at the guy next to me, but he was already whispering to the girl in front of him. In fact, it seemed everyone but me had a partner. This meant the teacher would pair up with me, or he'd force me into a three-way. Either way, I'd end up the focal point of the class—the one nobody wanted to partner with.

Mr. Duncan handed some papers to the first person in our

row. "When you guys are done, I want you to introduce your partner to the class. Clear enough?"

I kept hoping that one teacher out of the bunch would come up with a first-day activity I hadn't done a zillion times before. Or at least one that had some purpose.

Justin turned around and handed me the last questionnaire, a smile flickering at his lips. "You need a partner, don't you?"

I shrugged, not really knowing how to respond.

"Scoot your chair up," he said. "The more the merrier."

"Okay."

"She doesn't have a partner," Justin said to Kari as I moved my desk next to his.

"Aw, sure—yeah, join us," she said in a high voice. Too high. It sounded fake, even to me.

I had to look twice at the questions on the paper. They definitely weren't the normal set, like what's your name, favorite subject, etc. This one wanted to know our favorite vacation, the best book we'd ever read, what we wanted to be when we grew up, and the first thing we did this morning.

"These are really random," Justin said.

"Yeah, I had Duncan my freshman year," Kari said. "He's a nut job, but he's entertaining." She twirled a lock of hair around her finger, biting her lower lip. "We'll just go around in a circle. I'll ask you." She nodded at Justin. "You can ask Drea and whatever."

"That works," I said, glancing at the clock and counting the minutes left. Thirty-six.

"Okay." She poked Justin. "Tell me all about your favorite vacation."

Justin rolled his eyes up to the ceiling. "You'll have to give me a minute to think about that."

"Sure." Kari smiled at him. Her eyelashes looked like they belonged in a mascara commercial; every lash was perfectly separated and curled. I'd tried to use my mom's eyelash curler once, but it ended up being more of an eyelash eradicator.

"Do I have something on my face?" she asked me.

"No. I like your makeup."

The corner of her glossy mouth perked up. "Uh—thanks." She glanced at Justin, but he was doodling on his questionnaire. "Got an answer yet?"

He dropped his pen and folded his arms across his chest. "I guess it would be the summers I stayed in Milan with my grandma. She lived right by this gelato place, and they had a coconut and mango combo that rocked."

"I like coconut," I said.

"Hold up. You spent summers in Milan and all you can say is you liked the ice cream?" Kari asked.

"It ruined me on pizza in the States too. Can't eat it unless I use my grandma's recipe."

Kari wrinkled her nose at him. "Come on, you gotta give me more than that. Did your parents just, like, put you on a plane every summer?"

"Well, my dad worked for a company based out of Munich, so sometimes he took me with him. And Milan was only about a five-hour drive. Staying with my grandma was more fun than a hotel, you know?"

"Not really. My parents don't exactly frequent Europe much." Kari rolled her eyes. "We might see my aunt in Vancouver if they're feeling daring."

Justin looked down, drumming his hands on his desk.

"Do you speak Italian?" I asked.

Both their heads jerked up like they'd suddenly remembered I was sitting with them. Kari's eyes darted from me to Justin.

"*Sì.*" He smiled at me. "I'm a lot better at understanding it than speaking it, though."

"I have a bunch of language books at home," I said. "But they don't teach me how to say the weird stuff."

"Nah, you have to actually experience the place to learn the good words," he said.

"Do you study languages for fun?" Kari asked me.

"Yes."

"Interesting." She shifted her gaze to Justin and pursed her lips.

"Do you have a favorite language?" he asked me.

"Gaelic." I didn't even have to think about it. "It's really lyrical."

"Say something in Italian, Justin," Kari said, biting the cap of her pen.

"Like what?" He glanced at his hands again. His nails looked like the edges of broken glass. Maybe he bit them, like Naomi did.

She leaned closer to him. "Anything."

"*Sono strano.*" He gave me a side glance.

"You don't seem that weird," I said, hoping I got the translation right.

"That's because you don't know me that well yet." The way he said *yet* made my cheeks feel hot. Like he'd actually remember my name in a couple of weeks after he made friends here. Normal friends, like Kari.

By the time Kari was done prodding Justin, we'd learned that his favorite book was *Slaughterhouse Five*, he was interested in psychiatry because the human mind "fascinated" him, and he needed to make sure he still had teeth this morning. He'd dreamed that they'd all fallen out.

"So what was your favorite vacation, Drea?" he asked.

Considering my mom and I were always too busy moving to take vacations, I didn't have a lot to draw from. "My mom took me to SeaWorld once. I didn't want to leave after we saw the dolphins—so we watched them until the park closed."

"If that's your best vacation, you're even worse off than I am," Kari said. "Mine was when I snuck off with my ex during spring break. We drove along the coastline all the way to some town in southern California."

"Hey, it's Drea's turn," Justin said with a smile.

"I was just trying to speed this up." She grinned back.

"I want to be a sound designer, don't have a favorite book, and I tripped over a moving box this morning. Fast enough?" I asked. Next time I would have to come up with a better story for my vacation. Maybe one involving skydiving out of a plane with *my* "ex."

"For now," Justin said. "I'll just grill you more later."

Kari's favorite book was *Anne of Green Gables*, she wanted to be a journalist, and she'd hit the snooze button three times before she got up. My interview went a lot quicker because I didn't ask her to elaborate on her experiences. And Justin drew pictures of rectangles and eyeballs on his paper. I wondered if he was even paying attention to her answers.

"Guess we moved too fast," I said, looking around the room. Some students were using animated hand gestures, others were laughing, and many were writing furiously.

Kari leaned back in her chair, studying me. "So—when did you meet Naomi?"

"When I moved in on Friday. She lives across the street."

"What do you think of her?"

"She's nice." What else could I say? Mom told me to keep my answers to a minimum around people I didn't know, especially when they wanted to gossip about someone else.

"Yeah." Kari chuckled. "She sure seems that way, doesn't she? Watch your back around her."

Kari's words made me squirm in my seat. She was the second person in three days to warn me about Naomi. But almost everyone I met made me feel like a freak. They'd give each other these looks, much like the ones Kari gave Justin. I didn't notice the looks when I was little—the smirks and raised eyebrows. Not until the teasing started. Naomi never looked at me like that.

"She's my friend," I said.

Kari put her hand up and shook her head. "You need better taste in friends."

I opened my mouth to retort, but Justin reached under my desk and brushed his fingers against the back of my hand. It was a quick gesture, but enough to make me forget whatever I was going to say. Warm tingles shot up my forearm, and my stomach felt weird.

"Nothing wrong with loyalty," he said, giving me a smile.

NAOMI JUMPED IN FRONT OF ME and grabbed my shoulders as I left fourth-period biology. "Anyone?" she asked in a low monotone. "Anyone know what this is? Class?"

I pulled out of her grasp. "You're not making any sense."

She fell into step alongside me, her mouth hanging open. "Please tell me you've seen *Ferris Bueller*."

"I might have." It's not like I took notes on every single movie I saw.

"Okay, we're so watching that. There's a teacher in it who's just like the Bot."

"The Bot?"

"Yeah—that's what we call Mr. Harvey. He's the only bio teacher I've had who can make dissecting a fetal pig seem like a real estate seminar."

I hadn't noticed anything unusual about Mr. Harvey other than the spit flying out of his mouth with every hard consonant. He also smelled like an old closet—no wonder I had a front table all to myself.

Naomi pushed open a set of doors and led me back to the

fountain. Students poured out into the quad like ants zeroing in on a juice spill. "Is your lunch in there?" She nodded at my blue lunch box.

"It's in my backpack."

"Do you take that thing everywhere with you?"

My hand tightened around the handle. "Yes." Like Mr. Fuzzy the blanket, my box was a piece of home. It comforted me.

"Got anything I can eat?" She elbowed her way through a group of jocks and slid onto the cement wall, spreading her arms wide and leaning on her palms.

I plopped next to her, yanking a crumpled brown bag out of my backpack. "I've got a jelly sandwich and an apple."

Naomi wrinkled her nose. "Feeling extra fruity this morning?"

"The apple was Grandma's idea. You can have it."

She raised her eyebrows. "You got something against peanut butter?"

"Yeah, it's gross."

"But purple jelly between two pieces of . . . what the hell kind of bread is that?"

I shrugged. "Some twelve-grain stuff my grandma eats. I didn't have time to buy food this weekend."

She shook her head and sank her teeth into the green apple.

Drizzle sprinkled my cheeks, and the smell of wet pavement curled into my nostrils. I loved the scent of rain—if only it came in bottles. A couple of guys with messy hair and studded belts nodded at Naomi as they passed. She wiggled her fingers at them, and they nudged each other, smirking.

"Who are they?" I asked.

"Dumb and Dumber—the emo twins. I hooked up with the

blond one last year. Shortest lunch break I ever had." She grinned.

How was I supposed to respond to that? I swallowed a lump of jelly. "How come Kari doesn't like you?"

Naomi rolled her eyes. "I messed around with her ex-boyfriend. Only—I didn't know they were still together at the time. The dude in the red shirt." She pointed to a guy with a shaved head and biceps as big as my thighs. He stood near the school entrance, laughing with a couple other boys.

"Oh." I took another small bite of my sandwich. The seeds in the bread stuck to my teeth.

She nibbled on her thumbnail and gave me a sidelong glance. "It's not like I'm a slut. I've only had actual sex with three guys."

That sounded like an awful lot to me, but what did I know? The only people I talked to were net geeks online, and they never had dates either. "How old were you—the first time?"

She devoured the last speck of skin on the apple. "Fifteen. What about you?"

What made her assume I'd had sex? Maybe because she thought I had all these crazy-boy stories. "Um . . ." I tried to think of a good answer, but a hand squeezed my shoulder, making me jump.

"Hey." Justin smiled at us. "Mind if I join you?"

Naomi glanced from me to him. "Fine by me."

Justin sat next to me and unraveled a brown bag of his own, pulling out a couple pieces of vegetable pizza. The crust was super thin, like crackers. I wondered if it was his grandma's recipe.

"You gonna answer the question or not?" Naomi nudged me.

I leaned closer to her ear and lowered my voice. "Not now." Mom used to get on me about bringing up certain subjects around strangers, especially anything sex related. And talking about boys around a boy was just weird.

She leaned forward to look at Justin. "We were discussing our first time—when was yours?"

"Naomi!" I elbowed her. Maybe she needed a few social lessons herself.

Justin swallowed a massive bite of his pizza. "My first time . . . what?"

She squinted at him. "Don't be coy."

He crinkled his brow at me. "She always like this?"

Before I could answer, Roger shoved himself between Naomi and me. "Anyone game for Taco Bell?"

"Count me in," Naomi said.

Roger pushed his shades down his nose and peered at me. "What about you, Grannie Panties? You and your boyfriend want to come?"

I looked away. His presence and loud voice made me cringe. "Can you not call me that?"

"I'm just teasing. Don't get your panti—" He paused and laughed. "Oops."

"Why don't you drop it, man?" Justin asked.

Naomi's eyes widened, and she made an O shape with her mouth.

Roger held his hands up. "I'm just playin'. You guys coming or not?"

Justin raised his pizza crust at him. "Nah, I'm good."

"Aren't we supposed to stay on campus at lunch?" I asked.

Roger pulled my lunch box into his lap and inspected it.

I snatched it from him. "Don't touch that!" They wouldn't

understand my reaction. How could I explain the box was part of me—my space. I wanted to grab my stuff and run into the nearest bathroom stall. It was the only place at school that allowed me to lock people out. Sometimes it felt like the only place I could breathe.

Roger yanked on one of Naomi's purple pigtails. "Where'd you find this chick?"

She scrunched her nose at me and bit her lip. "I'm gonna split. But I'll see you in PE, okay?"

"Sure," I said, feeling Justin's eyes burning into me.

"Later," Naomi said, ruffling my red curls.

As Naomi disappeared into the crowd, I wondered why she'd want to spend so much time hanging out with a guy she didn't even seem to like.

"What a tool," Justin commented.

"Roger?"

"Who else?" He gave me a little nudge. "Naomi seems cool, though."

"Yeah, she's the first person who . . . never mind."

"Tell me." He leaned close enough for me to inhale a musky scent. Kind of like rain in a forest. It made my stomach tickle.

I counted the cracks in the pavement below my dangling feet. "She's really friendly—most people aren't."

"Maybe because you aren't very friendly to them."

I met his gaze. His eyes matched the cloudy sky. "What does that mean?"

"Well"—he glanced down at his long fingers—"you weren't exactly Miss Sunshine to me this morning."

"I'm sorry. Was I supposed to do a cheer for you?"

He rolled his eyes and chuckled. "No, but looking at me would've been nice."

"If I'm so horrible, why are you sitting here?"

"Because I think you're interesting."

Since when did guys like him find *me* interesting? "How can you say that? You don't even know me."

A smile edged at his lips, showing off a dimple on his left cheek. "I'm good at reading people."

I crumpled up my paper bag and shifted away from him. "Shouldn't you be hanging out with people more like you, then?"

"And who would that be?"

"Kari."

"How did you come to the conclusion that I'm like Kari?"

"Usually guys like you—"

"Guys like me? Spit it out, Drea. What little box have you stuck me in?"

His questions made my stomach shrivel, and my mind was at its limit. I couldn't even think. Nobody ever confronted me like this before. Usually I'd say a few sentences and they'd never talk to me again. Simple.

"I have to go." I snatched my backpack and headed toward the school building, tossing my bag in the trash.

"It's been a pleasure," he called after me.

My chest felt tight as I walked down the hallway in search of the restrooms. The never-ending rows of lockers bowed in and out, and my boots squeaked on the green tile floor. A group of girls stared at me as I passed them, their whispers like needles poking at my skin. Kari was one of them.

"Hey, Drea," she said with a half smile. Her dark eyes focused on the box swinging in my hand.

I muttered hi under my breath. A flutter of laughter followed me down the hallway.

"She looks like Raggedy Ann," one of the girls hissed. Another voice shushed her, and they went silent. I pictured their eyes on my back, analyzing everything from the way I walked to the size of my butt. Mom always did that. Compared herself to other women or criticized their outfits. When I'd hide in a bathroom stall, girls would stand in front of the mirror complimenting each other and insulting their absent friends. Always with lowered voices and soft giggles. Hatred and friendship seemed to go hand in hand.

The bell signifying the end of lunch break rang about five minutes later. My shoulders sagged as soon as I glanced at my schedule—PE. I'd purposely *forgotten* to bring a T-shirt and a pair of sweats, hoping this school wouldn't have a uniform. It wasn't like they could make me run around a field in a skirt.

I scanned the crowd for Naomi as I neared the brick gym building but found Kari instead. She had her hand on Justin's arm, and he was leaning toward her and laughing. I'd once read some lame magazine in a doctor's office that said casual touches and leaning toward each other were signs of romantic interest.

Kari's voice rose as she backed away from him. "See you in the parking lot, then?"

Justin gave her another dimpled smile. "You got Mrs. Baker for sixth period, right?"

She nodded, looking over at me. I realized I was gaping at them like an idiot.

"I'll meet you there after class." Justin turned and glanced at me. I opened my mouth to say hi, but he'd looked away and brushed past me before a sound escaped my lips. Nice.

"How's it going, Drea?" Kari asked, still staring at me from the entrance of the gym.

"Fine," I muttered to the ground.

"What?"

"It's fine," I said as I walked toward her. Where the hell was Naomi?

"Come on. I'll show you where the locker room is," she said, opening the graffiti-covered door.

Great—just what I needed. A guided tour of the locker room by a girl who hated my only friend here. "Thanks."

She led me down a hallway with a shiny wood floor and walls lined with trophy cases. "Did Naomi tell you we used to be best friends?" she asked.

"No."

"Didn't think so."

The smell of sweat and cheap perfume emanated from a blue set of double doors ahead, making me queasy.

"You'll have to see Mrs. Kessler to get your uniform first." She yanked open the heavy door.

Perfect, I thought.

The locker room was like every other I'd endured. Stained cement floors with matching walls, long skinny benches, and girls in various stages of undress. Some were hunched over, quickly yanking shirts over their heads. Others paraded around in nothing but fancy bras and underwear. The muggy air and high-pitched chatter made me dizzy.

Kari brought me to an office where a brunette woman sat. She looked nearly as small as I was—definitely not the norm for PE teachers.

"Newbie here, Mrs. Kessler." She jabbed her thumb at me.

"Thanks, Kari."

Kari shot me a quick grin and left me alone. Mrs. Kessler

handed me a uniform, went over the usual rules, and sent me on my way. She didn't even ask if I had questions.

Naomi stood outside the office, biting her lower lip. Her eyes looked glazed and sleepy. "Let's go find lockers." She grabbed my elbow and led me toward the back row. We scanned for a pair without locks and found a couple at the very top.

Naomi ripped off her black T-shirt and nodded at me. "Kessler is loads of fun, isn't she?"

"Sure . . ." I folded my arms over my stomach. I'd changed in the bathroom stalls at every other school. The other girls would smirk when I'd come out clutching my clothes. But it was better than standing around a bunch of half-naked strangers.

Naomi crinkled her brow at me. "Better get changed. Kessler is a real hard-ass about tardiness."

"Right." I stood up and backed away, pressing the clothing against my chest.

"Where you going?"

"Bathroom."

She unzipped her baggy jeans and let them fall to the floor. "Are you changing in the stall?" Her half smile told me she found that amusing. After all, she thought I'd had my share of boyfriends—surely it wasn't the first time anyone saw me undressed.

"I have to pee. But I guess I can change first."

"Whatever." She grinned and folded her jeans.

I glanced at the blue underwear riding low across her hips. The material was silky and thin. Nothing like the white pair that went up to my waist.

A couple girls walked into the aisle across from us—the same ones standing in the hallway with Kari at lunch. The blonde gave me a fleeting glance, but focused on Naomi. She was tall and big-boned with jowly cheeks and thin lips. She slid out of her tight jeans, showing off a satin thong. Her skinny friend wore one of those lace bras I saw in my mom's Victoria Secret catalogs.

I wasn't wearing a bra.

"Roger tried to make a move on me at lunch," Naomi said, slamming her locker shut. "You're definitely coming with me next time."

I pulled the gray sweats underneath my skirt. The scratchy material made my legs itch. "Why do we have to hang out with him at all?"

"Because he's got a car and he'll smoke us out." She wrinkled her nose at me as I slipped the T-shirt over my tank top. "Kessler usually makes us run a mile the first day."

"That's okay." I stuffed my skirt inside the locker and reluctantly put my lunch box inside. I never had much luck convincing PE teachers that I could run and play sports while carrying it.

"Someone should put biohazard tape over her locker," the blond girl across the aisle said loudly. She elbowed her friend and giggled at Naomi.

Naomi rolled her eyes at me. "Bitches."

The big-boned girl straightened and walked toward Naomi. God, she was at least six feet tall. "Did you say something?"

Naomi's shoulders tensed. "Nope."

The girl leaned within inches of her face. "You sure?"

Naomi pressed her back into the lockers, her hands curling into fists. "I didn't know, Casey. And I already apologized to her. What else do you want from me?"

Casey glanced down at Naomi's shaking hands and smirked.

She slammed her large fist into the lockers, missing Naomi's head by a couple inches. The thud echoed around the room like a firecracker, making me cover my ears. "Call me bitch again and I'll aim for your face next time."

"You got one minute!" Mrs. Kessler called from the front. "Let's go, ladies!"

Casey backed away and disappeared around the corner with her friend.

Naomi squeezed her eyes shut and let out a deep breath. "I totally forgot she'd be in regular PE this year."

"She looks like a football player," I said.

"No shit. She got kicked off the soccer team last year for sending a chick to the hospital."

"Why is she so mad at you?" I asked as we headed out of the locker room.

"Shhh." Naomi's eyes darted around the seemingly empty rows around us. She moved closer to me and leaned into my ear. "Because Kari will never be done getting back at me. Casey is, like, her personal fucking bodyguard."

"But that guy isn't even her boyfriend anymore, right?"

"It's not about that. I broke the girl code, you know?"

I nodded, but I didn't really *know*. Too bad there wasn't a dictionary for sixteen-year-old girl talk.

I nearly bumped into Justin when I found my sixth-period film class. He opened the door for me, but he didn't make eye contact.

I headed for the back row again—the seat closest to the window. Justin didn't follow me this time. In fact, he sat on the other side of the room near the front. I should've felt relief, but my chest felt heavy, and I slumped in my seat.

Our bald teacher fiddled around with a seventeen-inch lap-top at his desk. Every now and then, he'd look up and smile at the students wandering in. The bell rang, and I glanced around at the half-empty class. The two boys Naomi called Dumb and Dumber were sitting in the back row whispering to each other. Casey passed a cell phone to some guy with spiky hair behind her, and the pierced girl who'd complimented me on my skirt wrote in a journal. Justin drummed his fingers against the desk, gazing at the ceiling.

"Okay, guys." The teacher stood. He had buggy eyes and a lanky body, kind of like Gumby. "I'm Mr. Diaz, and obviously I'm new to Samish High. . . ."

He launched into a speech about teaching film at UCLA, and I stared out the window, tuning him out. Puffy clouds hovered over the dark blue bay, making my stomach growl. When I was little, I thought they were cotton candy.

"Why'd you come up *here*?" a nasal voice snapped me out of my trance. It came from the blond emo boy Naomi hooked up with.

"I like Bellingham." Mr. Diaz grinned at him. "Anyway, if you're hoping this will be a breeze, you might want to find another elective. I'm not going to expect any less from you guys than I did from my college students." He leaned against his desk and scanned the room. "How many of you like to watch movies?" When we all raised our hands, he continued. "Okay, how many of you like to see blockbusters at the big theaters?"

Justin, the pierced girl, and I were the only people who didn't raise our hands. I didn't like the crowds, the smell of the popcorn, or the stiff seats. Plus, the movies were always predictable.

Mr. Diaz nodded at Justin. "Why don't you like them, Mr. Nike?"

A small laugh escaped my mouth, and Justin glanced over at me before answering. "They lack originality ninety-nine percent of the time."

The teacher pursed his lips. "But hasn't every story been done before?"

"Doesn't mean it can't be told in a different way."

"Do you agree with him, Lilith?" Mr. Diaz motioned in my direction.

"My name is Drea," I answered.

He leaned forward. "Didn't hear you."

"Drea—my name is Drea!" The class snickered, telling me I'd said it way too loud. Justin was the only person not looking in my direction.

The teacher's eyes widened. "Fair enough. Do you agree?"

I looked back over at Justin, but he kept his eyes forward like I didn't exist. I hated him for it. "Yes, but I think it's kind of strange coming from someone wearing a Nike T-shirt."

"Why do you think he called you Lilith?" Justin asked. "Because you're so unique?"

"I don't know." I slumped farther in my seat.

"I suddenly feel like I'm in detention with Anthony Michael Hall," Mr. Diaz said. "Interestingly enough, *The Breakfast Club* is one of the first films we're going to watch."

Yet another movie I remembered hearing about but couldn't place. Several of the other students expressed their delight through muffled *yeah*s and hoots.

"Why do *you* think I called her that?" Mr. Diaz asked Justin.

"The black clothing, the pouting." Justin turned to look at

me. "Back row. Corner desk. Anti–brand name. Sounds like the stereotypical Goth to me."

Laughter filtered throughout the room. A guy mumbled something about being *owned*.

"What does that have to do with calling me Lilith?" I shot back at him.

"He could've gone with Raven too," Justin answered. "That's an even more played-out Goth name."

Mr. Diaz held his hands up and chuckled. "This is good. Because there will be a lot of disagreement this semester. Each of you sees the world differently, and movies are no exception. What one of you thinks is overdone and cliché, another thinks is groundbreaking." He pushed himself off the desk and paced the front of the room. "I'm not going to test you or throw out pop quizzes. But I will be keeping track of attendance and class participation. The bulk of your grade is going to be your final project. A five-minute movie of your own creation. It can be horror, action, comedy, a documentary, or even a music video."

"Sweet!" a guy with glasses said.

"Now," Mr. Diaz continued, "I want everyone except Drea and Mr. Nike to get out a piece of paper and write down your three favorite movies. You've got one minute." He looked down at his silver watch. "Go."

"What are we supposed to do?" Justin asked.

Mr. Diaz raised his bushy eyebrows. "Sit tight."

After the class handed their slips of paper to Mr. Diaz, he flipped through them with a smile flickering at his lips. "Now—here's the catch. The school bought only two camcorders, but they are PD-170s, meaning you don't want to break one. Trust me on that. And the lab will only let me reserve so many computers after school. Which means you'll need to work with a partner." He waved the papers in his hand. "Someone who has completely different taste than you."

The class groaned in unison.

"And you two"—he pointed at Justin and me—"already matched yourselves up. Good luck."

I glanced over at Justin, and he actually smiled and winked at me. Like he thought it was funny.

I was officially in hell.

5

THE LAST THING I WANTED was for Naomi to be there when Mom picked me up. I had a doctor's appointment after school, and I didn't want Mom mentioning it in front of her. The street in front of Samish High resembled the passenger drop-off area at a major airport. Horns honked, engines revved, and hands waved impatiently behind windshields. Most of the kids being picked up looked to be freshmen, no surprise there.

Mom's faded green sedan was about a block down the street. I broke into a sprint, hoping I could dive into the car before Naomi saw me.

"Wait up, Drea!"

No such luck. My shoulders slumped as I spun around to face Naomi.

"You need a ride?" She approached me with Roger in tow.

"No, thanks."

"Does your boyfriend always take other chicks home?" Roger asked, nodding at the street.

"What do you mean?" I glanced over my shoulder.

"Black BMW," Naomi whispered in my ear. "We saw him

pick up Kari in the parking lot," she continued in a louder voice.

My eyes focused on a shiny BMW inching past us. I could make out Kari's long hair in the passenger seat. He probably had a decent amount of horsepower in that thing. I used to be obsessed with car engines—drove Mom nuts.

"Twenty bucks says it's Daddy's car." Roger smirked. "Want me to kick his ass for you? Slash his tires?"

"Why would I want that?"

Mom tapped her horn three times behind me. I'd recognize that urgent tinny sound anywhere. "That's my mom. I have to go."

"Do you want to hang out later?" Naomi asked.

Grandma's voice echoed across the lawn, calling my name. "We have ten minutes to get to your appointment!" Of course Mom had to bring her.

"What appointment?" Naomi asked.

I sighed. There was no way out. "Just seeing a doctor."

Her eyes widened. "What for?"

"Um . . . stuff."

She nodded like she understood. "Oh, *that* doctor. Ew, I hate going there."

Roger chuckled. "Tell your mom you can get a ride from me and Naomi from now on, if you want."

"Sure, okay. Bye." I turned around and jogged to the car, ignoring whatever Naomi called after me.

Dr. Weber had about ninety different pictures of cats on her desk and a yellow rocking chair by the window. It was meant for kids, but I fit in it just fine. Mom sat cross-legged on the generic brown couch near the door.

"How are you today, Drea?" Dr. Weber asked.

I shrugged and stared at her shiny lips, wondering what kind of lipstick she used. Anything to ignore her squinty blue eyes and incessant writing. The lyrics to the Smashing Pumpkins song "Bullet with Butterfly Wings" roared through my mind every time I was in a doctor's office. *Despite all my rage, I'm still just a rat in a cage.*

Mom cleared her throat. "She always gets a little shy in these situations, but she's adapted remarkably well over the years."

The blond doctor flipped through my file and nodded. "She was diagnosed with ADHD?"

"Yes, in kindergarten," Mom rambled on. "Her last doctor thought she had AS, but her symptoms are so mild . . . I mean, it's not always obvious."

The doctor nodded. "Right. It's a difficult diagnosis. No two people with Asperger's—or with autism, for that matter—are the same. And females do tend to have less obvious symptoms."

"Do you have other patients with Asperger's?" Mom asked.

"Of all ages—children to grandparents." The doctor closed the file and looked in my direction again. She leaned back in her chair, folding her hands in her lap. "How'd your first day of school go, Drea?"

"It was school." I never understood that question. Did they want a synopsis of my entire day? Most people gave short answers like "great" or "fine" or "crappy." And telling someone I had a crappy day at school usually provoked the question "why?" But they didn't really want to know why because they'd end up interrupting me and changing the subject.

"Did you make any new friends?"

"Yes."

"There's a girl across the street that has taken a liking to her," Mom said. "It's the first time in a while—she hasn't had a friend in years."

"Why do you have to tell my life story?" I asked her.

"You don't like it when your mom speaks for you?"

"She has this need to tell everyone we meet that I have this *disorder*. But then she told me not to say too much about myself, because it might scare people off."

"I told you that in seventh grade, after what those girls did to you," Mom argued. "But your last doctor suggested that I inform the school, family members, and friends. People need to know what you're dealing with."

"Why does every guy you date need to know?"

Mom opened her mouth to protest, but the doctor broke in. "Does your new friend know?"

"No, and I want to keep it that way."

"She really has come a long way." Mom repeated herself, as always. "When she was little, she had a lot of run-ins with other kids, and I had a hard time getting her to bathe or—"

"Mom!"

"But now"—Mom uncrossed her legs and sat up—"she's doing better in school, and her, um, you know, grooming habits have improved, and—"

"You always got shampoo in my eyes. That's why I didn't like it."

"Even when I got you the tear-free shampoo, you still resisted. But that's not the poi—"

"No, it's not the point. Because I was five then, and I'm sixteen now. I take showers every day, I brush my teeth every night, I wear deodorant—even shave my legs. Because you wouldn't shut up about it. 'Comb your hair, Drea. Wear some perfume, Drea. Spend ninety million hours staring in the mirror like I do, Drea.' "

Mom rolled her eyes and sighed.

"If I may break in here," Dr. Weber said. "I think your mother is trying to tell you that she's proud of your progress."

"Exactly," Mom said, bobbing her head.

"Would it work better for you if your mom simply told you she was proud of you—rather than bringing up the past?"

"Yeah, because she never says that," I said.

"I say it all the time."

"No. You tell me to take my pills, you bring up things I did ten years ago, you remind me to brush my hair—but you never say you're proud."

"How's your mood been?" Dr. Weber moved on.

"Like it always is."

"Any negative thoughts or excessive worries?"

"Yeah, I've already been diagnosed with GAD. It's in the file." Doctors stuck me with generalized anxiety disorder in junior high when I began surfing the Web and self-diagnosing myself with everything from lupus to rabies and having panic attacks over it.

"I'm sorry," Mom said. "She's been really irritable with the move."

The doctor raised her eyebrows, nodding. "You've moved quite a bit, huh?"

And this would be the part of the meeting where Mom goes over our financial troubles and my lack of a father—all in an effort to excuse the fact that, as her friends say, *she changes cities like she does underwear.*

"How much of the XR is she currently taking?"

"When I can get her to take it, twenty milligrams," Mom said.

"How do you feel when you take it, Drea?"

"Like a zombie."

"Right when it kicks in, or is that something you feel later?"

"It gets worse later," I said.

"She gets more irritable at night—after it wears off," Mom chimed in. "But it really helps during the day. She's less impulsive and calmer."

"And I lose weight since it kills my appetite." I motioned to my body. "And let's face it, there isn't much to lose."

"Can you hop on the scale for me?"

I rolled my eyes and prepared myself for the inevitable questions—how did I feel about my body? Have I ever thrown up on purpose? Blah blah blah. Every doctor had to rule out eating disorders.

I stepped on the scale, and she peered over my shoulder, scribbling 100.5 in her little notebook.

"Well, I wouldn't want to see you lose any more weight. Go ahead and step off."

At least this doctor kept her comments to a minimum.

I plopped back into the yellow rocking chair and gazed out the window. Naomi was out there somewhere—probably having a great time. Who knew what Justin and Kari were doing. Probably kissing or more. I wondered what it would be like to kiss Justin. Ew, no. Scratch that thought.

"We've got a couple of options," the doctor said. "Some of my patients take the XR form in the morning and then an immediate-release tablet about eight hours later. It keeps them from crashing in the late afternoon."

"That won't keep her up all night?" Mom asked.

"It shouldn't. The IR is much shorter acting. Lasts an average of four hours. There is also an ADHD drug that isn't a stimulant—it may not suppress her appetite as much," the doctor rambled on. "I also think an SSRI would help, especially with some of the irritability and anxiety."

"I've been on antidepressants. I hate them," I said.

She glanced down at the papers and nodded. "How do they make you feel?"

"Like shit."

Mom put her face in her hands and shook her head. "I'm so sorry."

"It's quite all right. It's not easy trying out all these different meds, but sometimes it takes a while to find a combo that works." She went on to suggest the SNRIs, a newer form of antidepressants, because they tend to have milder side effects. "They increase your levels of norepinephrine as well as serotonin. That seems more effective in some people."

"What if none of them work?" I asked.

"Well, there's no magical cure out there. We're simply looking for a combo that benefits you most and causes the fewest side effects. A bigger part of the equation is how much you're willing to do for yourself, Drea."

I wondered if she'd ever tried multiple combinations of drugs.

"I'm starving," Mom announced as the three of us got back into her green Toyota.

"It's only three thirty, Juliana." Grandma was still grouchy because they had nothing but *People* magazine in the waiting room.

Mom rolled down the window and backed the car out. "So? We need to drop off Drea's prescriptions, and there's a phar-

70

macy right near a café someone recommended to me last night. Figured we'd go try it out."

"One of your square-faced dates?" The computer had replaced Mom's late-night trips to bars.

"Don't start, Drea. He seems really sweet."

"Of course he does. They all start off that way."

"Who?" Grandma asked.

"Mom's computer boyfriends."

"Drea." Mom squinted at me in the mirror.

"Computer boyfriends? Don't you ever watch the news? A young woman was just found murdered near the border. And do you know who the prime suspect is?" Grandma poked Mom's arm. The five- and six-o'clock news were her religion.

"I can't imagine." Mom shook her head.

"A man she met on her computer. And do you know what else they're saying? People can get your social security number, your bank account information, and"—Grandma yanked on Mom's elbow—"your *address*. They break into your computer and find all this."

"Yeah, but it usually only happens to dumb people who respond to e-mail scams or download viruses," I said.

"*Viruses?*" Grandma opened her mouth and closed it again.

"Anyway, he says they have a lot of vegetarian options, Drea," Mom said as we pulled into a parking spot downtown.

Grandma gasped. "Juliana! We're on Railroad Avenue."

"So what?"

"Are you crazy? We'll get mugged or killed. This is the worst part of town."

Downtown Bellingham consisted of a few brick buildings and rotting Victorian contraptions. Most of the inhabitants were college students with rainbow-colored hair and grungy people with acoustic guitars and tin cans.

"This is nothing, Grandma. You should hang out in downtown Oakland sometime."

"It's fine." Mom pointed across the street. "Look, there's a couple pushing a stroller, and some kids playing in the fountain over there."

"That's where they keep the drugs." Grandma lowered her voice and leaned toward Mom with wide eyes. "In the baby buggies."

"Okay, how about laying off the news for a while, huh?" Mom snorted out a laugh and got out of the car.

Grandma's sharp eyes didn't miss an inch of Café Mars when we arrived after dropping off my new prescriptions. By the time the hostess offered to seat us, Grandma concluded that the place was run by misfits. After all, it lacked sticky booths and fake sugar at every table.

The hostess showed us to a narrow table with stiff metal chairs. Grandma scrunched up her face and held on to the back of the chair, inching her compact body into the seat.

A familiar laugh made me glance up from my menu, and I found myself looking straight into Justin's eyes. Oh, God, no—of all places. He and Kari sat at a table in front of us, sipping milkshakes.

Kari looked over her shoulder and flashed me a quick smile. "Hi, Drea."

I sucked in my breath, focusing on the colorful menu in front of me.

"Who's that?" Mom whispered.

"Just someone from school," I mumbled.

"Well, say hi back at least."

"No," I said through my teeth.

"Blue walls are for baby nurseries, not restaurants," Grandma announced, scanning the room. "What kind of place *is* this, Juliana?"

Kari peeked over at Grandma and spun forward again, her back shaking with laughter. Justin stared at me, a half smile playing at his lips. I focused on my menu.

"Let's not worry about the décor for a change, okay, Mom?"

"And why do they have someone's trash all over their walls? That's the last thing I want to see when I'm eating."

Café Mars had records, photographs, magazine cutouts, antique toys, and even tires plastered to the walls. I'd been in a million places just like it in California—ever since Mom decided to go veggie.

"This can't possibly be the menu. It looks like a child designed it, for Christ sake." Grandma flipped it from side to side. "It's not even written in English."

Mom closed her eyes, sighing. "Yes, it is."

"A chix salad? *Chix?*" She banged her knobby finger into the menu.

"It's short for chicken." Mom smirked. Truthfully, *chix* meant veggie chicken strips—as in soy. She'd failed to mention that Café Mars had an all-vegetarian menu.

"She's going to know the difference," I told Mom.

"The difference of what?" Grandma asked.

"It's extra-lean meat here," Mom said, giving me a warning look.

"Oh." Grandma continued to scan the menu. "What is *fakin'* bacon? That a fancy way of saying Bac-Os?"

"Mmhmm." Mom nodded.

"Those are very high in sodium. Ten dollars for a salad?" Grandma chuckled. "What—they think we won't notice because they purposely misspell everything?"

"Keep your voice down, Mom."

A server with hot-pink hair and lip rings approached us with a big smile. "Hey, ladies. You ready to order?"

Grandma eyed her up and down, her mouth agape. "This isn't our waitress, is it?"

The girl's smile instantly faded as she narrowed her eyes at Grandma. "Would you like me to find someone else to wait on you?"

"Yes, please," Grandma muttered, focusing back on the menu.

Mom held her hand up and mouthed "Alzheimer's." The girl plastered another big smile on her face and nodded like she understood. "Okay, well, I'll give you ladies another minute." She walked over to Justin's table to let them know their meals would be out shortly.

"She doesn't have Alzheimer's," I said.

Mom kicked my shin hard enough to send an ache up my leg. "Ow!"

Grandma was too immersed in the menu to pay much attention. "Tofurky? Goodness."

The server returned a few minutes later. "Know what you want yet?"

Grandma squinted up at her. "You again."

The girl offered a toothy grin. "Yup. What can I get ya?"

"Just order." Mom rolled her eyes.

"Does this *chix* come from the breast?"

The server cocked her head, opening her mouth slightly.

"The breast," Grandma said louder. "Is it chicken breast meat?"

Kari let a high-pitched laugh escape before burying her head in her arms. Justin shushed her and covered his eyes with his hand. Other people were looking at Grandma now. Some with wide eyes and others on the brink of laughter.

Mom nudged Grandma. "Yes." She mouthed "sorry" to the pink-haired girl.

"I'll have the Chix Cobb salad. Nonfat Italian dressing on the side," Grandma said.

Mom covered her mouth and looked away.

Kari was still picking at her food when they brought out our meals twenty minutes later. Justin slouched in his chair and folded his arms across his chest, while she talked to him with animated hand gestures. He caught me staring at him and smiled. I nibbled on a seasoned fry, letting the spicy mush sink into my throat. It didn't have the right amount of crispness.

Grandma picked up her fork, prodding at various toppings on her salad. The prongs hovered over the egg halves for a second before she stabbed one and let it dangle off the fork. "These are pellet eggs," she decided.

"What?" Mom nearly choked on her bite of veggie burger.

"Pellet eggs." Grandma let the egg slice plop back onto the green leaves. "They're like rubber. And this chicken is awful."

Justin rose from the table, tossing a wad of cash over their check. Kari got up hesitantly, finding Grandma more interesting.

"See you later, Drea," Justin said.

I sank lower in my chair, contemplating the many ways I could avoid going to school tomorrow.

6

AFTER A SERIES OF DREAMS revolving around being dressed as
Barney in the boys' locker room, I woke up in need of a plan.
Or at least one less thing to be embarrassed about at school.

I tiptoed into Mom's room after she went into the bathroom and opened the top drawer of her wooden dresser. Piles
of underwear were tangled around silky bra straps. Organiza-
tion wasn't one of Mom's strengths either. A black pair of
underwear fell out, but I caught them before they hit the floor.
They were thin and sheer with a black ribbon encircling the
waist. Apparently, they would tie into little bows on the sides
of my hips. Cute, I guessed. I couldn't even consider the bras
since they'd fall right off.

The bathroom door across the hallway creaked open, and
I stuffed the underwear down my nightshirt. Mom walked in,
pulling her shoulder-length hair into a ponytail and singing
U2's "Vertigo."

"Hi, Mom," I said, heading toward the door.

She glanced from me to the drawer I forgot to close. "What
were you looking for, sweetie?"

"Nothing," I said, eyeing the hardwood floor.

"*Drea*—out with it."

"I'm out of clean underwear."

Mom shrugged. "Then we'll have to do some laundry."

"Oh, I forgot to ask you yesterday. Is it okay if Naomi and her friend Roger give me rides to school and back?"

She crinkled her brow. "Are they good drivers?"

I tensed. "I don't know."

Her lips stretched into a grin. "It's fine. I'm glad you're making some friends." She sat on the bed, crossing her legs. "I've got a job interview today."

"For what?"

She wrinkled her tiny nose. "Just a receptionist gig at a law firm. But it's better than nothing."

"Yeah." I studied her frown. "Maybe I should get a job too."

Mom sighed. She had shadows under her eyes. I wondered if she'd slept at all last night. "No, honey. I want you to really focus on school—so you can get into that music college you're always talking about."

"But it's in Boston, and it costs a lot of money."

She held her arms out to me. "Come here, baby."

I allowed her to pull me in and stroke my hair. There was something comforting about her touch—most people's hands hurt my skin. But I felt safe in Mom's embrace. It made me think of the hours we spent writing funny stories. The Noun and Verb Game, we called it—our own twisted version of Mad Libs.

"Who was that cute boy at the café?" Mom asked.

"A jerk. I have to work on a film project with him."

"Grandma really embarrassed you yesterday, huh?"

"They kept laughing at us."

Mom nodded. "She's never been really aware of what's going on around her. I think she's kind of like you in that she only knows how to say what's on her mind."

"Quit saying I'm like her. We are *nothing* alike."

A smile played at Mom's glossy lips. "You know what I like about both of you?"

"What?"

"You're strong—not afraid to be yourselves. There aren't many people I can say that about."

I looked away, not wanting to tell her how much I didn't want to be myself. How much I wished I had all these exciting stories to tell about guys I kissed or traveled down the coast with. How I was tired of being someone to laugh at.

"So, why is that boy a jerk? He seemed sweet. Was that his girlfriend with him?"

I shrugged. "That's Kari. She hates Naomi."

"Oh, I'll bet." She let out a hearty laugh. "Naomi's gorgeous—even with bright purple hair."

"His name is Justin—the boy. He's new too." I told her about how he'd approached me in the administration office and the things he said, including calling me stereotypical. When I finished, Mom could barely contain the grin on her face. "Why's this funny?"

She bit her lip. "It's not. I know. But here's the thing—you're a very pretty girl. Sometimes boys will talk to you because they really *are* interested. They aren't trying to be mean."

"I guess Kari interested him more."

"Maybe. Men are fickle creatures." Mom rolled her eyes. "Or maybe he wanted to make you jealous. In his mind, you rejected him."

"All I did was ask him why he wasn't hanging out with Kari. She's more like him."

"Yeah, but you don't like being compared to Grandma, right? Maybe he doesn't feel he's like Kari."

"That makes sense, I guess. Doesn't mean I have to like him."

Mom chuckled again. "Okay, well how about this? Apologize for getting off on the wrong foot and leave it at that. Then it won't be so awkward to work together."

"I don't have anything to apologize for."

"Be the bigger person. It'll make him feel like an ass." She winked.

"I'll try," I said, not entirely convinced I could even look at him, much less speak to him.

I didn't bother meeting Naomi after first period. Getting to English before Justin was imperative. With my luck, I'd end up tripping in front of him and Kari on my way to the desk.

Mr. Duncan told us that we were stuck in the seats we'd picked yesterday. Meaning I'd have to look at the back of Justin's head the entire semester.

I slid into my rock-hard seat by the window and waited. My stomach fluttered every time the door opened, but he still hadn't arrived a minute before the bell rang.

Then Kari walked in, and my fingertips went numb. She glanced up at me and smirked before sitting down and tossing a wave of hair over one shoulder. My cheeks went hot at the thought of Grandma's words in the restaurant. And Kari's high-pitched laughter. I couldn't get it out of my head.

The door swung open one more time, but I didn't recognize the guy who strutted in. And I definitely would've noticed *him* yesterday. His dark hair was tasseled and spiked, and he wore a black thermal with Robert Smith's face airbrushed on the front. My heart picked up as he headed for my row. Multiple zippers and rivets lined his black pants, and he carried a green lunch box with some cartoon character grinning on the front.

He met my gaze, his lips curving up in a smile. I'd recognize those gray eyes anywhere—even smudged with black eyeliner.

Justin lifted his arms and motioned to his clothes. "What do you think—too much?"

And here I'd been preparing myself to apologize. Forgive and forget, as Mom says. "Fuck you," I said, with a familiar ache in my throat.

Kari turned around, her mouth hanging open. "Smooth move, Justin."

He rolled his eyes at her and sat down, putting his hand on my arm. His fingers felt like an electrical current on my skin. Every nerve ached.

"Don't touch me," I said.

"Hey, I thought you'd laugh," he said. "Come on—I even begged my niece to let me use her lunch box."

"You're making fun of me. I get it, okay?" Out of the corner of my eye I could see Mr. Duncan walk in, but I didn't care. Part of me had hoped Justin was different—that he wouldn't make me the butt of another joke. But nothing had changed. Different school, same jerks.

"No—I'm—"

"Leave me alone!"

"What's going on back there?" Mr. Duncan asked.

Justin faced forward, and I looked up at the teacher. Every head was turned in my direction.

"Nothing," I said, my face on fire.

The teacher looked from me to Justin for a few moments before continuing. "I got the class syllabus printed off as promised." He fished a stack of papers out of his bag and began divvying them up among the rows. "As most of you know, I like to start the semester off with a bang, and I thought we'd tackle *Go Ask Alice* this year."

A couple of groans reverberated around the room. "Just say no!" a boy jeered.

"Sounds like you've read it," Mr. Duncan said. "And here I thought you guys were too busy watching *America's Next Top Model* or *Lost*."

"I read it in, like, seventh grade," a girl with long braids said. "It's a good book."

"Well, now you get to dissect it."

Justin dangled a stapled bunch of papers over his shoulder. I ripped them out of his hand, hoping to give him paper cuts.

"And you'll notice I'm still all about the journals."

More groans filtered throughout the room.

"Yeah, yeah. They're good for you. An entry is due every Friday. Tell me your thoughts on life. What you had for dinner, your favorite color or band. Whatever's on your mind. I won't be grading these—but I'll flunk you if you don't turn them in every week."

The thought of trying to organize my thoughts made my head hurt. I never got the point of journals. Why document things I already know? That's boring. Plus, most experiences weren't worth rehashing.

Most of the class whispered to each other as Mr. Duncan passed out the books. Justin held one over his shoulder for me, but he moved it every time I tried to grab it.

"Give me the book, jerk."

"And it looks like we're a couple short," Mr. Duncan announced. "I'll be right back."

Justin waited for him to leave before turning to face me. "Look, I'm sorry, okay? I'm not making fun of you."

"Yeah, right."

His eyes widened. "Do you have any idea how many boxes I had to go through to find these pants?"

"No, and I don't care. Can you give me the book now?"

He raised the book, but still kept it out of reach. "Come on, I'm wearing eyeliner here. I didn't even go this far when I *was* a Goth."

"Did you borrow that from your niece too?"

He smirked. "No, my older sister."

The image of Justin struggling to put on eyeliner *was* rather funny.

"Was that a hint of a smile I saw?"

"You look ridiculous," I said. Even though I kind of liked the way he looked. It was an improvement over the boring Nike shirt.

"You're hard to please," he whispered. "What look should I try tomorrow? Raver? Punk? How about a skater cowboy?" He set the book down on my desk and smiled.

Mr. Duncan tore back into the classroom and passed out the remaining books. Justin turned around and flipped through the pages.

A shadowed eyeball peered at me from the black cover. The face reminded me of Mom after she gets dumped. Her dark eyes get shiny and flat at the same time. I flipped to the first page and scanned what looked to be a journal entry. Whoever wrote it sounded young—my age maybe. She thought she had something worthwhile to say—but instead the diary had become nothing, like the rest of her life.

Naomi wasn't waiting outside my biology class. I found her at the fountain having an in-depth conversation with Justin. Seeing her throw her head back and laugh made my stomach hurt. Whatever he said couldn't have been that funny.

I marched up to him, preparing the perfect speech in my head. Something that would put him in his place and send him on his merry way.

Then he smiled at me and patted the space next to him, and I forgot how to speak English.

"You," I said.

"Me," he answered.

"Go away."

"And leave you to Roger? Never."

Naomi giggled. "Guess what? Justin plays piano."

I sat on the other side of her and ripped my lunch bag from my backpack. "I know."

"And he plays bass too. I was thinking—he could join our band. With him, we've got every instrument covered."

"I can play the bass just fine," I said, unraveling my jelly sandwich.

"But do you play the piano?" Naomi asked.

"Don't need to. I've got a midi keyboard and piano samples. I can just program the notes."

"And it sounds cold and robotic," Justin said. "Even electronica can use that human touch sometimes."

"Are you going to haul a piano into my grandma's basement?"

"How about a keyboard? My Bösendorfer isn't very travel friendly."

I dropped my sandwich in my lap. "For real? You have a Bösendorfer?"

He looked down at his hands. "Yes."

"Okay, what's a Bösen-dopper or whatever?" Naomi asked.

I gritted my teeth. "It's a really nice and expensive piano. But I have some samples of one on my computer."

"Oh, yeah." Justin snorted. "That'll beat the real thing."

"Are your parents, like, off-the-charts rich, or what?" Naomi asked him. "Because you've got a real nice ride too."

He bit into his sandwich and shrugged. "Something like that."

"Well, you're either loaded or you aren't," Naomi said. "Which is it?"

"My dad's a rap star."

Naomi rolled her eyes and elbowed him. "Okay, fine. Don't tell me." She whipped out her cell phone, pressed a couple buttons, and handed it to me. "Give me your digits. I wanted to hang out last night, but I was afraid your grandma would eat me if I dropped by too late."

Justin laughed softly into his sandwich, turning his face away.

"Where's Kari?" I asked him, punching in my cell number.

"I don't know."

"Yeah, I heard you guys hooked up last night." Naomi wiggled her eyebrows at him.

He squinted at me, shaking his head. "Having food at a café doesn't equate to hooking up. She offered to show me around town—I thought, Why not?"

"I didn't ask," I said. "Why are you here anyway?"

"I invited him. We've got fourth period together." Naomi took her phone from me and grinned at the number I'd plugged in.

Justin leaned around her to look at me. "I figured if we have to make a movie together—we might as well be civil. But I'll leave if you'd like."

"Okay," I said, pretending to savor a bite of my sandwich. The chunk felt more like a rock edging its way down my throat. I didn't really want him to leave, but I was afraid to let him stay. His presence gave me this tightness in my chest. Like I couldn't breathe. And I hated how I kept looking at his lips when he spoke—wanting to touch them.

"Don't go," Naomi said to him.

I could feel both of them looking at me, waiting for a response. All I could do was count the cracks on the pavement. Most of them were faint, but a couple were large and gaping. Ready to swallow me.

"It's cool." He crumpled up his bag and zipped up his backpack. "I'll see you in film, Drea."

"Call me!" Naomi yelled after him as he walked toward the steps.

He gave her a small wave before going into the building.

"What's your deal?" she asked. I didn't like the tone of her voice—it sounded more cutting than usual. Higher in pitch.

"He's a jerk."

"I haven't seen him be anything but nice to you. Confess already, huh? Who broke your heart?"

I stuffed my half-eaten sandwich into the bag, willing my mind to think of a brilliant answer. The thought of telling Naomi the truth made my teeth grind. She'd probably see me like everyone else did—sad, lonely, weird, even pathetic. When in doubt, I could always use Mom's experiences. "He cheated on me—well—a couple of them did."

She put her hand on my knee. "I'm sorry, sweetie." The warmth of her hand reminded me of our kiss, something neither of us had mentioned since it happened.

Roger sauntered up to us and tossed his backpack on the cement. "What's up?"

"Lunch is half over. Where the hell have you been?" she asked him.

"Got held up by my math teacher." He nodded at me. "What's up, Drea? You dump that loser?"

"He wasn't my boyfriend in the first place," I said.

He raised an eyebrow at Naomi, but she shrugged. "Guess it was just a fling," she said.

Roger leaned toward her, lowering his voice. "Scott got some killer bud last night. It's in my car."

"Sweet. Let's go." She grabbed my hand and pulled me with her.

I held back. "I-I don't—"

"Come on!" Her hand tightened around mine.

"But I don't want to go anywhere. We'll be late for—"

She rolled her eyes. "Chill, Drea."

Naomi and Roger scanned our surroundings as we walked around the side of the main building. Our shoes sank in the muddy grass.

"How long will this take?" I asked.

Instead of answering, she jogged after Roger toward a row of evergreen trees. They ducked behind the low branches, but I could still see Naomi's rainbow laces and Roger's dirt-smeared tennis shoes. The wet grass was like ice under my boots.

"Hurry up, Drea! You're gonna get caught," Naomi hissed.

Each step made me teeter to the left or right. I held my arms out for balance and took short, fast steps until I reached the trees. Then I dove under the branches and inhaled deeply. The air smelled like maple syrup and cigarette smoke.

A few students stood in the shade of the evergreens. Kari and Casey leaned against a trunk, narrowing their eyes at Naomi. Lipstick-stained cigarette butts smoldered near their feet. Kari met my gaze and leaned into Casey, whispering something. Both girls laughed, high and shrill.

"Ignore them," Naomi said, leading me through a break in the trees.

We passed a lip-locked couple—all tangled fingers and soft laughter. I wondered how that felt.

Roger's car was cream colored and shaped like an egg. The inside reeked of stale ashes and engine oil. Mom had a car like his once—even the brown upholstery was the same. Like cheap bath towels.

Roger reached over Naomi's knees and snagged his green pipe from the glove box. Then he pulled out a plastic baggy filled with what looked like herbs.

"Ooh, that looks good." Naomi grinned.

"Yeah, it's real smooth." He stuffed a pinch into the pipe and shoved the baggie back into the glove box.

"Good, because Scott's been getting bunk lately."

"You're still hanging out with Scott?" I asked. The contents of my stomach crept into my throat. Why did she insist on hanging out with these guys?

"He might've dropped by last night." She smiled wide and took the pipe from Roger.

He squinted at her. "He hooked up with Kelly this weekend, you know."

She bit her lip, shrugging. "So? He already told me."

"He was scoping out Drea on Saturday too."

"And he told me he was totally joking."

I swallowed hard and focused on the motor oil bottles below my feet. "Didn't sound that way to me."

"Do you buy everything he tells you?" Roger asked.

"Yeah, he said you'd say that too." Naomi thrust the pipe in front of me. "You get to do the honors, Drea."

"No, tha—"

"Why are you so into him?" Roger spoke over me.

Naomi rolled her eyes and wiggled the pipe at me. "You smoking or not?"

I took it from her, letting the cold metal sink into my palm. She settled back in the front seat and gazed out the window.

"Hey, there's Justin," she said.

"Where?" I asked, scanning the parking lot.

"In his fancy car. He's, like, taking a nap or something."

Justin's black BMW was two cars down, facing us. He had his seat reclined, and his head bobbed slightly—like he was lost in a song.

"Do you think he smokes?" Naomi asked.

"Yeah, right," Roger said. "He's got Momma's Boy written all over his sorry ass."

"Shut up. He's nice," she said.

He shook his head at her. "Is there anyone you don't want to bone?"

"Yeah—*you*."

Roger shifted in his seat and drummed his hands against the steering wheel. "Whatever."

Naomi slapped my knee. "Come on—use it or lose it, babe."

"You go first," I said, handing it back to her.

She stuck the pipe between her lips and ran the lighter over the end. Her face turned bright red before she finally blew the smoke out. The pungent odor stung my nostrils like Mom's overheated coffee.

"Nice." Her voice sounded hoarse. She squinted at me when I hesitated to take the pipe from her. "Why do you look so freaked?"

"I don't know." I took the pipe and the lighter from her. The warmth of the metal burned into my hand this time. Naomi and Roger watched me with half smiles—as if they knew I had no clue what I was doing.

And then the bell echoed from the school. "We should go," I said, dropping the pipe in Roger's lap.

"Watch it," he said.

Naomi rolled her eyes. "You got time for a toke, hon."

My throat tightened and my chest felt heavy. All I wanted to do was get out of that car. I fumbled with the lock, but the door didn't budge. "Let me out."

"Uh—*you* locked it," Roger said, shaking his head and clicking it open again.

"What's wrong with you?" Naomi asked.

"I can't breathe in here." I shoved the door open and flung my backpack over my shoulder.

"I'll catch up with you later," Naomi said.

I slammed the door shut and weaved through the parked cars. The drizzle had thickened into a soft rain, making me shiver. I was about to make a run for the school when someone grabbed my elbow and pulled me behind an SUV.

"Hey"—Justin spun me around—"it's just me."

I sucked in my breath and tried to break free, but he tightened his grip on my arm.

"Do you not see security standing about fifty feet away?" he asked.

I peeked around the rear of the large silver vehicle he was leaning against. A man and woman in blue rain jackets stood at the parking lot entrance. The man spoke into a two-way radio, and the woman began walking in our direction.

"She's coming," I whispered.

"Shit, I hate closed campuses." He slipped his hand into mine, leading me around the front of the SUV. I wondered if he'd been to as many schools as I had.

Rain tapped the hood of the car, drowning out the sound of the woman's footsteps. We squatted down beneath the headlights. Justin's cheek was only a couple inches from mine, but somehow it didn't feel close enough.

"What now?" I asked, my heart racing in my chest.

He put his finger to his lips as the sound of heels passed us by. I peered around the side of the SUV. The security woman moved slowly, glancing at the spaces between the cars. I looked back at Justin. Droplets had formed on the tips of his eyelashes, making them look even longer.

He met my gaze. "You smell like a concert."

"So?"

The beep of a two-way radio echoed nearby. "All is clear on my end," the woman said.

The radio crackled again, and a man's voice broke through. Most of his words were too distorted to make out. "Okay . . . check the . . . and bathrooms."

The hissing of the radio and her footsteps faded into the distance. Justin peered over the hood and stood up.

"They're gone," he said, ruffling his wet hair.

I used the bumper to hoist myself up, but my shaky legs made me stumble back.

He smirked. "Need some eyedrops?"

"What do you mean?"

"It's a pretty straightforward question." He tilted my chin, gazing at me. His left cheekbone was smeared with eyeliner. "Nah, you're good."

"I need to get to class."

"So go to class," he said softly, dropping his hand. His lips twitched like he was about to laugh.

But I didn't want to go to class. I wanted to ask him what was so damn funny, or if he really liked Kari, or if he'd ever smoked pot. Anything, really. "What were you listening to in your car?"

His smile faded, and he shrugged. "Probably someone you don't like."

"Tell me anyway."

"So you can hate me more?"

"I don't . . . never mind." I brushed past him and headed toward the school, but he didn't follow.

" 'Bus Stop' by the Hollies," he called after me.

I was glad he couldn't see the cheesy grin on my face. Mom always played that song when she was in a good mood. And we'd sing an off-key rendition on every road trip. It was the number-two most-played song on my iPod.

7

Monday, September 10

History is boring. ~~My teacher talks too fast.~~ What am I supposed to write about? I've been at Samish High for a week now. Naomi is my only friend here. She doesn't treat me like I'm a freak. And she loves to talk and sing. Her words fill the gaps in my mind. She's always smiling too. But I don't think she's that happy.

My mom is broke, so we're stuck living with my grandma. But I don't really feel like writing about Grandma. I see her enough.

~~There's this boy~~

"Andrea Horvath?" the teacher asked.

I glanced up, dropping my pen. "Yeah?"

"You're wanted in Jackie Bartlett's office. Take your things, please."

Great, the school counselor. I'd rather have listened to Mrs. Heinz's skewed perception of U.S. history.

Justin was leaving when I got to Jackie's office. He hadn't dressed like me again, thankfully. But he had a slightly different look every day. Almost like he fished things blindly out of a suitcase. Today he wore a gray thermal and a pair of tattered jeans.

I wondered why he had to see the counselor—maybe he needed help picking colleges or something. He gave me a small smile and brushed past me. Like I was just another student. Nobody. And for some reason, I wanted to matter to him.

"Hi," I said.

He turned around and raised his eyebrows. "Am I hallucinating?"

"What do you mean?"

"You haven't looked at me all week."

"I—never mind." I turned on my heel and headed into Jackie's office. It was true that I buried my face in *Go Ask Alice* during English class and hid out in the library when Naomi ditched campus at lunch. But I didn't know what to say when I felt his eyes on me. Everything I thought of sounded stupid— like I couldn't possibly be interesting to someone like him.

"How are you, Andrea?" Jackie asked. She was lanky with dark hair and big teeth.

"Call me Drea." I slid into the plastic orange chair, but kept my backpack on.

"Fair enough. Feel free to dump your backpack. Can't be comfy sitting there like that."

"I'm fine," I said, looking at the array of pictures on her desk. Everything from black-and-white arty photos to smiling teens in the sunshine.

"Twix bar?"

"I don't like chocolate."

"Ah." She banged her drawer open. "I've got SweeTarts for the chocolate haters."

I took a couple packages from her—at least she had good taste in nonchocolate candy.

"So, you've been here about a week now. How's it going for you?"

I ripped at the paper and dropped a green SweeTart into my mouth. "It's fine."

"Getting used to all the rain?"

I sank into the chair. "Can we skip all the preliminary questions? I'm not having any problems in my classes. I've found my way around school just fine, and I've even made a friend."

"Have you seen a lot of counselors before?"

"Of course. You guys think people like me always need the extra help."

"People like you?"

I hated it when they pretended not to know what I was talking about. "Yep, I've got AS and ADHD—and whatever other acronym assigned to me. I wouldn't be here otherwise."

Jackie leaned forward and clasped her hands together. "And what do those *acronyms* mean to you?"

"They're a constant reminder that I'm a freak. That there's something wrong with me."

"Do you think there's something wrong with you?"

"I feel like . . ." I shut my eyes, trying to think of the words. "Like I can't be me if I don't want to be lonely. Nobody takes me seriously when they know."

"Do you feel singled out?"

"It's not a feeling. I *am* singled out. My mom told all my

teachers when I was diagnosed. They started speaking to me really slow, like I was retarded. Then this jerk-off in my history class found out somehow, and he kept asking me if I was an excellent driver. Then he told me they'd made a movie about someone like me. *Rain Man*. So I watched it."

She took a sip of her coffee without taking her eyes off me. "What did you think?"

"I thought it had nothing to do with me. I don't repeat things over and over. I don't count toothpicks. I know how to subtract fifty from a hundred."

"There are many different types of people on the autistic spectrum. Some end up being very successful out in the world— just like anyone else."

"Yeah, I know—so why do I need a label?"

"Have you ever Googled Asperger's? There's—"

"Yeah, it listed a bunch of random symptoms. Bad social skills, lack of eye contact, can't understand tone of voice, being overly interested in something—which makes no sense to me. Isn't wanting to learn a good thing? I think everyone should be passionate about something."

Jackie shut her eyes slightly and nodded. "What I was getting at was there are online communities for people with AS. A lot of people who probably feel like you do. If you want, you can just browse the boards. See what others are saying."

"I belong to a lot of music communities. I do just fine on those. We basically stay home all night and talk about our gear."

"And that's fine. But I still recommend you check out some online communities for Asperger's."

"I'll think about it." But I had already thought about it, looking for others online. I was afraid they'd be so weird I'd

feel as lost as I did at school—which meant I didn't fit in anywhere. "How often do I have to come here?"

"Once a week for now, more if you'd like. But it doesn't
sound like you need it."

"How about less?"

"We'll consider it. Any other questions for me?"

"Why was Justin Rocca here?"

She smiled and leaned back in her chair. "Surely a guidance
counselor veteran like yourself knows I can't tell you that. Is
he a friend of yours?"

"Not really. He's my partner in film class. But maybe he
told you that."

Jackie shrugged. "So what if he did? Does it matter?"

"No, I was just curious."

Her dark eyes combed my face for a second. They made
me squirm. "Then why don't you ask him?"

"I'm not comfortable doing that."

"Why?"

"We don't really talk that much." I wove my fingers
together and pressed down on my knuckles.

"Is that because you don't want to talk to him?"

"I don't know what to say to him." I looked away—I'd
already said too much. "He makes me feel stupid."

She cocked her head at me, giving me that concerned doctor
look. "How?"

"Sometimes it feels like he can see inside my head. Like he
knows that . . ." *I can't stop thinking about him, or that I
watch him in class sometimes.*

"Are you going to finish your thought?"

"No, forget it. I don't know what I'm saying."

Jackie lifted her blue mug again. "I think you do. You know, people aren't as closed off as they seem. Sometimes all it takes is a smile or a hello to break the ice. He probably finds you just as intimidating."

"Did he say that?"

"I have a dare for you, Drea. Say hello to someone today—it can be anyone. See if you get a response."

"That's dumb."

"Why? It's hello—simple, straightforward. No strings attached."

"I already said hi to Justin on his way out."

"How'd that work out for you?"

"He was surprised."

Jackie tapped her nails against her cup. The sound made me cringe. "Hey, it's a start."

I fought the urge to hide behind my book when Justin walked into English. I stared at his white tennis shoes as he approached his desk, straining to open my mouth. But hi came out more as a grunt.

He slid into his seat and turned to look at me. "You say something?"

"I said hi."

He smiled. I noticed a faint freckle on his upper lip. "Poe sucks." He motioned to my T-shirt.

"*You* suck." Poe was one of my favorite female artists. And she actually produced her own music—couldn't say that about most pop stars.

He poked my arm. "I was only kidding. My sister said she's amazing live. She saw her back in 2001."

"What's your favorite album?"

"*Haunted* is pretty awesome—can't say I've heard anything like it."

Kari looked at me over her shoulder. Her eyes moved to Justin. "Hey." She tapped her polished nails against his desk.

He turned to face her. "What's up?"

"You never called me back."

"I know, sorry. I—"

She moved closer and lowered her voice. "Can we talk at lunch?"

Mr. Duncan began his lecture before Justin could answer her. Kari rolled her eyes and spun around. I'd never been so glad to hear a teacher speak.

I stood in the parking lot like an idiot after school. Roger's egg car wasn't in its usual space. Just perfect.

Naomi wasn't by the fountain at lunch, and she never showed up to PE. My wrist still ached from volleyball. Choosing to slam one's flesh into a hard ball seemed wrong. How anyone enjoyed that was beyond me.

"Hey, Drea," a sharp voice said behind me.

My heart pounded as Kari approached me. "Hi," I mumbled.

"Have you seen Justin?"

"He was talking to the film teacher when I left class. Probably still there." I eyed the ground, hoping she'd go find him and leave me alone.

Out of the corner of my eye, I could see her studying me. Her arms were folded tightly across her stomach, toe tapping on the pavement.

"So"—she shifted her weight—"are you guys, like, seeing each other?"

That particular phrase always threw me. Whenever Mom said she was *seeing* someone, I always thought—well, duh.

"Not like *that*."

She wrinkled her nose at me. "What do you mean like *that*?"

"I mean, he's not my boyfriend."

"That's not what I was asking."

"I don't understand."

Kari rolled her eyes and pursed her lips. "I'm not in the mood for games. Did you guys hook up or not?"

I backed up a couple steps. "He's just my partner in film."

A white sedan pulled up, and the driver tapped the horn twice. I could make out Casey's long blond hair and broad shoulders.

Kari held a finger up, asking Casey to hang on. "If you see him on his way out, tell him to call me." She shook her head and got into the car, slamming the door. Casey revved the engine and sped out of the parking lot.

Slow footsteps emerged behind me, and I got the prickly feeling of someone staring at my back. I looked over my shoulder and met Justin's stare. What a convenient time to show up.

"Hey," he said, peering in the direction Casey's car went. "Sorry about that."

"About what?"

"That she was interrogating you about me." He shoved his hands into his pockets and kicked a rock.

"Are you hiding from her?"

He sighed, rolling his eyes up to the dull sky. "Kinda—yeah."

"Bad date?"

A smile tugged at his lips. "That's the problem. It wasn't a date."

"Why? Did you *want* it to be a date?"

He crinkled his brow at me and shook his head. "You're an odd duck, Drea." Before I could ask what the hell that meant, he continued. "I signed up for a camera the weekend after next. Mr. Diaz said everyone waits until the last minute, so I figured we'd beat the rush. Any ideas?"

"Not really. The only movies I've made are of sea lions, clouds, and my mom's retarded ex with my crappy HI-8."

"Hey, it's better than nothing." He scanned the parking lot. "You need a ride home?"

"It appears that way. But I can call someone."

"Someone, huh? You've got a lot of friends in a town you just moved to."

I looked away, my stomach tensing at the thought of being alone with him.

"Okay, suit yourself," he said. "Later."

Then again, getting a ride home from Justin seemed a lot more exciting than waiting for Mom or even worse—Grandma. "Wait," I called after him. "You can give me a ride home."

He turned around and walked backward with a grin. "Oh, can I? Thanks, I feel privileged."

I followed him to his car, scanning the shiny black paint. M3 gleamed back at me in silver. It looked like a 2006—333 horsepower. Not bad.

He held the passenger door open for me. "Don't worry, I don't bite on the first ride home."

I hesitated. "Huh?"

Justin rolled his eyes and waved me in. "Never mind."

I slid into the black leather seat, breathing in the faded stench of cigarettes. Probably from Kari. I didn't like picturing her in this seat.

He got into the driver's side and started the engine. A song with grinding guitars and piercing synthesizers roared through my ears, but he quickly turned it down and mumbled an apology.

"They've got a V-8 M3 now," I said.

He backed out of the parking space. "You don't strike me as a car fan."

"I used to read *Car and Driver* and *Motor Trend* a lot. Now I'm more into sound design."

"You've got some interesting hobbies. So—where do you live?" He pulled onto the main street.

"Make a left at the light."

"Can you give me a general area?"

"It's near the bay. That street you make a left on—"

"Holly?"

"Yeah. Keep going straight and then Holly turns into something else after you pass this really big church. I live three streets down from that."

He glanced over at me with wide eyes. "Oookay. Let me get this straight. I hang a left on Holly, and Holly turns into something else, hopefully another street. And you live on the third cross street after the church."

"Yeah, it's either the third or fourth."

He shook his head, smirking. "Please tell me you know the name of your street."

I looked out the window, my cheeks growing hot. I never paid attention to names—only landmarks and how many left or right turns it took to get there.

He touched my shoulder before shifting again. "Don't worry, we'll figure it out."

A few moments passed before he tapped a button on his wheel, turning the music back up. The beat was danceable, and

I liked the mix. Most modern songs overdid the compression to the point of killing any dynamic that once existed—they were just loud. Period.

"Who is this?"

He squinted at me as we pulled up to a red light. "Why—you hate it?"

"No, I kind of like it, actually."

"It's a band called Black Lab. They don't normally do electronica. It was kind of an experiment, but I like bands that take risks."

"Me too."

"Do you consider yourself a music snob?"

I couldn't help but smile. "Yes."

He raised his eyebrows at me. "Same here. *And* you lost points for not knowing Black Lab."

"Don't play the music game with me. I'll win." At least I did every time someone challenged me online.

"Oh." He shook his head. "*This* is gonna be good. Try me. Throw some names out."

"Porcupine Tree."

"I'm torn between 'Deadwing' and 'The Sound of Muzak' for my favorite song, but I think *In Absentia* is a better album."

"It was a little mellow for me. I preferred *Deadwing*—it was more visceral and dark."

"Of course." He rolled his eyes. "Okay, here's one for you. Puracane."

"My favorite song is 'Shouldn't Be Here.' "

"Because it's *dark* and *visceral*?"

"No, I can relate to it for some reason."

"Why? You wake up on a lot of random couches?"

"No, I just get it."

He tapped his finger against the steering wheel and gave me a sidelong glance. "Yeah, I know what you mean. Some melodies just talk to me. The lyrics don't matter."

We drove in silence for a minute. Brick buildings, kayak places, and bike riders whizzed by.

"So if you love cars so much, how come you don't drive?" he asked.

I focused on two older women in the car next to us. One had purple hair. "I don't have a license."

"Why not?"

"I kind of flunked the test." I didn't want to tell him there had actually been six of them.

"Kind of? We'll have to fix that."

"Are you going to take it for me?"

He chuckled. "No, but I'll give you free driving lessons."

"Um, I drive pretty bad. You really don't want to do that."

He pointed to my right. "There's the church."

"It's the street right after the white-and-black house."

"Drea, there are several that color."

"The one with all the yellow flowers in the yard."

He nodded and sped up. Maybe he just wanted to get rid of me.

"You live on Daisy Street for future reference," he said after we turned the corner.

"Thanks. It's that ugly, yellowy-green house on the right."

"I like your neighborhood. It's got character."

"It's just old."

He sighed, shaking his head. We pulled up next to the curb, and I was relieved to see Mom's Toyota missing from the driveway. She'd ask a million embarrassing questions if she saw Justin drop me off.

"So, um . . ."

"We need to figure out what we're doing for our film project," he said.

I avoided his gaze. "You could come in, I guess." After all, I *did* tell Mom we were working on a project together.

"I didn't mean now."

"Oh, okay. Well, bye, then." I pushed the door open and climbed out, sliding my backpack over my shoulder.

"Hey, I didn't say no." He ejected the Black Lab CD out of his player and waved it at me. "Want a copy?"

I attempted to smile even though my knees were shaking. "Yeah."

He shut off the car and hopped out, gazing at the trees lining the street.

I unlocked the door and prayed Grandma wasn't home. "Hello? Grandma?"

No answer. My muscles relaxed.

Justin followed me to the basement and made an approving sound when he spotted my guitars and Mac Pro. "Nice." He nodded at the computer. "Is that an eight-core?"

"No, it's an older dual-core. Got it off eBay." The setup had cost me years of birthday and holiday checks.

"Cool."

"I've got Final Cut, so we can edit the video here—i-if you want to."

He grinned and walked over to my work desk, scanning the effect pedals, wires, and boards in various piles.

"I'm, um, building some pedals. Hopefully, I can sell them later."

"I can see that." He seemed to have a permanent half smile when he was around me.

"Is that funny to you?"

"Not at all. If I played guitar, I'd ask you to build me one."

I walked over to my computer and jiggled my mouse to wake it up. The silver tower revved like a car engine—I loved that sound. Justin came up behind me, close enough to smell the gel in his hair. Just feeling his warmth made my knees weak again.

"Here," he said, slipping the CD case into my hand.

"Thanks." I stuck the CD into the drive, trying to block out the burning sensation on my skin. Mom told me I had a much bigger space bubble than most. Certain people really set it off, like Roger or some of my mom's boyfriends. The feeling wasn't much different than a spider crawling through my hair. But Justin was different. Just as intense, but warmer somehow. More pleasant.

"I thought we could do a music video for our project," he said.

"Yeah, we could work on a soundtrack and . . ." I didn't know if I wanted to work that closely with him. It would be easier to just stick a random song over the top, but there was no way I'd settle for that.

"But that would require working on music with me," he said. "Sure you can handle my greatness?"

I glared at him. "Let me be the judge of how *great* you are."

"Fair enough. Guess I'll have to use your crappy midi to prove my point."

"It gets the job done."

He sat in front of my midi keyboard, shaking his head. "You just don't get it."

My phone bellowed out of my backpack, making me jump.

"Does your cell always scare you?"

I ignored him as I dug the contraption out of my bag. He

really didn't need to know that my mom was the only person who ever called me.

"Hello?" I answered.

"Am I interrupting anything juicy?" Naomi's voice exploded into my ear.

I held the phone a few inches away. "I don't understand the question."

She sighed. "Uh, I'm standing right next to Justin's car. Did you guys decide to form a band without me?"

"No, we're discussing our film project."

Justin shook his head, grinning. Naomi's voice was loud enough for him to hear every word.

"Discussing it, are you? So proper."

"Why are we talking on a phone?" I asked, heading up the stairs. "I'm opening the front door." I snapped the phone shut.

Naomi stood on the porch wearing big sunglasses and a cheesy grin. Her purple hair jutted out in various directions.

"Did you get electrocuted?" I asked.

"No. I've been at Scott's for the last couple hours." She threw her arms around me, making my entire body stiffen. Her fingers dug into my back, and she rubbed her cheek against my velvet top. "You're soft, like a kitty."

I pushed her off me and backed away. "You're being weird."

"How's it going, Naomi?" Justin leaned against the wall behind me, his arms folded across his chest.

Naomi walked over and hugged him. "You feel nice too. Your thermal is all fuzzy." She ran her hands down his arms.

He frowned and gave her an awkward hug back. "What are you on? E?"

"Maybe." She giggled and headed downstairs.

"What's going on?" I asked.

Justin rolled his eyes at me. "If you have any bottled water, bring it downstairs. If not, use the tap."

After he followed her, I rummaged through Grandma's alphabetized pantry and found a jug on the floor. I'd remembered hearing girls talk about E back in San Francisco. It usually involved stories of being up all night or messing around with some *hot* guy.

"This is all I could find," I said, making my way downstairs.

Naomi was doing what looked like ballet moves across the cement floor. Justin grabbed the water from me and peeled off the seal.

"Sip on this." He raised the bottle at her and set it near the steps.

"Yeah, I know. Scott told me to drink lots of water, blah blah." She continued to twirl like she did in the greenbelt.

"Who's Scott?" Justin asked, sitting in front of my midi keyboard.

"A loser," I said.

"Yeah, but he's a loser who gave me two of these for free." She walked over to me, opening her hand to reveal two small pills with weird etchings on them. "Want one?"

Great, more pills. I had enough of those in my life. "Th-those never really worked for me."

"God, am I like the last person on earth to try E? You want one, Justin?"

He glanced at me and then turned around, busying himself with the silent midi keys. "No, thanks."

"You guys suck." She shrugged and stuffed the pills back into her jean pocket. "More for me."

"Don't take them all at once," Justin said.

"Okay, Dad." She wrinkled her nose at him and grinned at me. "Have you ever had sex on it?"

I glanced at Justin, knowing my cheeks were probably bright red. There had to be something I could say that didn't make me sound like a total loser. "My ex-boyfriend took me skydiving once."

Naomi's eyes widened. "Whoa."

Justin squinted at me. "Don't you usually have to be eighteen for that?"

"I don't think so," I said.

"Right." He smirked. "Are you going to give me sound here or what?"

I leaned in front of my computer and opened Logic, the recording program I used. "I've got a bunch of samples—want me to use the Bösendorfer?" My hands shook. I didn't understand how people could lie all the time; it took an immense amount of energy.

"It doesn't matter. They all sound like shit to me. Just put a little reverb on it."

"I can make it sound good," I insisted, sticking the sampler on a track and fiddling with the EQ.

"I've got the real thing, Drea. Don't try too hard."

"Do you prefer bright or dark 'verb? Probably bright, huh?"

He grinned. "You're the expert."

It felt weird to have someone watching me, seeing my process. Naomi didn't seem picky, but what if Justin hated my style? What if I hated his?

Naomi came up behind Justin and rubbed his shoulders. She'd perched her sunglasses on top of her head. "And I have no clue what you two are talking about."

He shut his eyes and smiled. For some reason, that really bugged me.

She leaned toward his ear. "Can I ask you a personal question?"

"Do you ask anything *but* personal questions?" He tried out a couple notes and nodded at me. "Not bad—I'll give you that."

Naomi leaned over and whispered something in his ear. I couldn't quite make out what, but it had my name in it.

He pulled away from her touch and focused on the keys. "How about I give you something to dance to?"

She squatted next to him with a smirk. "You're a virgin, aren't you?" It sounded more like a statement than a question.

He played an E-minor chord. "Go dance, Naomi."

I wondered if he felt embarrassed like I did when she asked those questions. Maybe he was like me and didn't want people to know what a dork he was.

"It's okay." She pinched his cheek. "Drea's a great kisser—I speak from experience. I'm sure she can show you a few other things too."

"Naomi!" At that moment, I really wanted to die. Or maybe hit her with a baseball bat. "Would you shut up?"

Justin raised his eyebrows, an odd smile on his face.

Naomi rolled her eyes at me. "It's not a big deal, Drea. It probably turns him on."

"Not really," he said, tapping the high keys gently. "Do you think you're the first straight girl to kiss another girl for shock value?"

"We were by ourselves. And what makes you think I'm straight?" she asked.

"Because I've got amazing gaydar."

"I don't put labels on myself," she said. "I just am."

"Okay, so go *be* over there." He waved toward the open space in front of my bed.

Naomi ruffled my hair before collapsing on the bed, her legs dangling over the side. I settled into my computer chair, hoping she'd be quiet for a while.

Justin began with a chord progression that instantly connected with me. My fingertips buzzed with anticipation, and I heard a billion different guitar melodies over the top. Maybe a gentle synth—bell-like without the piercing edge. He closed his eyes as each chord rang out, letting them bleed together and create the perfect mix of colors. Blue entwined with varying shades of gray. Like the drizzle outside. Comforting but a little sad. Then he played a fast, erratic melody with his right hand. Every note made me shiver, each one building into something even more amazing.

Naomi rolled off the bed, humming a melody of her own over the top. She walked up behind Justin and tapped his shoulder. "Can you play just the chords?"

"Sure," he said, going back to the original progression.

She closed her eyes, fingers tapping against her ripped jeans. Her lips moved slightly with each chord change. "She smiles with grace, but no one recalls her face," she sang. "Invisible . . . carved between the walls."

I guessed at Justin's tempo, setting it around 100bpm, and fished around for some drum samples. Most of the time I'd start with a loop that felt right—couldn't explain why. Then I'd EQ the sound so it fit the tone of the song and add more drum samples from there. This song had a real trip-hop feel to it— slow, dark, and catchy. I found a bouncy beat and distorted the drums a bit. Naomi could play a live beat later, and I'd combine the two.

"I like that," Justin said to me.

"Tempo okay?"

He nodded. "I can work with it."

Naomi still had her eyes shut, nodding to the beat now. "She knows her place in this world. She can tear down its walls, and still nobody knows her name."

Justin stopped playing and shook his head. "You've got an incredible voice, Naomi."

She bit her lip, eyeing both of us. "Really? I don't sound stupid?"

"No," I said. "You're giving me chills—both of you are." I walked over and opened the case of my twelve-string acoustic. Another cheap and rare find from an online acquaintance.

Justin raised his eyebrows at my guitar. "Interesting choice."

"Start again," I said, setting the drums to loop mode and cranking the volume.

Layering the guitar chords on top of the piano gave the song a dreamy atmosphere. But Justin's melody and Naomi's vocals took the song to a place I could never go on my own. It tore at my gut and haunted my mind until all I wanted to do was get lost in it for hours. After our third time through, I decided to record the piano and guitar. Naomi insisted on reworking her lyrics before recording.

"Okay, Drea? If you don't let Justin join our band, I'm seriously going to smack you," Naomi decided.

I stared back at my computer screen, wanting nothing more but too afraid to ask. "You can join—if you want to."

"Nah, I've got better things to do," he said.

I swiveled to look at his grinning face.

"Smile, I'm only kidding."

I didn't find it very funny. He obviously had no idea how hard this was for me.

"But I'm only joining on two conditions," he said. "One, I get to use my keyboard. And two, nobody shows up to practice wasted."

"Fine by me," I said.

"Hey," Naomi pouted, "I sang better today than I ever have."

"That's what it seems like. Trust me, I've been in bands before. It always becomes a problem." He looked down at his hands. "Anyway, I'm digging our sound so far. Reminds me a little of Portishead."

"What did you play before?" I asked.

"You name it. Mostly metal, though."

"With a piano?" Naomi picked up the water bottle and took a big gulp.

He shrugged. "Why not? Sounds like you need to expand your horizons."

"She does."

Naomi held her hands up. "Hey, I already told you I'm clueless, Drea." She scanned the room. "So, why aren't these walls painted yet?"

"I was going to pick up some paint this weekend and do it."

"Okay, I'm *so* helping! I'll bring *Ferris Bueller*—we'll make a slumber party out of it." She smiled at Justin. "Wanna join us?"

He chuckled and stood up. "No, thanks. I've gotta work."

Her eyes widened. "You work?"

"Yeah, believe it or not. The rich boy works. Speaking of which"—he looked down at his watch—"I'm already running late."

"How'd you score a job here so fast? I've been looking all summer," Naomi said.

"My brother-in-law runs a computer repair shop on Lakeway. I'm his newest tech."

I ejected his CD out of the computer and handed it back to him. "Well, um, thanks for the Black Lab and the ride and stuff."

He studied me for a moment, his eyes intense with something I couldn't even pinpoint.

"She's kind of adorable, isn't she?" Naomi asked.

I focused on his tennis shoes. Dirt was caked around the rims, and one of his laces was coming loose.

"Yeah, she's kind of a lot of things." His voice was soft, like he meant it as a compliment. But a lot of things could mean, well, *anything.*

"You should double knot your laces." I pointed at his shoes.

Naomi giggled and plopped on my bed again, and Justin let out what sounded like a soft laugh. I looked up at him hesitantly.

"I'll keep that in mind," he said, smirking. "I'm off Friday, though. We should—"

"Make out!" Naomi shouted.

Justin rolled his eyes. "Practice. And come up with a name for our band." He brushed his fingers against my arm. "See you later."

"See ya." The sensation of his brief touch traveled to my fingertips.

Naomi had the decency to wait until he left before announcing her thoughts. "Oh my God, he totally wants you! You are so lucky."

8

ON WEDNESDAY, Naomi insisted on getting a pint of cookie dough ice cream after Justin dropped us off. I hated that he had work. All I'd wanted to do since Monday was make music with both of them.

Naomi kept trying to tickle me as we walked to the grocery store. It made me feel like crawling out of my skin.

"Stop!" I said finally.

Her hands went up. "God, you don't have to freak out like that."

"I really hate being tickled."

She kicked a rock in front of her. "I feel like there's something you aren't telling me."

My heart sped up a little. We got to the end of our street and rounded the corner. "What do you mean?"

She moved a little closer to me. "Well, if you ever want to talk about, you know, whatever, I'm here, okay? You can tell me anything."

Right then, I wanted to tell her. But the thought of trying to explain everything I wasn't made me cringe inside. All it would take was for her to hear the term *autistic*. And she'd think the worst, like that kid in my class last spring. What if she thought I was retarded? I couldn't risk it.

Naomi decided she wanted rocky road when we walked into the ice cream aisle. She grabbed a pint, studied it, and then put it back. "Actually, cookie dough still sounds better. You like that, right?"

"It's got chocolate chips in it."

She rolled her eyes. "Okay, what kind will you eat?"

"I like vanilla."

She wrinkled her nose at me. "But what do you put on it? Granola? Strawberry sauce?"

"I just eat it plain."

"Oh my God, no! That's so boring. I'll go crazy."

"Then get whatever. I don't need to eat it."

She grabbed a vanilla pint out of the freezer and tossed it in the basket. "No way am I pigging out alone. I'll just get some chocolate sauce to put on mine."

I plucked it out. "You shouldn't grab the first one."

"Okay, *why*?"

This wouldn't be easy to explain. It was just something I had to do. Somewhere along the line I'd convinced myself that the first package on every shelf was contaminated or damaged somehow. The SNRI the psychiatrist prescribed was supposed to help with my more obsessive behaviors, but antidepressants took weeks to start working. "This one was leaking," I said, shoving it back in the freezer and reaching for the next pint.

She took it from me, shaking her head. "It looked just fine to me."

"Wait." I snatched the pint back and scanned it. "You should always check the date on food before you buy it."

"Drea, it's ice cream. It doesn't expire."

"Yes, it does. See? Right here."

"Awesome, can we move on now before it melts?"

I nodded and tried to mimic one of her wide smiles. She didn't grin back that time.

When we got back to my house, I made Naomi go downstairs. If Grandma saw us eating ice cream before dinner, she'd flip out. Not to mention, no food was allowed outside the kitchen.

I had about two spoonfuls before the nausea set in, and I sat against my headboard. The new ADHD meds had yet to improve my appetite.

Naomi devoured another bite and squirted chocolate sauce in her mouth. "No wonder you're so skinny. You never eat." She sat on my bed and licked the remaining sludge from the spoon.

"I eat. I'm just not hungry right now."

She took another bite, closing her eyes. I wished I knew what that felt like—to really enjoy something. Grandma's cooking was horrid, but liking something meant I tolerated it. The texture or spices didn't make me gag.

Naomi put the ice cream on the floor and scooted next to me, close enough so our shoulders touched. "Want to make out?" she asked with a smile.

"No."

"Gee"—she leaned harder into me—"tell me how you really feel."

I moved away so we had a few inches of space between us. "I just did."

"I was only kidding. You don't do it for me, either. Can we still be friends?" She giggled.

I looked at her. The sparkles on her eyelids matched her blue irises. "Of course. You want to, right? Be my friend?"

Her grin faded as she studied my face. "Duh. You're real, you know?"

"Last time I checked."

Naomi laughed and rested her head against my shoulder. It made me stiffen at first, but I relaxed as she spoke.

She told me about the cross-country roadtrip in her head. It involved a fast car with the top down. Didn't matter what kind of car, just as long as it was black and fast. A guy with dark blue eyes and *golden* hair, not blond, would be driving. But he'd let her take the wheel at least half the time. They'd get lost in the mountains at least once and keep each other warm all night. And they'd take pictures of every cool moment. The trucker dives, the cheap motels, the scenery whizzing by—everything would be recorded forever.

"And when we fought," she continued, "we'd have amazing make-up sex in the back seat."

My body tensed at her words. That wasn't something I wanted to picture.

"Then afterward," she sighed, "we'd split a doobie and fall asleep under the stars—or on a rickety hotel bed. Whatever we could afford that night."

"A doobie?"

"Yeah, yeah. No drugs for you, right?" She nudged me. "Little Miss Squeaky Clean."

I looked away, clutching the cover underneath me. "Drugs don't do for me what they do for you."

"What's *your* dream?" she asked.

"My dream?"

"Yeah, what is one thing you want to do before you die?"

I wanted to get through another day without being found out. I wanted Naomi and Justin to like me. I wanted to experience a real kiss and see those stars everyone talked about. "I'm pretty simple, really. I want to produce music and make it sound just the way I hear it. So many songs are missing that vibration, the kind that moves through my body and makes the world vivid. I want to see colors I never knew existed."

She stared at me for a few seconds, running her finger along her mouth. "That's exactly what I love about being high. I guess music is your drug of choice."

I nodded and smiled. It was good to feel understood, even for just a moment.

After she left, I got back to work on my wah pedal. But my brain wouldn't shut off enough to focus. I kept going over the whole afternoon with Naomi. How I could've acted cooler, more relaxed, like her. Words just flew out of her mouth. She didn't have to think about what she said or make anything up. But I was constantly on edge, trying to cover my mistakes. I had to think about *everything*.

Keep my voice neutral. Sometimes people thought I was being snippy when I wasn't. Remember to smile. Laugh when she laughs. Pretend to know about boys.

My entire body felt weak and my eyes scratchy. Trying to be *normal* was tiring. I sat in front of my computer and stared at the Google logo on my browser. I wondered what other people in my situation did.

I typed in the words and bit my lip. *Asperger's community*. Maybe there was nobody who completely understood. But I had to find out.

I found a link to a message board that had many different sections, one being relationships. A thread called Friendship with an NT caught my eye, so I clicked on the heading and scanned the page. Apparently, NT stood for *neurotypical*, which was a term that referred to the so-called neurologically normal. I liked the second half of the word—typical. Some of the things people said about NTs made me nod and smile, especially when they talked about how an NT could be obsessive too. Why was it considered normal for a girl to live for fashion and makeup, but not car engines or bugs? And what about sports fanatics? My mom had a boyfriend who would flip out if he missed even a minute of a football game. Wouldn't that be what doctors considered autistic behavior?

My eyes caught the topic Coming Out. I clicked on the link, skimming the post.

I told my NT friend about me yesterday. Now she's asking a million questions. She keeps adding "do you understand?" at the end of her sentences. I told her I was the same person she met three months ago. She said she knows, but wants to make sure I get everything she says. And if I don't, to tell her. I hate it. I hate that she treats me like a completely different person.

I let my breath out slowly. Not what I wanted to read.

Naomi decided to blow off our band practice for Scott on Friday, leaving Justin and me alone in the parking lot. This sucked, since Justin had offered to help us move her drum set to my basement.

"Maybe I should give you those driving lessons instead," he said.

"I really don't think that's a good idea."

119

He opened the door for me. I was beginning to savor the earthy smell of his seats. "Why? Can't drive a stick?"

"Um—I have issues with the gas and the brake."

He smirked and pushed the door shut. This was the fourth time he'd given me a ride home. But Naomi was with us the last two times. She usually did most of the talking.

Justin slid into his seat, still grinning. "Does your mom drive an automatic?"

"Yeah, why?"

"Would she let us borrow her car?"

"Possibly, if we stay in a very empty parking lot. She said that's the only way she'd get in a car with me."

He scrunched up his face and started the engine. "Ouch."

I was beginning to enjoy driving down Holly Street and watching all the people milling around on the sidewalks. Shopping bags, dreadlocks, grins, steaming coffee cups, and "give me money" signs—all of it streamed by like a peep show into another world. "We could work on a song. Naomi can do the vox later," I said.

"I'll drop you at home so you can prepare yourself for a grueling driving lesson." He looked over at me as we stopped at a red light. "Then I'll run back to my place and get my keyboard. We'll jam later."

"We can go to your place now." I rolled my eyes. "I don't need time to prepare."

"Nah, I live in the opposite direction. Take a shower or something—I'll be back in no time."

I tilted my head to sniff my armpits. Did I remember to put deodorant on this morning? "I want to see your Bösendorfer."

"You will one of these days." He shifted down and bit his

lip. "My house is kind of a mess right now." We made a right onto my street a little faster than necessary.

I pushed the door open after he pulled up to the curb. "See you in a bit, then?"

He winked. "Give me ten minutes."

I was going to head straight for the shower. Maybe he was hinting at something. People did that.

But Mom greeted me at the front door. "Your friend has a nice car."

"I guess." I pushed past her.

"Where are you going?"

"Bathroom," I said, picking up speed. "He'll be back— we're going to work on our film project."

"I see."

I looked over my shoulder and cringed at the grin on her face. It was like she knew exactly how I felt around him. She'd always told me that it would happen. *One of these days, some lucky boy is going to give you butterflies in your stomach. Just wait.* I'd told her to keep dreaming.

Warm rays of water trickled down my neck a few minutes later. Part of me couldn't help but think what if—what if Naomi was right and Justin *wanted* me? I'd think he would've told me or asked me out at least. Maybe Naomi was wrong. She was definitely wrong about Scott.

By the time I got out of the shower, Justin was sitting at the kitchen table with Mom. Just great.

"What are you guys talking about?"

Mom gave me that knowing smile again. "I was going over the rules with your driver's ed instructor here."

I glanced from her to Justin. He smiled at me like nothing

was different, but I never did pick up on subtle body language. For all I knew, she had told him all about my refusal to take baths when I was younger. "You're letting us borrow your car?" I asked Mom.

She nodded.

Justin downed the glass of water in front of him and drummed his hands against the table.

"Can we go now?" I didn't want to give Mom the chance to say anything more to him.

"Sure," Mom said. "And you're welcome."

I looked away. "Thank you. . . ."

"Be careful. Pay attention to what he says." She stood up and tried to give me a hug.

I pulled away from her. "Mom, please."

I studied Justin's face after we got into the car. He handled her keys like they might break and carefully turned the ignition.

"What did my mom say to you?"

He gave me a sidelong glance. That dimple appeared on his left cheek. "She showed me some of your baby pictures. There was one with cake all over your face and one with bubbles on your head in the tub. Too cute."

"*What?*" If I had a picture with bubbles on my head, it needed to be destroyed immediately.

He backed out of the driveway and chuckled. "I'm kidding. She told me to stick to parking lots only and to bring her car back in one piece."

"Did she say anything else?"

"Why? Is there something she should've told me?" He raised his eyebrows.

"No. She says stupid stuff sometimes, that's all." I looked out the window. We were heading uphill toward the freeway.

"She worries a lot, huh?"

"Did your mom freak out over letting you drive?"

Justin didn't look at me this time. He focused on the car in front of us. "I'm sure she would've."

"Would've?"

We pulled up to a red light. "She died when I was twelve."

My mouth fell open to speak, but I didn't know what to say. The only person I knew who died was my grandfather, and I knew him as the guy who sat in a wheelchair and wore diapers. I didn't depend on him or talk to him every day like I did Mom. "Why? I mean, how—what happened?"

"Lung cancer—and no, she didn't smoke." He drummed the steering wheel, still not looking at me.

Sometimes I avoided eye contact when I didn't know how to answer a question. Maybe he didn't want to talk about his mom, like Naomi didn't want to talk about hers. "Where are you taking me?"

A little smile played at his lips. "You'll see."

We headed south toward the mountains. Trees lined every inch of the highway. Some of the leaves were fading into shades of orange and yellow. Justin slowed as we neared a sign that read LAKE PADDEN.

"There's a trail that goes around the lake. It's really pretty," he said.

Walls of evergreens sheltered the parking lot we pulled into. A baseball diamond and tennis court sat in front of an oblong lake. The water resembled glass under the low clouds.

Justin got out of the driver's side to switch with me, but my legs froze. I couldn't tell my left from my right when I got nervous. Sometimes I'd start laughing or I'd go into a full-blown panic attack. I'd failed all six driving tests within the first five minutes.

He held the door open for me, a comforting smile on his face.

"Maybe we can go for a walk instead?" I suggested.

"You can do this. Now scoot over or I'll sit on your lap."

Before I could protest, he gripped the edges of the seat and moved toward me. Our faces were inches apart. He had gold flecks in his eyes. They were like spots of color in a black-and-white photograph.

"I mean it," he whispered.

I lifted my shaking limbs over the shifter and settled into the driver's seat.

After we got the car home, miraculously in one piece, Justin deemed me a parking lot master. He'd made me park and back out what seemed like a billion times—then he had me do something called a donut. That was fun at least.

We went down to the basement so Justin could rerecord the piano part to our first song. Naomi had decided to call it "Invisible."

"I think you're ready to cruise the neighborhood," Justin said, setting up his keyboard.

I shook my head at him, a laugh escaping my lips. "Weirdo."

"I stockpile my cheesy lines just for you." He smirked and sat down in front of his keyboard. "I'm ready when you are."

I created a new track in Logic and hit record. "Go ahead."

Justin dove right in, playing softly at first. I closed my eyes and allowed the melody to wash over my skin. Good music was something I could feel from head to toe. It calmed me, made me feel safe. I wouldn't have minded if he wanted to do a hundred takes. But he settled for three.

"I thought up a good band name," I said when he finished. "M3—like your car. Since there's three of us and stuff."

"It's simple. I like it." Justin picked up his chair and moved it next to me. "Naomi better finish the vocals. This song is going to be incredible."

"We should make a band page on MySpace and some other music sites. I belong to this indie music site called Slip Music. It's a really supportive community."

"I'm game." He nudged me and motioned to my computer screen. "So what do you do in Logic? Show me how a producer works."

I smiled—if there was one thing I had no problems talking about, it was music production and synthesis. I soloed Naomi's vocals and explained how I'd go about making them sound better. "In this case I added reverb to the track—gives it more space. And then I added some delay, but automated it to only work on certain words."

Justin leaned in. The heat from his body made the hairs on my arm stand up. "I like that. It adds a lot of depth to her voice."

I clicked on the guitar track with a shaky finger. "There's this program called Guitar Rig, which is like a virtual guitar studio. I can approximate most guitar sounds with it, but nothing beats playing through a loud amp."

"Cool." His voice was soft, but inches from my ear.

My breath quickened. I moved on to how I created synths. "I see sounds in colors, and oscillators are like my primary colors.

I start mixing them together, then I add a filter or two and get the core sound. Effects, LFOs, and modulation matrixes—"

"Drea"—he put his hand on my arm—"you lost me."

"Oh, sorry. Sometimes I get started and can't shut up." Another laugh escaped my mouth.

"Hey." He touched my cheek, running his fingers along my jawline.

A shiver ran down my back. I hoped my breath didn't smell like the Doritos I ate after PE. Mom always carried a pack of gum on dates.

He dropped his hand and smiled. "I think you're pretty damn amazing, regardless."

"Oh, um . . ." My knee slammed against my keyboard. "Thanks."

His lips parted as if he wanted to say something else.

"So . . . ," I said.

Justin stood up, looking at the staircase. "I need to take off. Thanks for the mini lesson though. I enjoyed it."

The air suddenly felt cold around me, and my shoulders sagged. I got up and tried my best to smile at him.

Without warning, he wrapped his arms around my waist. I sucked in my breath, nuzzling my head against his chest. His thermal smelled sweet, like fabric softener.

"Have fun this weekend." His lips brushed against my ear.

"You too." I tightened my grip, not wanting to let go.

"See ya." He pulled away and headed up the stairs—two steps at a time.

9

Even Grandma couldn't stop me from smiling Saturday morning. I devoured the grainy cereal she'd put in front of me and thought about Justin—how he made me feel.

Grandma looked at my empty bowl, her eyebrows pinched together. She pointed to the pink capsule she'd set next to my food: my SNRI. "You haven't taken that yet."

I put the pill in my mouth, choking it down with water.

She narrowed her hazel eyes at me. "That helping you any?"

"I don't know. I just started taking it." I took my bowl and put it in the sink.

"What's it supposed to do?"

"Make me less anxious and depressed. But most of them just make me tired."

"I'm going to start assigning you chores, Andrea. My back isn't as good as it used to be. Maybe that'll wake you up."

I turned, facing her. "What?" Mom used to tell me stories about Grandma making her scrub the kitchen floor until every inch sparkled. One time she forced Mom to remake her bed ten times.

"You heard me." She smiled. It looked wicked. "I saw your mother doing your laundry last night. Sixteen years old and you don't know how to wash your own clothes?" She clucked her tongue.

I shrugged. The truth was Mom never trusted me with the clothes. Not since I got bleach spots on half her jeans and turned every white pair of underwear pink.

Grandma pushed a folded piece of paper across her glitter-ridden table. "I wrote down what I want you to do today. And gave you directions on how to do it."

I sighed and picked up the yellow paper. Her purple cursive neatly spelled out each step.

"I'd follow that to every crossed *T* if I were you. Because I'll make you do each thing over again until you get it right."

Hushed voices in the entranceway caught my attention. I peered around the corner to see Mom hugging some guy with dark hair and a white shirt. She held a blue robe tightly around her body and pecked him on the cheek.

"What are you looking at, Andrea?" Grandma's voice was loud enough to get their attention. Mom pointed in Grandma's direction and put a finger to her lips, telling me to stay quiet. The man smiled and waved before edging himself out the door.

I couldn't believe Mom was sneaking around like she was my age. I wonder why they didn't go to his place. Mom came up behind me, squeezing my shoulders. I pulled away from her because I could smell *his* cologne. Whoever he was.

"You're up early," she said to me.

"Did your guest leave?" Grandma asked. She scrunched her lips into a tiny circle.

Mom tucked a lock of messy hair behind her ear, and her cheek twitched. "My guest?"

"Yes, Juliana. The strange man who was going through my refrigerator at one A.M."

"Oh, Mom." She rolled her eyes and chuckled like it was no big deal.

"What were you thinking? He could've killed all of us in our beds. Have you checked your purse? He might have stolen your wallet."

"He's a local dentist, and he drives a Benz. I highly doubt we have anything here he'd want."

"I don't want strangers spending the night in my house. You have no idea—"

"Point taken. Let's move on." Mom rubbed her eyes and poured herself a cup of lukewarm coffee.

Grandma cleared her throat. "I've given Andrea some chores today." She shifted her glare to me. "You can start by vacuuming the living room and hallway."

Mom took a sip of coffee, wrinkling her nose. "She can't tolerate the noise."

"Can't or won't?"

"I'll do something else, but I'm not vacuuming." Every time Mom vacuumed, I'd shut myself in my room and put headphones on. The high, whiny noise pierced every nerve in my body and made my hair stand on end. And the crackling sound really got to me. Like tiny electric shocks. When I was little, I'd cover my ears and rock in the corner until it stopped.

"That's the most ridiculous thing I've ever heard," Grandma said. "This is why we have kids like Naomi Quinn running wild—no discipline. No responsibilities."

"It's not about that, Mom. Drea doesn't process sound normally."

I tossed the paper on the table and left the kitchen, heading right for the basement. They'd had this discussion at least six times since we moved in. Being spoiled versus having a disorder. I didn't like either argument. What was so wrong with just being me? Disliking vacuum noise wasn't any more bizarre than hating pickles or roller coasters.

I speed-dialed Naomi's number on my cell and counted the seconds until I heard her voice. She'd make some joke about Grandma or tease me about Justin. But she never tried to fix me.

"Hello?" Naomi's voice was hoarse and muffled.

"Hey, you should come over now."

"Huh?" There was a loud rustling sound. "God, Drea. It's nine A.M. Call me later."

"I thought you wanted to hang out today."

She cursed and sighed into the phone. "Yeah, *later*. I've been asleep for, like, three hours." With that her breathing was cut off.

"Hello?" I glanced at my phone. Call ended, it read. I'd messed up again.

"Drea, honey?" Mom's slippers padded down the stairs.

"What?"

She walked over to my bed and sat down with that squinty look in her brown eyes. Usually it meant we were moving again, or she'd lost her job. "Grandma's not bending on this one." She handed me the yellow slip of paper.

Chores to be done every morning:

1. Make your bed.

2. Clean up any mess you've made in the bathroom getting ready. That includes putting your dirty clothes in the hamper.

3. Unload the dishwasher. Then reload it with any dirty dishes before you leave.

This was followed by a page-long description of how to vacuum.

"Fine, I'll do that other stuff, but I'm not vacuuming."

Mom put her hand over mine. "Maybe you can wear some headphones—turn the music up real loud. I've got some ear plugs you can use."

"Just tell her I'm not doing it."

She rubbed her temples, exhaling sharply. "We need to keep the peace until I can afford a deposit on an apartment, okay?"

I nodded, knowing what she'd say next. Same old story. Compromise or live in her car.

Mom reached down and squeezed my hand. "You deserve better, baby." Her voice was strained and muffled.

"Quit saying that."

"I just wish I could give you more. The depression hit me bad in San Francisco. I couldn't pull out of it. And I really am sorry."

"I know." I twisted my green quilt around my finger until it went numb.

She wiped her eyes. "I got that job at the law firm. Start Monday. We'll be out of here soon. And I promise that we'll stay put for a while. Do you want to finish high school here?"

"Don't make promises you can't keep."

Mom cupped my face with both hands, forcing me to look into her watery eyes. "I promise I'm going to do everything I can to keep us here. The paralegal there is retiring soon, and she offered to train me. That would be a really good thing for us."

"Do you even want to be a paralegal?"

She dropped her hands and shook her head. "It's a lot better than any other options I've had in the past. And the pay isn't bad. Enough to live on our own—just you and me." Mom sighed and tousled my hair. "I'm going in the shower. Let me know if you need any help."

I could handle the vacuum noise for about five seconds before I had to shut it off. Even with sound-canceling headphones blaring my favorite songs, the squeal cut through, making me feel like I was being zapped from the inside. My skin itched, and I feared that the bulging bag would explode. I sat on the couch and hugged myself.

"Doesn't sound like you're making much progress out there!" Grandma called from the kitchen. She had a mini TV with antennas on the kitchen counter. The buzzing from the crappy signal filtered throughout the house.

I pulled my phone from my pocket and thought about calling Naomi. But she'd already hung up on me once. Justin's name stared back at me from my address book. The letters alone made my stomach flutter. We'd exchanged numbers a couple days ago, but he'd yet to call me. Would it be weird if I called him?

I pressed dial and squeezed my eyes shut.

"Hello?" he answered.

I opened my mouth to speak, but nothing came out.

"Drea?"

"Um, hi!"

"What's up?" His voice sounded deeper on the phone.

"I have to vacuum."

"That's . . . nice?"

"Does your family ever drive you insane?"

"All the time."

"Andrea, I still don't hear that vacuum!"

He laughed softly. "I dig your grandma."

"Why? I want to buy her a muzzle."

"I like how she just doesn't care. But I can see how she'd drive you nuts."

"You've never met her."

"What can I say? The comment about garbage on the walls at the café won me over."

Silence. He was probably wondering why I called him.

"You and Naomi still doing that movie night thing tonight?"

"I think so. She's asleep." *Ask questions, Drea.* "Are you doing anything after work?"

"Why?" His voice got softer. "You asking me out?"

My heart jumped in my chest. "Like on a date? No, I wouldn't do that. I mean—I've done that, but I wasn't asking you. Um . . ." It was official. I sucked at the phone thing.

"So let me clarify. That's a no, right?"

"No. I mean—yes. Yes, that's right."

He chuckled again. "I've never met anyone like you."

I swallowed hard. "Is that bad?"

"No and—yes."

"Um . . ."

"No, because I really like that about you. And yes. For the same reason."

"Huh?"

He sighed into the phone. "Nothing. It's not bad, Drea."

Grandma appeared in the living room, hands on her bony hips. "Mobile phones don't vacuum living rooms. Get off right now."

"Sounds like you should go," he said. "I'll talk to you later."

"Okay, bye." I flipped the phone shut and looked at Grandma. "I can use this phone when I want to—it's mine."

"And that's a big part of your problem. You're used to getting your way all the time."

"If that was the case, we wouldn't be living with you."

Grandma's mouth dropped open, but Mom walked in before she could speak. "She didn't mean it. Right, Drea?"

"She needs a good paddle on the behind," Grandma said.

"Give me that phone," Mom said, holding her hand out to me.

"What? No." I hid it behind my back.

"I said give it to me!" Her voice made me jump. She rarely yelled like that.

I slowly held the phone out to her, avoiding her dark eyes.

Mom ripped the cell from my hands. "You'll get it back when you finish your chores. And only then." I opened my mouth to protest, but she cut me off. "Apologize to Grandma."

"For what? She interrupted my phone conversation."

"Say you're sorry, or Naomi can't come over later."

What was the point of that? It wasn't like I'd mean it. "But I'm not sorry."

Grandma shook her head. "You should make her stay in her room for the rest of the weekend. And unplug her computer too."

"Mother, please. Just let me handle this, okay?"

"I'm not going to tolerate this in my house, Juliana." Grandma retreated into the kitchen, turning up whatever news program she had on.

Mom walked over and knelt in front of me. "Drea, please," she whispered. "Stop pushing her."

"Don't make me say things I don't mean."

"Remember what we talked about in San Francisco? About letting things go? Apologizing to her will keep her out of your hair."

"I don't care."

"Drea, she took us into her home, and she didn't have to. Do you understand that? She's tough to be around, yes. But right now, she's all we have."

I understood why I was supposed to appreciate Grandma. And I did—a little bit. But it didn't mean she could force me to do things. "Fine, I'll do it. For *you*."

"Thank you."

"But I'm not vacuuming. I can't. It hurts."

She sighed. "Okay, I'll talk to her. But you have to finish the rest of your chores." She held up my phone. "Then you'll get this back."

Grandma ignored me when I walked into the kitchen. That's how I knew she was really angry. She almost always had something to say.

I focused on the beige tile below my feet. Pale brown lines carved out triangles and squares. "I'm sorry I said that to you. I appreciate you letting us stay here."

She nodded but kept her eyes on the television. Her shoulders were hunched, and her mouth turned down at the corners.

I waited for a few moments. Nothing. She didn't even look in my direction. It made my stomach hurt. "I said I was sorry."

"I heard you," she said, still not looking at me.

"Okay." I turned around and left to clean the bathroom.

My day didn't get much better when Naomi finally showed up. She insisted on dragging me to the mall with her, which was as bad as Grandma making me scrub the bathtub three times—if not worse.

"I hate malls," I said, avoiding eye contact with the hordes of people walking in the opposite direction. All the faces and chatter made me dizzy.

Whoever came up with the idea of food courts needed their head examined. The smell of sugary dough did not mesh with teriyaki sauce. Add cheap tomato sauce to the mix, and it had the same effect as ipecac.

"Scott wants to hang out tonight. I need something sexy to wear."

"What about painting and the movie?"

Naomi rolled her eyes. "It's only five thirty. Scott isn't coming to get us until at least eleven or midnight."

"Us?"

She grabbed my arm, pulling me close. "Yep. He's racing tonight."

"Racing?"

She let me go and bit her lip. "You'll see. There will be lots of hotties there."

"I'd rather just stay home like we'd planned."

"What? And do each other's makeup and hair all night? God, Drea, I was only kidding about the slumber-party thing. We aren't ten."

A lump formed in my throat as I followed her into a store filled with fancy underwear, bras, and lingerie.

"I know you think he's this big jerk," Naomi said. "You know how guys are, though—they talk like pigs to each other, but they don't mean anything by it." She rummaged through the piles of underwear, plucking out a lacy red pair.

"Justin might like these." She thrust them into my chest, grinning.

I dropped them back into the pile. "Well, I don't like them."

Naomi tore a silky black slip from a hanger and held it against her body, fingering the plastic security tag. "What do you think? Pair it with some thigh highs maybe?"

I checked the price. "It's almost fifty dollars."

She leaned into my ear. Her breath smelled like mint gum and cigarettes. "No worries—they've got the cheap non-ink security tags here. Easy to remove."

"Can I help you ladies with anything?" a girl with bleached teeth asked. She eyed Naomi from head to toe, pausing on her baggy jeans.

Naomi grabbed a pink gauzy thing and what looked like a doll gown off the rack. "Yeah, can you start a fitting room for us?" She handed the garments over to the clerk.

"Certainly—two rooms?"

"We can share," Naomi said.

The girl scanned me up and down before flashing a quick smile. "Let me know if you need anything else." She walked away.

"Okay, bitch," Naomi whispered. "Did you see the way she looked at us? It's why I don't feel bad ripping them off." She glanced at the other clerk before stuffing the black slip down her jeans. "I just wish this place was busier. It usually is on Saturdays."

"What are you doing?"

"Shhh." She looked over her shoulder before cramming a white lacy slip down the other side of her jeans. The oversized band T-shirt she wore covered the bulge.

Mom said she'd never resort to stealing. Even if that meant living on gas-station food. I picked up a silky corset with fraying laces—$110. "I could make this stuff for a lot cheaper. You don't have to steal anything."

"I was going to ask if you made your clothes," she said in a louder voice. "They're really awesome." The salesclerk who'd started our fitting room had come back out. She straightened racks a few feet from us.

"Kinda have to—not much fits me otherwise."

She nodded at my white skirt. "Did you make that?"

"I added the lace hem to this one." I leaned closer to her. "Put them back, Naomi!"

She put her finger to her lips, her eyes widening. "So what do you think Justin would like? I'm betting on something innocent."

Heat ran up my neck at her words. "Do you really think he likes me that way?"

"I swear, Drea. Sometimes you act like you've never had a boyfriend before."

"I've had plenty of boyfriends." My pulse throbbed through my ears and my fingers ran cold. She'd caught me.

"And didn't you have to make the first move with at least a couple?" She took my hand, pulling me toward the fitting rooms. "We're ready," she called over to the clerk.

The salesclerk smiled. "Okay, let me know if you need a different size."

We squeezed into the fitting room. It smelled like roses and sweat.

Naomi pulled the white lacy slip out of her jeans and tossed it at me. "This will look so good on you. Sweet and sexy."

I unraveled the light material. A pale ribbon swirled around the high waist, and it was barely long enough to cover my butt. What exactly did she expect me to do with this? "How do I act like I've never had a boyfriend?"

She took off her T-shirt and gave me a sidelong glance. "Mostly, it's the way you act around Justin. You blush a lot—and you get all shy and giggly."

"He's different from most guys I've been around." At least that much was true.

"I figured. Were most of them jerks?"

"Yeah." I thought back to some of Mom's boyfriends. "A couple drank a lot, and they'd get violent and break stuff sometimes. One of them stole our—my money and gambled it all away."

Naomi smoothed the black slip over her baggy jeans and raised her eyebrows at me. "Like, online?"

"In Vegas."

"Was he older?"

Oh, crap. "Yeah."

She nodded. "I've dated a couple older losers too."

"Like Scott?"

"He's really sweet when we're alone together. Oh my God, I didn't tell you what he did last night." Naomi's cheeks practically glowed as she twisted in the mirror, eyeing her behind. "He brought yellow tulips—my favorite—and took me out to this really nice restaurant in Seattle. Like the kind that gives you warm bread before the meal." She gazed up at the ceiling. "Anyway, he told me he wouldn't see other people if I don't."

"I'd rather a guy not see other people because he doesn't *want* to."

"You and every other girl. Guys just think differently, you know?" She sucked her stomach in. "Do you think I've got too much tummy for this?"

All I saw was a huge chest, a small waist, and curvy hips—the perfect female figure. Everything mine wasn't. "You look beautiful," I said.

"Aw. Try yours on."

"No thanks. I've got no reason to wear it."

"Drea! Boys or no boys, there's always a reason." She winked. "I think Justin suffers from FGS, by the way."

"What's FGS?"

Naomi giggled and peeled the slip off. "It's a term me and Kari came up with—we used to be joined at the hip."

"She told me."

"Yeah, anyway—it's Former Geek Syndrome. Guys who are late bloomers and don't get hot until their junior or senior year. Most of the time they aren't aware of it yet, so they haven't gotten all arrogant. They usually make the best boyfriends but have no idea how to make the first move." She nudged me. "So do it already."

"There's more to life than boys. I'd rather write more songs."

She pulled a flathead screwdriver and a small pair of pliers from her pocket.

"What is that for?"

Naomi put her fingers to her lips. "The security tags," she whispered. "Make some noise, okay? Talk loud or something." She slid the screwdriver in where the tag gripped the clothing.

"I'll make you something. Don't do this."

"Quit worrying," she whispered. "I'm not exactly new to this."

"I'm leaving," I said, reaching for the door.

Naomi grabbed my arm and yanked me backward. "Chill the fuck out. You're going to get us caught."

I avoided her gaze, which seemed to burn into me. Her nails dug into the skin of my arm.

"Please, Drea. Just help me out, okay?"

I yanked my arm out of her grip and slid to the ground. It was so hot in here. I couldn't breathe.

"Look underneath the door," she whispered. "Tell me if someone walks by." She started to sing the lyrics to "Invisible" as she grasped the tag with the pliers. It snapped a couple seconds later and she handed me the remnants, which included a sharp pin. "Hold this. Anyone coming?"

I glanced under the door and shook my head, my breaths coming out fast. Naomi put the black slip back on, tucked it inside her jeans, and then pulled her T-shirt over it.

"Now yours." She took the white lacy slip from my hands and repeated the process, still singing. "Put this on under your clothes."

"I don't want it."

"Fine, whatever." She stuffed it down her jeans, then grabbed the broken security tags from me and tossed them under the divider into the adjacent fitting room. "Let's get out of here."

When we opened the door, the salesclerk came around the corner smiling. "How'd it go?"

I felt like there was a knife twisting in my stomach.

Naomi handed her the doll gown and the unidentifiable pink thing. "Neither of these were me. Maybe next time."

"Would you like to try a different size or color?"

Naomi took my hand, pulling me forward. "No, no. The cut just didn't work."

We'd almost left the store when the salesgirl asked us to stop. I glanced over my shoulder and saw the security tags in her hands.

"Run." Naomi took off in a sprint.

I tried to follow, but running through crowds was near impossible. Every time I avoided one major collision, someone else appeared out of nowhere. Two security guards were jogging in my direction. I sucked in my breath and froze, watching them close in on me.

A hand grabbed my arm and pulled me into a hallway with a green exit sign. "Come on!"

I chased Naomi toward the sign, but I could hear the buzz of radios and voices behind us. The two guards entered the hallway just before we reached the doors.

"Found two females matching the description," a breathless guy said. "They're running out the south exit. Over."

Naomi pushed the door open, and I dug my heels into the pavement, using every last bit of muscle to get to her dad's car.

"Duck," she said, bending over and weaving between the cars. The sound of opening doors and footsteps rang out behind us.

"Search the southeast parking lot," a guy said. One set of footsteps ran in another direction.

Naomi pushed the unlock button and opened the silver door of her dad's SUV. "Scrunch down in the seat so nobody will see you," she whispered.

I squeezed the handle, and the passenger door creaked open. It sounded more like a scream. They must've heard it. I'd gotten us caught.

Naomi threw a blanket over my head as I climbed in, closing the door with as little force as possible. I squeezed my eyes shut despite the darkness. All I could hear was Naomi's labored breathing and the roar of the car engine.

"We'll be okay," she said over and over again. A metal song blared out of her speakers, and she tapped her hands against the wheel.

The endless turns made me dizzy. Stop. Go. Stop. Crawl. Stop. Every second seemed like an eternity. And the screaming vocals certainly weren't helping the mood.

Finally, Naomi let out a wicked laugh and tore the blanket from my head. "That was such a rush."

I gaped at her grinning face. "Are you crazy?"

"Probably." For whatever reason, she seemed proud of this.

We made a right onto the main street and got onto the freeway on-ramp. "We should go back and return the stuff. They saw us—and they probably have cameras."

Naomi shrugged. "I didn't see any. Besides, it's not like we robbed a bank. We stole some overpriced lingerie."

"*We* didn't do anything."

She rolled down the window, sticking a cigarette between her lips. "You can't tell me your friends back in San Francisco or Vegas or *wherever* never ripped anything off."

"We went to parties and clubs and stuff."

Her blue eyes lit up. "Ooh, you got a fake ID?"

"No."

She sped up to eighty-five. "How'd you get in? Did you flirt with the bouncer?"

"The speed limit is sixty."

"I had no idea. Tell me again." Her smile faded, and she pressed harder on the gas.

"The speed limit is—"

"Do you take everything literally?"

I glanced down at my shaking hands. They looked pale and small in my lap. "I don't understand the point of saying something you don't mean."

"I don't understand the point of a lot of things." She turned up the radio, and we rode the rest of the way home in silence.

10

We waited for Grandma to go to bed before we lined the floor with newspapers and cracked open the paint. Naomi rambled on about Scott, the time Kari got lice, and a bad acid trip she had as if she'd completely forgotten the incident at the mall. I got this gnawing pain in my gut every time I looked at the stolen lingerie on my floor.

"You do realize this is a hideous color, right?" Naomi slapped the roller onto the wall, splattering paint across her cheeks. "Oops."

"It's a happy color."

"Says the girl who almost always wears black. I like the smell of paint, though—makes my head all nice and fuzzy."

"Hey, Drea." Mom headed down the stairs. She was wearing a fitted black dress and matching heels. "Oh, God." Her eyes widened at the lime green paint. "Grandma is going to kill us both."

"I'll paint it white again when we move out."

"Damn it, Drea. You should've asked me first." She sighed.

"We'll deal with it tomorrow. I'm going on a second date with that dentist tonight."

"Ooh," Naomi said. "Is he hot?"

Mom grinned and crossed her arms over her chest. "Very."

I wondered if Mom wished I was boy crazy like Naomi. Maybe she'd talk to me more—like, tell me more about the guy in the first place.

"Anyway, make sure you keep the windows open and don't sleep in here overnight."

"I'm not a complete idiot." I rolled my eyes. "I'm sleeping at Naomi's."

Mom gave me a hug and a kiss on the cheek. "Have fun, sweetie. See you later, Naomi."

"Bye." Naomi wiggled her fingers at Mom and slapped the wall with the roller again.

"You're not supposed to beat the wall with it."

She blew her purple bangs out of her face. "My arms are getting tired."

I shook my head and dipped my roller in the pan. The jittery tunes of Imogen Heap's "Goodnight and Go" wafted in the background. The song put a grin on my face because it reminded me of Justin. I sang along.

Naomi snorted out a laugh. "Okay, Drea, I think you're a wonderful human being." She sighed and met my gaze. "But you can't sing."

I moved closer to her and sang louder.

"Stop!" She covered her ears. "Get your mind off Justin already, will ya?" She smirked as if she'd read my mind.

I focused back on the wall. "It's not on him."

"It *so* is. You're thinking about the many ways you can rip his clothes off and ravage him."

Giggles escaped my throat. "Nooo."

"You should invite him tonight."

"He's got work."

"At midnight? I highly doubt it. But maybe it's past his bedtime—he does seem like he's every mother's dream." She laughed and slapped more paint on the wall. "I bet he helps little old ladies cross the street in his spare time."

"Why do you think that?"

"He just seems a little too nice, you know?"

"I don't think he's fake, if that's what you mean." Usually people smiled too much or asked pointless questions in a high voice when they were being fake. Justin never did that.

She grinned and flung paint at me. "You're so hooked."

I loved moments like this with Naomi. They felt close and warm. If I could put this moment between us in a box, I'd hide it under the bed and take it out whenever I could. And I'd throw out the incident at the mall and Scott. I wished this was enough for her. I wished *I* was enough for her.

We watched *Ferris Bueller* with achy arms and grumbling stomachs. Saturday night wasn't the best night to have a pizza delivered quickly. Naomi's blue floral couch smelled like cat pee, and Lizzie insisted on playing with my hair.

Naomi was laughing at a scene where this guy Cameron didn't want to leave his dad's Ferrari at a parking garage in downtown Chicago. He listed all the bad things that could happen to it, which made perfect sense. But his friend Ferris didn't think it was a big deal, even though they took the car without permission.

"You remind me of Cameron," Naomi said.

"Why?" I detached Lizzie's claws from my hair.

"You freak out over little stuff."

"I wouldn't call getting caught stealing *little*." I was happy when she'd taken the clothing and stuffed it in her dresser. Out of my sight.

"Uh, how about throwing the pipe at Roger because the bell rang?"

"I didn't throw it at him. And I told you—I needed air."

"Or how about freaking out over ice cream expiration dates? Plus, you're pouty like Cameron is."

"I don't mean to be." Lizzie made smacking sounds next to my ear. "Why is your cat eating my hair?"

Naomi hoisted the cat from her perch and kissed her head. "She likes you. Don't you, Lizzie Wizzie?" Lizzie meowed in response, her dreamy green eyes blinking once.

Keys rattled in the front door lock. Lizzie scrambled out of Naomi's lap and squeezed her chubby body under the couch.

"It's just my dad. He went camping with some buddy of his."

The door swung open and a tall man wearing a blue T-shirt and jeans walked in. He had sandy hair and thin arms—almost scarecrowlike.

I looked back at Naomi. She focused on the movie. Two parking attendants were stealing the red Ferrari.

"How are you, Kari?" Her father was peering at me from the dim entranceway.

"It's Drea, Dad. Our new neighbor. I told you she'd be coming over."

"Oh, right. Sorry." His voice was almost too soft to hear. "Naomi, I'm taking . . ." The roar of the car on TV drowned out his words.

Naomi hit the mute button. "You can come in here, you know. I can't hear you."

Her father cleared his throat and inched into the living room, giving us a tight smile. "I have to cover for Brenda this week, but I've got the first two weeks of October off. We'll car hunt then, okay?"

"Why not leave me a check and I'll do it myself?"

"You said you wanted me to help you."

"Yeah, but then Lisa might need to go on maternity leave. Or Vickie might get pneumonia. Or maybe you'll decide to work those two weeks just because. I'll need a car regardless."

He glanced at me before shaking his head. His eyes were a mess of shadows. "I'm not going to do this in front of your friend. We'll talk later."

"Yep, it's always later. What if you wake up and find there's no tomorrow, Dad?"

He ignored her and climbed the steps with slumped shoulders.

"Sorry about that. He really pisses me off sometimes." Naomi nibbled on her thumbnail.

"Where does he work?"

"He's a flight attendant."

"That seems like a cool job."

"Sure, if you don't mind never being home." She shrugged. "I could scream in that man's face for hours and he wouldn't even flinch. He responds to my words, but he never actually *hears* me, you know?"

"Maybe he doesn't understand what you're saying."

"No, he just doesn't care. Anyway, enough about him." She smiled, but her eyes looked darker than normal. "If the pizza doesn't get here in the next five minutes, I'm going to eat the delivery person too."

"I doubt that would taste very good."

She laughed and paused the movie. "It's nine thirty. I bet Justin is off work by now."

"So?"

"You should call him."

"No."

"Fine, give me your phone. I'll call him."

"Use *your* phone."

"It's upstairs charging. Come on, fork it over." She made a grabbing motion.

I opened my lunch box and fished my black cell out. "Don't do anything embarrassing."

Naomi batted her eyelashes, taking the phone from me. "Never." She pressed speed dial and put the call on speaker. I sank into the couch.

It rang three times before he picked up. "Hello?"

"Hey, baby." Naomi made her voice higher. More breathy. More like mine.

I tried to grab the phone from her. "Stop!"

She pulled away and ran into the bathroom, shutting the door. "I've been thinking about you all night."

I pounded on the door. "That's not me!"

"Oh, yeah?" Justin's voice echoed inside the bathroom. "You've been on my mind a lot too." His voice sounded different. Lower. It made me stop knocking.

"What are you wearing?" Naomi continued.

"A pair of tube socks. What about you?"

"Just some lacy nighty I found in a gutter somewhere."

I slid against the door, putting my face in my hands. This was a nightmare. He'd never talk to me again.

"Wow," he said. "That's hot."

"You should come over and check it out."

"Sure—on one condition."

"Anything."

"You take me off speakerphone and give Drea her phone back."

"You're no fun," Naomi said in her normal voice. "And that's technically two conditions." She opened the door.

"Sorry, Drea's yelling in the background kind of gave you away. Plus, you're a shitty impersonator."

"Hey, I was the prank call queen in junior high. I could do anyone's voice."

"It was her idea to call you," I said. "I didn't want to bother you again."

Naomi raised her eyebrows at me. "Again? Oh, my."

"Did you finish watching your movie?" Justin asked.

"Not yet," Naomi answered. "We're getting antsy because our pizza hasn't shown up yet. Seriously, you should come over. My boyfriend is taking us to a race tonight, and Drea needs a buddy."

"I'm not going," I said.

She rolled her eyes. "You're going. Can't punk out on me now."

"A street race?" Justin asked.

"Yeah," Naomi said.

"Where is it?" he asked.

"Why—you wanna race?"

"No, I just didn't think it was possible to drive more than twenty-five miles an hour in this town."

Naomi rolled her eyes. "Oh, I know—people are, like, allergic to their gas pedals here."

Justin exhaled a laugh. "Anyway, can't go. I'm babysitting my niece."

She scrunched up her nose. "Sounds riveting. You going to bake cookies for your grandma too?"

"Probably."

The doorbell rang, and Naomi's eyes widened. She tossed the phone at me. "Pizza's here!"

"Um, hi," I said.

"You want to take me off speakerphone now?"

I pressed the speaker off button. "Sorry if we bothered you. It . . . it really wasn't my idea to call."

"I know."

I pictured him with that half smile. "So—"

"Hey, if you don't want to go tonight, don't go."

I watched Naomi take the pizza into the kitchen. "I don't want to be stuck in a car with her boyfriend," I whispered. "He's a creep."

"Is he a bigger tool than Roger?"

"Yeah."

"She needs better taste in guys."

"No kidding. Maybe *you* can ask her out."

He chuckled. "Does that mean I have your seal of approval?"

"I like you. I mean—better than Scott." I rolled my eyes. Why was this so hard?

"Don't worry. You had me at *I like you.*"

Naomi poked her head out of the kitchen. "Say bye to Prince Charming. Pizza is getting cold."

"Sounds like you need to go again."

"Yeah."

Naomi ran a hand through her hair, tilting her head back. "Oh, Justin! Your voice is so sexy."

I covered the mouthpiece, heat creeping up my neck.

"Is she on something again?" he asked.

"I don't think so."

Naomi continued to moan his name and roll her eyes up to the ceiling like she was having a seizure.

"That girl's a trip," he said. A child's voice rang out in the background. "I gotta go, but, hey, if you decide to go and her boyfriend gets weird, call me, okay? I'll pick you guys up."

The nausea eased some. I really didn't want to go, but I didn't want to let Naomi down, either. "I will. Thank you."

"Anything for my new bandmates. Talk to you later."

"Bye." I flipped the phone shut and glared at Naomi. "Do you really need me to go?"

She swallowed a large bite of her pizza. "What else are you going to do tonight?"

"I don't know." There was a curious part of me that wanted to be wild and crazy with Naomi. Live the life I'd overheard so many people talk about. The parties, the hookups, the "you just had to be there" moments, and even the hangovers. But so far I'd spent more time being uncomfortable. "Don't you want to be alone with Scott?"

"He'll be busy prepping his car. I'll make him take us home as soon as it's over." She stuck out her lower lip at me. "Please? It would mean a lot to me."

"Fine, I guess."

She did a corny dance and thrust a slice of pizza in my face. It smelled like cardboard. "Eat."

The pizza was cold and slightly chewy, but Naomi's smile made it taste better.

Scott showed up just as Naomi stuck the last pin in her hair. She smelled like a fruity flower, and her lips were the color of red wine.

"What's up?" Scott said after she let him in. He reeked of cigarettes and aftershave. Naomi threw her arms around him, and he stared at me over her shoulder.

I looked at the stained green carpet.

"How's it going, Drea?"

"Fine," I said. My lips were sticky with the brownish muck Naomi claimed looked good with my red hair.

"I brought you a present," he said in her ear.

"I've got something for you too," she whispered before glancing over her shoulder. "We're gonna go upstairs for a couple minutes."

I nodded and sat on the couch. Their footsteps thudded up the stairs, and Naomi let out a squeal after they closed the door. More laughter followed. A few thumps. And then silence. It wasn't too late for me to get up and go home. Especially if she was going to be girly with Scott all night.

But I was still sitting on the couch when they came down a decade of minutes later. Like a good friend.

"Sorry, we got a little detoured," Naomi said. The hair she'd spent hours curling and pinning up was a limp mess around her shoulders, and her lipstick had been smeared to one side. I didn't get it. Why spend two hours getting ready just so some guy can obliterate it all in five minutes?

"Okay," I said, looking down at my black sneakers.

Naomi plopped next to me with a compact mirror. She wiped the remnants of lip color off with the back of her hand and redrew a line around her lips.

Scott ruffled her hair. "We don't have time for that."

"Hang on," she said. Her hands shook as she applied the lipstick. I wondered if he made her nervous.

Scott nudged her head forward so she missed her mouth by an inch.

"Hey, jerk." She looked over at me and grinned. Her eyes looked like black saucers.

"Let's go!" Scott headed for the front door and yanked it open.

Naomi jumped up, smoothing out her rumpled denim skirt. "Okay, cranky bear."

Cranky bear didn't even begin to cover Scott. I followed them out to the car, telling myself that it was good to be out on a Saturday instead of sitting at home online. Even so, I missed my computer, my pedals, and the berry candles I'd normally be burning.

Scott sped off with the same grace he had a couple weeks ago. The leather of the back seat gave me goose bumps. I should've brought a jacket.

We flew past the silhouettes of boats in Squalicum Harbor. They looked like rows of toothpicks under the full moon. Still and lifeless as if they'd been there forever. Railroad tracks ran parallel to us on the other side, disappearing into nothing but blackness.

At some point we merged onto the freeway, but we only drove a couple exits north before Scott got off and made a right. The streetlights evaporated, as did the stores and the gas stations. Scott floored the Mustang as soon as we hit a dark stretch of road, and the trees blurred into odd shapes and jagged edges.

"Is that all you've got?" Naomi asked him.

"Gotta save some energy." He grinned at her, taking one hand off the wheel and resting it in her lap.

She tilted her head back and closed her eyes, laughing. "Come on, step on it."

"You really want me to?"

We were already going so fast. Too fast. The white road bumps had become a solid line, curving into nothing ahead. "I think we should slow down," I said.

But they didn't hear me. Too much wind from the open windows. Too much drum and bass from Scott's crappy speakers. I tapped Naomi on the shoulder.

"What?" Her eyes were sunken holes in her face, and the rest of her features were indistinguishable. She'd become nothing more than purple hair and pale skin.

"Make him slow down."

"No way. Are you kidding?"

The tires skidded around a sharp curve. Trees swallowed the car, blocking out any remaining moonlight.

"Please," I said. "I can't see anything."

"That's because we're in Hicksville. Only life around here is Farmer John and his harem of cows!" Naomi laughed again. It was too loud. Too out of control.

Warmth was building behind my eyes, and my chest felt tight with fast breaths. I rocked back and forth, telling myself that it was just another anxiety attack. Naomi and Scott weren't monsters that were going to dump me in the woods somewhere. But it sure felt like it. The way he kept tugging at her arm. She'd try to bite his hand. And she kept talking so fast—like a tape stuck on fast-forward.

The engine growled, jerking my body left. Then right. Left again. My head slammed against the seat with every downshift, and the tires squealed a little more with every turn. Scott said something about a homestretch and crunched on the gas. The car sounded like a freight train. I squeezed my eyes shut, bracing for impact. But Scott hit the brakes, and I opened my eyes to a sea of headlights pointed in every direction.

11

Naomi and I huddled under some trees with a few other people. Most of them were girls taking puffs of cigarettes or giggling about their boyfriends. One guy told another his money was on Scott. I inhaled the smell of cow crap and car exhaust.

Scott's Mustang sat alongside some blond girl's red Honda. Both cars faced a flat stretch of road that bled into the darkness. The blond girl peered under Scott's hood, pointing at various things and laughing. Scott's gaze dropped every time she bent over to look at something.

"Why doesn't she just lift up her skirt and flash him already?" Naomi said through her teeth. Her eyes narrowed at the girl, and her fingers twitched against her denim skirt.

"Why would she do that?"

She rolled her eyes at me and took another sharp drag of her cigarette. "You ask really dumb questions sometimes."

I sank back into the shadows of the trees. Her hands clenched into fists every time a girl talked to him—even if it was just hi. And her eyes were different too. Always darting from one thing to the next. Hungry.

"How long will this take?" I asked.

She shrugged, flicking her cigarette into the gravel. "I'm not a psychic."

I hugged my body, shivering in the damp air. Autumn definitely hit Washington earlier than California. A police scanner bellowed out of a car nearby. Two guys sat inside—the neon dashboard made their faces look alien.

The racer girl gave Scott a playful punch in the arm, and Naomi edged forward. When he leaned in to whisper in the girl's ear, Naomi walked up to them, gesturing wildly. Some of the people around me chuckled and talked about a catfight.

I moved forward until I could hear what was going on.

"Maybe you should get your girlfriend a leash," the racer girl said, shaking her head at Naomi.

Naomi lurched forward, bringing her face within inches of the other girl's. "Maybe you should wear a skirt that covers your fat ass."

Racer girl swung at Naomi, but Scott and a guy in a baseball cap pulled the two girls apart. Scott pressed Naomi against his car and took off his hoodie. "I told you not to do so much. Go for a walk or something, okay?" He handed his jacket to her.

Naomi's entire body shuddered like she was cold. "You promised," she said.

"I didn't do anything." He gave her a stiff hug and patted her on the back. Kind of like the hugs I gave Grandma.

"You were flirting with her."

Scott laughed at this. "We were just talkin'."

"I'm ready when you decide to lose the ball and chain," the racer girl said, getting into her car and slamming the door.

Naomi spun around to say something, but Scott squeezed

her face with one hand and lowered his voice. "I'm not gonna deal with this psycho-bitch shit."

"I'm sorry," she said, nuzzling her face into his hoodie.

He dropped his hand. "Get off the car."

Naomi moved away and looked at me for the first time. Her eyes were like oil slick in the headlights.

"Are you okay?" I asked, my legs shaking.

She wrapped her arms around me, burying her face in my shoulder. "No."

A guy with a walkie-talkie strolled past us and stood between the two cars. Both engines revved like dueling bass lines.

Naomi's heart pounded against my chest, and her breaths were shallow. "I'm so jacked up, Drea," she said. "I can't even breathe."

The guy stuffed the radio in his belt and held his hands up like a conductor. I stroked her hair, hoping it would calm her as it did me. "What did you take?" I asked. "Do you need a doctor?"

She sniffled into my ear. "No, I . . ." The growl of the cars drowned her voice out.

The conductor guy dropped his hands, and both cars skidded off, leaving us to choke on the stench of burnt rubber. The crowd shoved past us, shouting and hooting like a bunch of baboons in a cage.

Naomi's breaths quickened, and I pulled her away from the street. She squatted in the darkness, chewing on her ring fingernail. "My heart won't stop pounding, Drea. It won't stop."

I sat on the grassy roadside and winced as a cold wetness seeped into my ivory skirt. "Just sit down."

"I can't—I can't sit. I can't do anything."

I reached for her hand and pulled her toward me. "Lay your head in my lap and close your eyes." It was the only thing I could think of. Whenever a noise would bother me as a kid, Mom would tell me to lie in her lap. She'd sing to me or stroke my hair and talk about something that made us both laugh. Usually all the practical jokes she played on Grandma when she was little.

Naomi put the hoodie in my lap and rested on top of it. I ran my fingers through her damp hair, and she clenched her jaw.

The crowd's cheers were off in the distance now. Someone had won, but I didn't really care who. "You know what my mom did to my grandma once?"

"What?" she asked weakly.

"Grandma would always go on these cleaning rampages. Tear the whole house apart and put it back together again. And the whole time she'd be complaining about *everything*. Anyway, Mom decided to record her one time. Then she put this happy organ music to it—like the kind on a merry-go-round."

"Oh my God—I can totally hear that."

"She made a series of these things. Even gave them titles and stuff. "Mom and the Plunger," "Mom's Thoughts on Hairballs." I could feel Naomi's chest shake with laughter. Her breathing slowed some. "Then she wrapped them up and gave them to Grandma for a birthday present, telling her it was this old blues singer she loved. Well, they had some dinner guests over—neighbors mostly. Grandma puts it on, and the first thing everyone hears is her yelling about dirty sheets."

"Your mom is awesome. Seriously, you're really lucky."

"Sometimes I don't feel that way." I let her hair sift between my fingertips.

"Everyone wishes they had different parents, I think. But at least you know she cares about you—like when she told you to keep the windows open tonight. That was cute." She exhaled slowly. "I can't even remember the last time my dad bothered to ask where I was going."

"Do you guys ever eat together or watch TV?"

"I got him to watch the first five minutes of *CSI* a couple months ago. Then he fell asleep. It was easier when my brother was around—I had someone to share my misery with."

"Where's your brother now?"

"Who knows? Probably somewhere a lot more exciting than this place." Naomi reached up and squeezed my hand. "I'm sorry I freaked out on you."

"It's—" I was interrupted by what sounded like a herd of horses. People were running to their cars and slamming doors.

Naomi grabbed the hoodie and jumped up, her eyes darting around the street. "Shit, they must've heard something on the scanner. We gotta find Scott."

Cars sped off in every direction as we jogged along the side of the road. I was sure at least one would end up hitting us. Naomi ran into the street just as a black Mustang approached us. It skidded to a stop, and she yanked the front door open.

"Hurry up!" Scott said.

I dove into the back seat, and Naomi barely had enough time to slam the door before Scott floored the gas.

Scott insisted on taking us back to his apartment. He claimed that he was *beat*, and our houses were *too far*. Even though they weren't more than ten minutes away. Naomi didn't put up much of a protest.

"Don't worry—he's got a comfy couch," Naomi said as I got out of the car.

Scott headed upstairs to his apartment without speaking to either of us. Most of the ride here consisted of him bragging about winning the race, and Naomi nodding and staring out the window.

"I want to go home." I checked the time on my cell. One thirty A.M. My mind was racing, but my body felt achy and weak. I needed sleep. "Maybe we can call Justin."

She put her hands on my shoulders, grinding her teeth. "He's probably asleep. Look, I need to talk to Scott for a few minutes, and then I'll see if I can get us a ride. Roger is probably still up."

I followed her up the cracked steps to Scott's apartment. Naomi pushed the door open and let me in first. A gigantic flat-screen TV with massive speakers sat opposite a black leather couch. The kitchen bar was lined with bottles of wine and hard liquor. He even had art hanging on the walls—which struck me as odd. The apartment complex itself was pretty ghetto. The kind Mom and I could only stay in for so long.

"Nice digs, right?" Naomi smirked.

"How does he afford all this?"

She raised her eyebrows. "How do you *think*?"

I shrugged. For all I knew, he robbed banks.

Scott paced around the kitchen, talking on the phone. Tattoos covered his shirtless back. Most of them were black and red with sharp edges and wavy lines. "What am I—Domino's? Fuck that. Come over and I'll show you," he said.

Naomi walked over to a shelf of CDs and pulled a few out, scanning the track lists.

"Hey." Scott walked into the living room, covering the mouthpiece. "Put those back where you found 'em."

She rolled her eyes and shoved a couple back into their slots.

"So walk," Scott said into the phone. "Your transportation issues aren't my problem." His eyes met mine and a small smile crept across his face. "Yeah, it's worth it."

I looked down at the dark brown carpet, staying near the front door. Scott mumbled a word that sounded like *later* and hung up.

"You gonna sit down?" he asked me.

I shrugged, keeping my elbows close to my body.

"We're going to take off," Naomi said, standing up. "But I want to talk to you first."

"Yeah?" He walked over to her and wrapped his arms around her waist.

She pulled away. Her hands were still shaking. "Not like that—I mean it."

"Thought you were staying over." Scott raked a hand through his shaggy blond hair and motioned in my direction. "Your friend can take the couch. Or she can join us." He poked at her ribs and laughed.

Naomi flipped him off. "Why do you have to be such a pig?" She pushed past him and settled into the leather couch.

I backed into the cold wall, wishing I could disappear.

Scott folded his bulky arms across his chest. His grin faded into a thin line. "I don't have time for your drama, Naomi. You wanna go home, go. Take your weird friend with you."

I sucked in my breath. "I'm not weird."

He cupped his hand behind his ear. "What was that?"

My heart thudded in my chest. "You don't deserve Naomi," I said. "You're a jerk."

Scott shook his head and walked over to me. I squeezed my eyes shut.

"You wanna look me in the eye and say that?"

"Leave her alone," Naomi said. Her voice was behind him now.

"No. I want to hear what this stuck-up little bitch has to say." His breath smelled sour and bitter—like old cigarettes.

My throat felt like it was closing up on me. "I want to go home, Naomi. Now."

"*I want to go home, Naomi,*" Scott said in a high voice. "Word of advice—don't run your mouth off about something you know nothin' about."

"Scott," Naomi whispered, "let's go in your room and talk, okay?"

His hot breath fell on my forehead. I bit down on my tongue until it ached—anything to hold in the scream building inside me.

A few more seconds passed before their footsteps moved toward the bedroom.

"That chick is a fuckin' freak," Scott said, shutting the door behind them.

My knees gave out and I slid against the wall until my tailbone hit the floor. I nuzzled my face into my knees and exhaled a breathy scream. The tightness in my throat unraveled some, but there was so much left. So much I wanted to say and couldn't.

Their voices rose behind the door, and my fingers went cold. Naomi cussed. And Scott cussed back. She kept asking him why. And he wouldn't give her a real answer. I fished out my phone and stared at Justin's name. He'd told me to call him, but did that mean in the middle of the night? I shut my brain off and pressed dial.

He answered after the first ring. "Hey, Drea."

"Did I wake you up?"

"Nah, I was writing in that journal for English."

"They're fighting in Scott's room. I want to go home, but I don't want to leave her alone with him."

"What's the address?"

"Crap, I don't know." I got up and parted the blinds hanging over Scott's window. "It's too dark to see the sign."

"Does he have mail lying around somewhere?"

My knees wobbled as I wandered into the kitchen. A mess of papers covered the table. I fished an envelope out. It was sticky with something.

"Found a telephone bill," I said. "It's 1401 Madison Street—apartment 239."

"Got it. I'll be there as soon as I can."

Someone banged on the door about four minutes later. I was sitting at the kitchen table, still clutching my cell phone. Too early to be Justin—unless he lived on this side of town. Every nerve in my body turned to ice.

Scott barreled out of the bedroom and glared at the phone in my hand. "You call the cops?" He made a move toward me, but the banging continued. He snuck up to the door and looked into the peephole. His shoulders relaxed at whoever was standing outside.

"Don't pound on the door like that, jackass," Scott said, opening the door.

This was followed by male laughter. Two guys walked in. One had long, frizzy hair and the other wore a beanie and about a billion facial piercings. Frizz Head made himself at home on the couch, and Beanie Guy followed Scott into the kitchen.

"What's up?" Beanie Guy nodded at me.

I looked down and hightailed it to the front door. Their eyes burned into me.

"I think she's retarded or something," Scott said.

"Dude, that was *cold*." Beanie whispered something else I couldn't hear, and they both laughed.

"Hey," Frizz said from the couch, "you gonna let him talk about you like that?"

"Naomi?" I called, keeping my eyes focused on a hole in the wall. "Where are you?"

"I'm coming," she said, tearing out of the room. "Sorry." Her eyes darted from the couch to the kitchen.

"Justin's coming to pick us up," I said.

"Hey, Naomi!" Beanie called. "What's wrong with your friend?"

She rolled her eyes. "She's got standards."

Scott leaned toward him. "That's all she does, man. Stands in corners all hunched over. You say hi to her and she does this twitchy thing like—"

"We can hear you!" Naomi said.

"She's kinda hot, though," Beanie said back. Like I wasn't even in the room. Like I didn't matter.

Naomi wrapped her arms around me. "Ignore them."

Frizz switched the TV on, cranking up the volume. Some cartoon roared through the apartment.

Scott walked over and clicked it off. "I got neighbors that bitch if I fart too loud, okay?" Another knock echoed around the apartment. "Who's that?"

"Maybe you should consider a new line of work," Naomi said. "You're paranoid as hell."

I hoped it was Justin.

Scott looked into the peephole again and yanked the door open. "Yeah?"

"Drea here?"

"Never heard of her." He went to slam the door, but Naomi shoved him.

"Let him in—it's just Drea's boyfriend."

"But he's not—" I began.

Naomi put a hand over my mouth and looked back at Scott. "He's cool, okay?"

Scott opened the door, studying Justin from head to toe. Justin walked in with his hands shoved into the pockets of his jeans. He stared back at Scott before turning to us and smiling. The Björk shirt he wore almost made me smile back. I loved Björk. But I didn't love this situation.

"Drea has a boyfriend, apparently." Scott walked back into the kitchen. "And he likes Ba-*jork*."

"My little sister loves her," Frizz said.

All three guys looked at Justin and snickered.

Justin rolled his eyes and nodded at the door. "Can we get out of here?"

"Yes, please," I said, grabbing Naomi's hand.

"Give me a minute, okay?" She looked back into the kitchen.

"How much for an eighth?" Beanie asked.

"Eighty," Scott answered.

Beanie Guy shook his head. "I'll give you fifty."

"It's weed, not used cars. Take it or leave it."

Frizz joined them, and they continued to argue. Eventually, Scott went into his room and came out with a baggy. Naomi leaned against the couch, tapping the heel of her boot against the carpet.

Justin slipped his arm around my shoulders. I stiffened with his touch.

He pulled his arm away. "Sorry. You okay?"

I shook my head and leaned into him. His warmth felt amazing. He wrapped both arms around me, running his hands down my forearms. Naomi crinkled her brow at us, her mouth turning down at the corners. I wished I knew what she was thinking.

"Why don't you call him later, Naomi?" Justin asked.

"No, he needs to know." She dug her nails into the back of the couch. "He needs to know he can't just treat me like I'm nothing."

Justin lowered his voice. "The guy's a dealer. Were you expecting love poems and walks on the beach?"

Naomi clenched her jaw again. "Just go. I'll be fine."

I looked at her twitching face and hands. In that moment, she looked like a scared child. "I'm not leaving you here alone," I said.

Beanie and Frizz headed for the door, telling Scott it better not be crap like last time. Scott assured them it wasn't and escorted them out.

He looked at Justin after he shut the door. "You buyin' something?"

Justin pulled back from me and leaned against the couch. "No—just waiting on Naomi."

"Then get out. She's crashing here."

"I want you to apologize," Naomi said.

"For *what*?" Scott asked.

Justin stood up. "This isn't going anywhere." He put a hand on Naomi's shoulder. "Let's go."

Naomi moved away. "Back off, Justin."

Scott walked closer to him, but Justin didn't move back. For a second they looked like they might kiss.

Justin looked down at Scott's clenched fists. "Maybe you should stay out of your own stash."

Scott shoved him into the couch. "Get the fuck out."

Justin straightened and held his hands up.

Naomi tugged at Scott's elbow, pulling him away. They moved into the bedroom and left the door open. She talked in a loud whisper, but I couldn't make out most of the words.

"Because you're up my ass twenty-four seven," Scott said.

"Scott, I need you. Scott, come over. Were you checking her out?"

"First you tell Roger you want to hook up with Drea." Naomi's voice cracked. "You told me it was a joke—fine, whatever. Then I hear about Kelly."

"And? We weren't together."

They continued to fling words back and forth, voices rising and falling. And then they fell into low whispers.

Justin leaned back against the couch and shut his eyes. His fingers tapped sharply against his jeans. "We can't make her go." He brushed his other hand against mine.

That's when we heard a crash against the bedroom wall. Naomi screamed. We ran around the couch and into the bedroom in time to see Scott slug her. His knuckles made a loud, popping sound when they hit her jaw, and he shoved her to the ground.

"You pushed it too far." Scott jabbed a finger at her. "Too far!"

Justin lurched at Scott and twisted his arms behind his back. He shoved Scott against the wall, struggling to keep him contained. "Get her out of here, Drea!"

I helped Naomi off the floor. Her lip was cut and her face was stained with tears.

Scott pulled out of Justin's grip and sent a fist into his face. Justin punched Scott's nose and rib cage, his features contorting into a mess I didn't even recognize. The sound of cracking knuckles and struggling feet echoed in my head. Naomi yelled for them to stop. I dropped my lunch box and covered my ears, taking fast breaths.

Scott protected his bloody nose with one hand and kicked Justin in the gut. Justin winced and clutched his stomach. But Scott raised his fist again. He wasn't going to let up.

I ran at Scott. Mom always said if a guy attacked me, go for the balls. I brought up my foot and kicked him twice, as hard as I could. I just wanted it to stop. It had to stop.

Scott hunched over and screamed a bunch of stuff that blurred together. Justin moved between us and spread his arms wide, shielding me. The room became silent, except for heavy breaths. Sirens wailed in the distance, barely audible over the ringing in my ears.

Scott cursed and scrambled over to his bedroom window.

"I gotta get out of here," Justin said, heading for the door.

I grabbed my lunch box and ran after him. I thought Naomi was behind me, but I wasn't sure. The world was nothing but a throbbing pulse in my ears and the impact of my footsteps on the pavement. It felt like a dream. Like nothing was real. All I knew was I didn't want to stay there.

We piled into Justin's car, and he took off with the same vigor Scott had during the race. I could see flashing blue and red lights several blocks down the street. The sirens were loud enough to be heard over his music. It was even a song I liked. And then I started laughing. Couldn't stop.

"Are you laughing?" Naomi asked from the back seat.

Justin shifted with a jerk and tore around a corner. He backed the BMW between two cars on a nearby residential street and cut the engine.

"What are you doing?" Naomi asked him.

"Didn't want to risk passing them."

"How do you know they're even going to Scott's?" Naomi asked. "I hear sirens all the time over here."

"Did you want to stick around and find out?" he asked.

I continued to laugh—even though I felt anything but happy. My entire body shook, sweat covered my back, and my temples were throbbing.

"Well, Drea's amused," Naomi said.

"I think it's her way of dealing," Justin said, looking over his shoulder. A police car screamed by on the main street.

"I'm sorry. I can't stop." The words came out in short bursts of breath. I rocked myself, focusing on long, deep breathing through my nose. Back and forth, in and out. A doctor told me to do that once.

Justin reached over and stroked my hair. "It's okay—you're just in shock."

"Laughter is a lot better than tears." Naomi poked the back of Justin's head. "Why are you so afraid of cops?"

His jaw tensed. "Besides the potential assault charge and being in a dealer's apartment?"

"You were defending me—I would've told them the truth. And Scott doesn't usually deal out of his apartment, unless his friends want something small. So he never keeps much there. He probably just flushed anything he had left."

"You don't have a lot of experience with the cops, do you?" Justin squinted at her in the rearview mirror. "I could tell you were tweaking as soon as I walked in the door." His voice sounded different to me. Rougher, angry even.

I wanted to ask them what tweaking meant exactly, but I could guess. The rabid look in Naomi's eyes was hard to miss. I'd spent my entire life fighting to be *normal*. An array of medication every morning, every six hours, every evening—a prisoner of rashes, headaches, drowsiness, and other fun side effects. All so I could be who everyone else wanted me to be. Nobody ever gave me a choice. But Naomi had a choice, and she didn't even seem to care.

"Where did you learn to throw punches like that?" Naomi asked.

Justin shrugged, but he gripped the steering wheel harder. I studied their shadowy faces. They were like two strangers to me.

Naomi glanced down at her nails. "I hope they arrest him."

"Me too," I said.

She looked up at me and smiled, but I sank into my seat. It wouldn't be that easy for her this time.

Justin started the car and put a hand on his stomach, wincing. "Let's hope for the best."

We pulled up in front of Naomi's house ten minutes later. Justin didn't speak or look at us the entire way back. He'd tensed up every time headlights approached from behind.

"Home, sweet home," Naomi said, shoving my seat forward and squeezing out. "Thanks . . . Justin."

He nodded and waved, but kept his eyes forward.

I stared at his profile for a few seconds. His cheek was like marble under the dim streetlights. I swallowed, wincing at my dry throat. "You want to give me a driving lesson tomorrow?"

"I don't think so, Drea."

"Why n—"

"I need to go," he said.

I waited for him to say he didn't mean *right now*. Like he did when he drove me home the first time.

"Drea, please just go." He looked at me, but I couldn't see his expression. Shadows hovered around his eyes and mouth. "And trust your instincts next time."

The pizza I'd eaten earlier crept up my esophagus. There was something in his words that made me think I'd never see him again.

I climbed out of the car, and he sped off after I shut the door. No second thoughts. His taillights disappeared into the early morning fog.

12

Monday, September 17

Something has been caught in my throat all day. Heavy. Impossible to dislodge. Naomi left five messages on my cell phone yesterday. I pressed 7 as soon as I heard her voice. Delete. I don't know what to say to her. I told her I wanted to go home, and she didn't care. But I cared enough to stay and wait for her. So did Justin. Now he hates us both. He won't answer his phone or return my calls. He's not even at school today. I've never felt like this before. So empty.

Grandma woke me up on the couch yesterday. She tried to get me to repaint the walls and even threatened to kick us out. I couldn't take it anymore. I asked her why. Why couldn't I have one thing that makes me feel at home? It's just a color. But it means the world to me. So we worked out a trade. I keep my walls green, and I have to help her set up a garage sale this weekend.

"I'm sorry." A backpack slammed onto the table. Naomi hovered above me—in the library of all places.

I flipped my journal shut. Sorry wasn't enough.

"I'm done, Drea," she said, yanking out a blue plastic chair and sitting down. "No more Scott. No more partying."

She sounded like she meant it. But it would be like me saying "no more music." It didn't make sense.

"I don't know if I believe you."

"I know I really screwed up this weekend, because I'm stupid." She rested her chin in her hand, covering a yellowing bruise. Her face looked pale and worn. "But he crossed the line. I'm done."

"I don't know what you want me to say."

"You're the only person who gives a shit. The only one I trust." Her eyes were large and red rimmed. "Please tell me it's not too late. Tell me there is *something* I can do."

I stared back at her for a long time, my lips glued together. She had offered her friendship to me. No questions asked. And I'd lied to her. I wanted to tell her the truth. To start over— reintroduce myself. *Hi, I'm Drea. World-class dork. I'm not cool. I'm not even normal. Do you still want to hang out with me?* And she could've done the same, told me she didn't have anyone either. If we'd both admitted how alone we were, maybe everything would've been different.

But I couldn't form the words. She trusted me. Nobody had ever said that to me before. Not even my mom. "No more stealing?" I asked finally.

She let out a shaky breath. "No more. I want to focus on music. We rock together, Drea. I don't want to lose that."

"Me neither." I tried to smile, but I didn't know if it translated to my lips. "Do you know if Scott got arrested?"

"Roger told me it was the old bag upstairs who called the cops, and she calls them, like, nine times a month for stupid shit. Like, one time she thought a stray-cat fight was a kid screaming for help. Anyway, Scott told them he tripped and smacked his nose on the coffee table playing Wii. And they apparently bought it. But who knows."

"Promise me you won't see him again?"

Naomi smiled and looped my pinkie with hers. "I won't even mention his name."

I wanted to believe her, but an ache in my stomach warned me against it. Still, I didn't want to lose the first friend I'd made in years or our music. "We decided on M3 for the band. I think I forgot to tell you."

"I like it—a lot, actually. Where's Justin?" '

I dug my pen into my notebook, scratching a tiny star in the corner. "He didn't show up today. I think he hates me."

"I don't think that's it, babe. People don't run from the cops unless they have something to hide. I told you he seemed a little *too* nice."

"He told us why." My chest felt tight again. I didn't want Justin to be one of the bad guys, but I couldn't get his contorted features out of my head.

"Do you know where he lives? Maybe we can drop by after school," she said.

I shook my head. "I need to find him, Naomi. I need to know. . . ."

She put her hand over mine. "It'll be okay. He can't skip school forever. You'll get another chance."

That wasn't good enough for me. I went to the bathroom before class and left my mom a voice mail, telling her I was going out with Naomi and I'd be home late.

I had an appointment with Jackie during PE. I wished I had the ability to hide my emotions.

"You look troubled today, Drea. Rough weekend?"

I shrugged, trying to stop my knee from jiggling.

"SweeTart?"

I nodded, and she tossed a couple of packs to me.

"How do you know if someone is telling the truth?" I asked, letting the candy sizzle on my tongue.

Jackie's dark eyes drifted to the ceiling. "That's a tough question." She leaned back in her chair. "I'd say the best proof is when their actions back up their words."

"What if they tell you they aren't going to do something, and it seems like they really mean it, but your stomach tells you they don't?"

"I think you're talking about instinct. Has this person lied before or gone back on a promise?"

"Not exactly. You know how people smile even when they aren't happy? Like salesclerks?"

Jackie chuckled. "Yes, it's kind of a silly idea, isn't it? Smile wide and maybe people will buy more."

"It annoys me. They don't even know me, so how could they possibly care how my day was?"

"I'm with you there. We'll ask if we want something, right?"

I nodded.

"Problem is, people don't always say what they want," she said. "Maybe they're too afraid to ask. Or sometimes they simply don't know. If you had to guess, what would you say your friend wants?"

"Love. She wants someone to care about her." I sucked in

my breath. Stupid me. She'd be able to figure out who I was talking about.

"Don't worry, Drea. Everything you tell me is confidential unless you tell me this person poses a danger to herself or others."

Well, she had an ex who'd harmed her, but I'd learned early on that being a tattletale wasn't cool. Dustin Jenkins threw rocks at me for a week after I'd told the teacher he'd peed his pants. Not to mention numerous other incidents that resulted when I opened my mouth. "Okay," I said.

"I think the best thing you can do is watch out for her. If you get that ache in your stomach, ask her how she's feeling. Tell her that you're there for her. And really, that's all you *can* do. It's up to her to ask you if she needs help." She went on to tell me that I could always talk to her or a trusted adult if the situation got out of hand. But I'd already tuned her out because "out of hand" was subjective, and I had no idea where to draw the line.

We piled into Roger's car after school. Naomi immediately ejected his CD and put in the mixed one I'd made her. Snow Patrol's "Somewhere a Clock Is Ticking" filled the stuffy car with a soft guitar melody.

"Aw, come on. Do we have to listen to this foofee stuff?" Roger asked, glancing longingly at the death metal CD Naomi had stuck in his binder.

"Deal with it." Naomi plopped her feet on the dash.

"Do you know where Lake Padden is?" I asked them.

"No, I've only lived here my entire life." Roger rolled his eyes.

"Can you take me there?"

Naomi turned around, frowning. "Why?"

178

"Justin told me he likes to go there a lot."

Roger merged onto I-5 south. "Scott is looking to pound that guy."

"You better keep your mouth shut, then," Naomi said.

"Hey, he hit you. I'd kick his ass myself if I wasn't sure I'd lose. That guy benches at least three fifty."

"Uh, yeah. Slight exaggeration there, Roger." Naomi chuckled. "Besides, little Miss Kung Fu back there kicked him in the balls. Twice."

I stared out the window. That was a moment I wanted to forget.

"Whatever. I told you he was an ass," he said.

"Yeah, but I'm still not going out with you."

"I never asked."

"Uh-huh." She glanced at me and wrinkled her nose.

My stomach tensed when I saw the sign for Lake Padden. The odds of Justin being here were slim, but I had to know he wasn't some dream in my head. That the nice guy I knew actually existed.

"What do ya know, Drea's a psychic," Naomi said. "Isn't that his car?" She pointed out her window.

I followed the scattered cars until I spotted a black one in the far corner. Roger drove past it, and my heart sped up when I saw the silver M3 on the back.

"Doesn't look like he's in there. Maybe he went for a jog," Naomi said.

"You guys can drop me off. I can have my mom pick me up."

"Uh, you sure?" Roger asked. "What if the guy is a psycho killer?"

"You sound like my grandma," I said.

"I can go with you," Naomi offered.

"I need to do this alone."

She opened the door and let me out of the back seat. "Good luck. And call me if you need us to come back."

I took a deep breath as the squeak of Roger's fan belt faded into the distance. The screams and giggles of children rang out from the small park, and the jingle of leashes could be heard from dogs walking the trail. The sun had graced Bellingham with its presence today, lighting snippets of water and making me squint. My eyes paused on the baseball dugout. A figure with dark hair was hunched over, reading something.

I headed across the damp grass, my shoes growing heavier with each step. Just as I reached the dugout, my foot slipped, and icy mud bled through my sock.

Justin's head jerked up. The skin under one eye was the color of a plum. He closed his book and set it on the bench. "You really should try wearing jeans. They're more dirt friendly."

Brown sludge covered the hem of my white underskirt. "They're too scratchy and confining," I said, clutching the metal fence and stepping inside the dugout.

He glanced at my feet and smirked. "I hope you don't expect me to give you a ride home."

"I don't expect anything other than an explanation. You can't just be there for someone and then disappear." I sat down but kept my distance from him.

"I missed one day of school. Why are you talking like I left town?"

"Because that's what guys do—they disappear. And most of the time, I don't care. But when they're really nice . . ." This wasn't where I wanted to go.

"Don't hold me up too high, Drea. There's a lot I haven't

told you." He rested his head against the wall, keeping his eyes downcast.

I stared at my muddy shoes. "Why?"

His face turned in my direction. "Because I like you."

I forced myself to look at him. "I like you too."

We stared at each other with parted lips and nothing to say. Did his *like* mean the same as mine? I wondered if his stomach fluttered when I was around. Or if he thought about me before he went to sleep. Either way, we needed to stop hiding from each other.

"You know what I love about music?" I asked. "It doesn't lie, even if the lyrics do."

"Are you a Hendrix fan?" he asked.

"Yeah. His solos just say, This is who I am. You can take me or leave me."

"Me too. My mom had a record player in our living room. I'd go in there and play air guitar to 'All Along the Watch Tower' over and over." He looked down, smiling.

A laugh escaped my throat. "I'm sorry I missed it."

"Don't be. I have two left feet, and my sister said I looked constipated. Guitar playing just wasn't in the cards for me." He glanced at me and smoothed his ruffled hair back. The sleeve of his T-shirt rode up, revealing a hint of black ink on his arm. A tattoo—not something I expected.

I looked at his jagged fingernails and the bruised knuckles of his right hand. "I want to know you, Justin. Even the parts you don't think I'll understand."

He exhaled sharply and drummed his feet against the ground. "Bellingham is my clean slate—my second chance. I can't screw it up."

I waited to see if he'd offer more. He didn't. "Is that all you're going to tell me?"

He followed my gaze to his knuckles and covered them with his other hand. "I didn't use to be much different than Scott, okay?"

"You sold drugs and hit girls?"

"No, but I got wasted a lot. And I used to race. Only we were a bunch of rich private-school guys—we didn't even care about the cash."

"Then why did you do it?"

"I needed the rush and the distraction. After my mom died, I didn't want to feel anything. I wanted to hit the fast-forward button and skip to the part where my stomach stopped hurting. When the dreams stopped. When everything I looked at didn't remind me of her. I wanted to pretend she never existed."

"Did it work?"

"No."

Justin told me about his freshman year. He wore a lot of black and smoked pot behind the library with his friends Kermit and Jake. They'd write lyrics about robots and global warming for their industrial band. But Kermit got kicked out later that year for selling his mom's painkillers. And the band went to hell.

He joined a metal band sophomore year. They met a chick from the all-girls' school down the street who could roar like the guy from Mayhem. He fell in love with her and with speed that year, but she used him to make the lead guitarist jealous. The rest of the year was a blur—moving walls and trails in his eyes. Sometimes he couldn't even tell what was real anymore. He got suspended for coming to class high and then expelled for breaking some guy's nose. But he couldn't even remember the guy's name, much less why they fought.

He went to public school his junior year, and his dad tried to keep him housebound when he wasn't in class. So he ran away—lived out of his car until he met up with his old buddy Kermit. He joined Kermit's band, and they played gigs around town. But mostly they sat around Kermit's mom's apartment and got wasted.

"I was with Kermit the night he got busted," he said. "He was selling weed to some girls behind the mall and these un-marked cars came racing up. Doors flew open, and I just ran. I heard them grab Kermit, but I was too high at the time to even realize they were cops. I got away and flagged down a cab. Went back home, asked my dad for help. He called the cops. I can't get the look in his eyes out of my head. He was fucking terrified of me." He took a deep breath before continuing. "They found speed on me. Charged me with possession and obstruction, all that fun stuff. They tried to pin an intent-to-sell charge on me, but it didn't stick. My dad told the judge he didn't want me back home. So I got to spend more time in juvie, then rehab. My sister took custody when I got out—made me promise I wouldn't let her down. And here I am, repeating my junior year like a dumbass."

I couldn't imagine my mom calling it quits on me like that. Despite my issues and our fights, she never walked away from me. "Are you angry with your dad?"

He looked over at me and shook his head. "I was at first, but not anymore. It wasn't like he didn't try. He put his job at risk so he could be home with me last year. We were never close, though."

I moved nearer to him and put my hand over his. "You're nothing like Scott."

"I was waiting for you to get up and run."

"I'm not going anywhere."

He weaved his fingers with mine, brushing his thumb along the back of my hand. "Good."

The warmth of his touch traveled up my arm. I looked away, trying to hide a smile. "What was your mom like?"

"She was always cooking something atrocious." He shook his head and chuckled. "I mean, really bad. But she loved it. Never gave up. And she never let us give up, either."

He talked about how she required him and his older sister to practice their passion for an hour every day—piano for him and everything from martial arts to hairstyling for his sister. "When she got sick, it happened so fast," he continued. "One day she was humming in the kitchen, full of energy, and then she wasn't."

I laid my head on his shoulder and squeezed his hand. There wasn't anything I could say—words wouldn't take away his pain. His heart beat slowly against my ear, and he rested his head against mine. We stayed like that for a while, taking in the sounds around us. The lake whispered in the distance, calming my racing thoughts. There was cheering from a nearby soccer game and laughter from people eating charred burgers at picnic tables. Things I normally hated because I didn't feel part of them. Sometimes it was like watching aliens in their habitat from behind a glass wall. But Justin's warmth against my cheek made it okay.

I sat up, closing my eyes. "I have . . ." My lips tried to form the word, but I couldn't quite do it. "I don't know how to say this."

"Sometimes the only way is to stop thinking of how you'll say it, and just say it. It's kind of like ripping off a Band-Aid."

I opened my eyes and faced him. "I have ADHD and

something called Asperger's syndrome. At least that's what they tell me. It's kind of like—"

"I know what it is. My niece is autistic."

"Oh. Well, it's milder than autism. Like, in my case, the doctor said I didn't need special classes or anything, because my grades are pretty good."

His arm pressed into mine. "You're just a geek. Like me."

"You don't seem surprised."

"I'm sorry." He smiled. "Was I supposed to do a cheer for you?"

"My mom told you, didn't she?" Somehow I felt that—no matter how well he was trying to hide it.

"Yeah, when we took her car out." He put his hand on my knee. "She was just looking out for you, I think. She didn't know what my intentions were."

"And that's my whole problem. She treats me like I'm retarded, like I can't do things for myself."

"Drea, she's a mom. You know mine didn't let me cross the street by myself until I was, like, ten?"

"Why didn't you tell me you knew?" I looked away, folding my arms across my stomach.

"Because I know it's a lot bigger deal to you than it is to me. And I wanted to hear it from you."

"How can it not be? It's not like I'm confessing to needing eyeglasses here."

"It's just a word, Drea. A definition for a certain way of thinking. There's nothing wrong with it. My niece does some pretty brilliant things."

I glanced up at him. "Most people don't see it that way."

Justin ran the back of his hand down my cheek. "I know. But I'm not most people, so stop trying to put me in a box."

"I'm working on it." I let a grin escape, but it quickly faded when I reminded myself I had to tell him everything. "You and Naomi are the first friends I've had in a really long time. And I made that skydiving thing up. I've never actually had a boyfriend."

"Why did you think your dating history mattered to us?"

"Because you guys were the first people to treat me like nothing was wrong with me. I've had labels thrown at me my whole life. Teachers calling me socially immature, kids calling me a freak, doctors checking off symptoms so they could plop a diagnosis in my lap. All because I don't understand some invisible set of social rules. Lie about this, but don't lie about that. Smile—even when you aren't happy—but don't smile too much. Too much is weird. Look people in the eye but, again, not too much. That might freak them out. It's like acting in a play. I've tried to learn my lines, but I'm not very good at it. And with you guys, I wanted to be good. I didn't want you to start looking at me like everyone else."

"Well, if it makes you feel any better, I've never been in a relationship, and I don't have many people I'd consider real friends."

"What about that girl you fell in love with?"

He squinted at the lake. "We messed around, but we were never together. And after that, I didn't want to get close to anyone. Committing to anything or anyone scared me. It still kind of does."

I thought about asking what *messing around* entailed, but I decided to drop it. It bothered me—made me feel more alone. Like I was the only person my age who hadn't experienced a real kiss. The kind that made people see stars.

186

"Naomi doesn't know about me yet. I wanted to tell her today, but I couldn't," I said.

"Why not?"

"She said I was the only person she trusted."

"All the more reason to tell her."

"Don't say anything to her until I do. Please."

He leaned closer to me, brushing a strand of hair out of my face. "I wouldn't do that."

I turned away from his stare. "What does your sister think of you missing school?"

"She allowed it for today only. This weekend brought back a lot for me. I needed some time to think. But then you went and found me."

"Sorry," I said.

"Don't be." He put his arm around me, giving me a quick hug. "Let's get you home so you can wash that skirt."

We took the long, no-muddy-grass-involved way to his car. When he opened the door for me, I stopped and looked at him for a second. I wanted him to lean in and kiss me, like they did in an eighties movie Mr. Diaz showed. They kissed in the pouring rain—I thought that was cool.

Justin raised his eyebrows. "You getting in?"

"Yeah, guess so." I collapsed into the seat, feeling frustrated and relieved at the same time.

Justin didn't say much on the way home, but I was okay with that. I never got why people had issues with silence, especially with good music playing. He gave me a hug and said he'd see me tomorrow. And that I'd better be prepared to jam.

I was more than ready.

Mom shuffled away from the living room window when I walked in. "I thought you said you were out with Naomi."

A lump formed in my throat. I wanted to tell her everything—what happened over the weekend, the things Justin said. How lost I felt. I wasn't used to keeping things from her. "She had stuff to do with Roger."

A smile flickered across her lips. "I see."

"Why did you have to tell Justin about me?"

She sighed. "I'm happy that you're making friends here, baby. But new friends bring new experiences, and I want them to understand you, why you may not always react how they expect."

There she went again. Talking to me like I couldn't handle anything on my own. "How can anyone really understand anyone? We aren't in each other's heads," I said.

"Well, that's true, but—"

"Why do I need a disclaimer? It's not like I'm hurting people . . . or myself. And it's not like I don't try. I try really hard."

Her dark eyes softened. "I know you do. And I am proud of you. I hope you know that."

"Then why do you have to tell everyone that I have Asperger's?"

"It's not a dirty word, Drea. It just means that you have a unique mind, which is something you should embrace. The world needs more people like you."

"Then why are you always trying to change me?"

Mom moved closer to me, shaking her head. "I'm not. I'm trying to teach you ways to cope—how to communicate with people who don't think like you do. It's a good skill for anyone to have, a necessary one."

I looked away, clasping and unclasping my hands. She'd told me this before. It seemed rehearsed, like lines she'd memorized out of a book. "I wish you'd give me a real answer for once."

She rubbed her temple, her mouth turning down at the corners. "Okay, Drea. What is it you'd like me to say or do? I'm only trying to—"

"Help. I know. But you aren't helping by treating me like a baby, by telling people that something is *wrong* with me before they even get to know me. Let me decide if I want them to know or not."

"I don't use the term *wrong*. I just explain your diagnosis and how it affects you. But"—Mom held her hand up, giving me her stop sign before I could interrupt—"I won't tell anyone else without your permission."

"That's all I wanted."

She wrapped her arms around me, squeezing me tight. "I know you want to work a lot of this stuff out for yourself, but it's hard for me to let go. Be patient with me, okay?"

I nodded and swallowed hard, thinking about Justin, wondering if his mom had said the same stuff to him. I couldn't imagine Mom not always being around. "I love you," I said.

Her chest shook. I couldn't tell if it was from tears or laughter. Maybe it was both.

O N THURSDAY, Mr. Diaz showed his favorite example of a long shot—Godard's *Week End*. This included a horrendous traffic jam and a continuous barrage of horns. Apparently, they thought honking made traffic move faster in 1960s France. This little black car managed to weave its way through, while the other cars sat in line.

Justin turned in his seat and whispered, "This has to be the most boring and interesting clip I've ever seen."

I glanced at Mr. Diaz and leaned forward. "That made no sense."

"It's getting really repetitive, but I keep expecting Godzilla to show up."

The last bit showed mangled bodies in the grass and some guy walking around them like they weren't even there. I used to see people do that to the homeless in the city. Half the time they looked dead, but Mom said they were probably passed out drunk.

"Okay." Mr. Diaz flipped the TV off. "What did you guys think?"

At least half the classroom was asleep, drawing, or otherwise preoccupied with something on their desks.

The dark-haired emo boy raised his hand. "I don't get the point. If people were so pissed about the black car cutting through, why didn't they slug the driver? They just stood there waving their arms like idiots."

"Yeah," another guy chimed in. "They kept getting out of their cars like they were gonna give him a beat-down and then nothing happened."

"I thought it was obnoxious," Casey said.

"All good points," Mr. Diaz said. "Why do you think they held back?"

I raised my hand. "It's a picture of society. How nobody tries to help each other—it's everyone for themselves."

"I think the black car is breaking free from the rat race in a sense," Justin said. "All these people were lined up for the daily grind, and the driver of the black car said, Screw it, nobody is going to stop me."

"Nobody wanted to see them get ahead, but their persistence eventually paid off," I said.

Mr. Diaz nodded at us and smiled. "It's good to see you two working so well together."

A couple people giggled, and Casey shot me a dirty look. I sank lower in my chair.

Mr. Diaz opened his mouth to speak, but the bell cut him off. "We'll continue this tomorrow! Don't forget to write up your movie reviews for this clip. They're due tomorrow—first thing."

Justin waited for me as I shoved a binder into my backpack. Casey hovered around her desk, watching us.

"It was good to hear your voice today, Drea." Mr. Diaz

said. "I can tell from your reviews that you understand a lot more than you think you do."

"Thanks," I mumbled, my cheeks growing hot.

"We've got the camera this weekend," Justin said.

I flung my backpack over one shoulder. "Crap, I promised my grandma I'd help her with a garage sale."

He grinned. "Maybe there will be some fun customers to film."

"Hey, Justin," Casey said as we passed her, "Kari wants to talk to you. She's waiting out front."

Justin's jaw tensed. "Okay."

The two of them walked ahead of me toward the school parking lot. Naomi grabbed my shoulders from behind, pulling me back a couple paces. My lunch box slipped out of my grasp and crashed onto the floor. The contents—my iPod, loose change, crayons, lip gloss, and two maxi pads—scattered across the green tile.

"Can you not do that?" I knelt down and grabbed my iPod.

"God, cranky much?" She got on her knees and picked up the quarters.

A couple guys walked by, laughing. "Are those the extra-absorbent kind?" One of them kicked a pad over to me.

I snatched it and shoved it inside the box. Apparently the fiasco had caught Justin's attention because he handed the other pad to me and picked up some of my crayons. I really wanted a blanket to hide under.

"Why don't you use tampons?" Naomi asked.

"I'll wait for you guys outside," Justin said, getting up. He jogged after Casey.

"I really hate you right now, Naomi." I slammed my lunch box shut. "Why do you have to embarrass me in front of him?"

"Uh, Drea. Most guys our age know we get periods. It's not like a big secret or anything."

"My mom says guys get weirded out when you talk about it."

"I know." She gave me a big smile. "That's why it's fun. I like to watch them squirm."

I shook my head and headed toward the double set of doors. "Why? That's a pointless goal."

She walked ahead of me and shoved the door open. "Don't you ever get tired of being such a priss?"

"Whatever that means." I hadn't told Naomi the truth yet. Her words kept spinning in my head. *The only one I trust.*

Justin leaned against the trunk of his car, eyeing the ground. Kari did most of the talking, using animated hand gestures that resembled sign language. Casey paced behind them with a cell phone glued to her ear.

"Drama-queen alert." Naomi tugged me along. "Let's go spy."

I followed her. At least we wouldn't be in Kari's line of vision that way. We slouched over and crept behind a pickup truck next to Justin's BMW.

"You didn't strike me as a coward," Kari said.

"I didn't know what to say—it was awkward."

"Only because you made it that way."

Naomi let out a snort and covered her laugh.

I elbowed her in the side.

Justin shoved his hands into his pockets. "I told you, Kari. It's not you."

"Are you gay?"

"I just don't want to hook up with anyone right now."

"Is that why you and Drea are attached at the hip?"

"We're friends."

"Right. You should hear the way she salivates over you in the locker room. Good luck with that." She shook her head and walked off with Casey.

I really wanted that blanket.

Naomi jumped up. "For the record, we merely admire you—our salivary glands aren't involved."

I followed her, keeping my eyes on Justin's tires. Looking at him would be too intense. Too embarrassing.

"Good to know," he answered. "We recording?"

"I'm game. Did you mic my drums yet, Drea?"

"Yep." We'd finally moved her drum kit over yesterday, but she'd played for only five minutes before Grandma had major issues. No drums after sunset, she said. I guess she feared they would attract vampires or something.

"Sweet! I can't stay for long, though. My dad is taking me out to dinner tonight," she said.

"That's good, right?" I asked.

She shrugged. "As long as he shows up."

I insisted on riding in the back today. The thought of being so close to Justin made me nervous. If he didn't know how I felt before, he certainly did now. Kari sucked. And so did Naomi for teasing me so much in the locker room.

"So, did you totally shoot Kari down, or what?" Naomi asked as we turned onto Holly Street.

"She made a move on me, and I told her I wasn't interested. Took her home."

"Let me guess. She either gave you a shoulder rub or just leaned in and kissed you. I'm guessing the first one—she uses that on the good boys."

I peeked at Justin in the rearview mirror, and his eyes met mine. I hadn't told Naomi about him.

"Neither," he said. "Anyway, she took it personally and wouldn't let it drop. So I've been avoiding her."

"Sounds like Kari." Naomi tapped her knuckles against the window. "Be forewarned—that girl can hold quite the grudge."

"I'm not losing sleep over it."

I tried to hold back a smile but failed.

"You don't think she's hot at all?" Naomi asked. "Because everything else with a dick does."

"Sure, but she's not my type."

"You prefer brainy redheads with music addictions, right?"

I kicked the back of her chair.

"Ow, hi. Base of my spine here." Naomi shifted in her seat.

"As long as it's *good* music," he said, glancing at me in the rearview mirror again. His lips twitched with a smile.

I stared out the window for the rest of the car ride.

I deconstructed Naomi's face with my HI-8 video camera, moving from her full lips to the crinkle in her brow. The beauty and the flaws—every unique freckle. This was how I saw people.

"She smiles with grace, but no one recalls her face." Naomi swayed in front of the microphone, shoe tapping the floor. "Invisible. Carved between the walls. She can scream your name, but you don't hear her at all."

I moved the frame to the right. Justin's fingers hammered their way into the chorus. His eyelashes fluttered against his pale cheeks and his shoulders gently swayed. Black or white— he owned every key.

I loved watching them create their magic. That's what it was to me, really. I could hear everything wrong with a mix, produce a vocal to death, and create a billion different sounds, but I couldn't play a melody that made me shiver.

Naomi tilted her head back. Her face contorted with each word. "She knows her place in this world. She can tear down its walls, and still nobody knows her name. Yeah, she knows her place. But she's not going down . . . without a fight."

Too bad today was just practice. I was getting some great shots.

She tore the headphones off and hooted. "Okay, that rocked."

I turned back to the computer and made sure the vocal track recorded properly. "You really nailed this take, Naomi. I think I can pretty much use the whole thing."

"Pretty much?" Justin asked. "Use it all—in its entirety. The flaws make the emotion come through even more."

I double clicked on the track. "Yeah, but—"

"Yeah, but nothing," he broke in. "Put your 'verb and delay on it—just don't chop it up."

Naomi squealed. "I can't wait to hear the whole thing! I like the bass line you did, Drea." She wrapped her arms around my shoulders and kissed my cheek. "It's groovy."

"Thanks," I said, wiping the wet spot she left behind.

She plopped in Justin's lap and sighed. "You, sir, are a piano god."

He winced as she gave him a juicy kiss on the forehead. "Are you on something again, Naomi?"

"I'm high on music. Lighten up, *Dad*." She stood up and did some kind of dramatic pose.

"I think she's happy about seeing her dad tonight," I said.

"No, no," she said. "It's the music. Hey, we should play 'Dawn' for Justin. I want to record that next."

"You up for it?" I asked him.

"I play by ear. No preparations needed." He smiled.

I grabbed my green acoustic and sat with it in my lap. "It's a little slower in tempo, but more upbeat." I told him.

This song called for fifths in the verse. Two power chords played twice each with a muted pick rhythm in between.

Naomi grabbed the mic, nodding her head to my strums. "Sweet little Jane was caught in a rut. She went too far and never paid up. And the street corner won't give a dime to Daddy's little girl with the misty eyes."

I glanced over at Justin. He stared back with the hint of a smile on his face. My fingers slipped. "Oops."

She launched into the bridge, a spoken-word part repeated twice. "There's no God fear and no sky to reach. Are my words silent shadows or just obsolete?"

I avoided Justin's gaze as I shifted into the chorus. It wasn't punchy like the verse, calling for more of a dramatic riff.

"She waits for the dawn . . . with her lace gloves on. She said revolution. Cleanse the streets, unveil the mask of sweet pollution. Yeah, she waits for the dawn. Her time will come."

Justin played three high notes on the piano and colored them in with two bass chords. It gave the song a little more elegance. He kept it simple, as if he knew too much sugar would ruin the mix. I really liked that about him.

"What time is it?" Naomi asked suddenly.

"It's just after five," Justin said.

And from the sour odor wafting down the stairs, dinner would come too soon.

"I gotta go." She snatched her backpack. "You going to put 'Invisible' up tonight?"

"Planning on it. I just have to do a little mixing and

mastering," I said. What I really wanted to say was, Don't leave me alone with Justin. I can't even look at him right now.

"Cool." She gave Justin and me a quick hug before sprinting up the stairs.

The door clicked shut. I faced the computer.

"Do you want to work on something new?" he asked.

"That's okay. I think this will keep me busy for a while." I labeled Naomi's latest vocal.

"Should I go, then?"

No, I like being around you. Yes, because I think I like it too much. Maybe, because I don't know what else to say. "Do you want to go?"

His footsteps came up behind me. Soft and hesitant. "No."

I bumped the mouse, undoing my last action. "Um, okay." Edit-redo. "Just so you know, what Kari said about the locker room thing. I don't talk about you. Naomi does and—"

His breath tickled my ear. "I don't care."

I accidentally deleted my bass track. Undo. Wait, wrong menu. "What would you like to undo? I mean, do?"

He looked at the computer over my shoulder. "I could watch you work your magic."

"I need the earphones for that." *Think, Drea.* "But I've always wanted to learn how to play the piano."

"Sweet." He grabbed the back of my chair and rolled me toward the keyboard. "Door-to-door service."

I gripped the armrests. "Um, thanks."

He moved his chair to my right. His arm pressed into mine as he sat down. "What song do you want to learn?"

"How about one of yours?" I tried to keep my voice even. Interested. But it probably came out over the top.

"Okay, I'll teach you the first one I wrote. It's really lame, but easy to learn."

"I doubt it's lame."

He took my left hand and pressed my fingers into three notes. "This is A-minor. Your first chord. Just keep playing A-C-E-A-C-E."

I played each note as he directed until I found a rhythm.

"You got it." His hand hovered over mine again. "Now move your pinkie back to the G and play G-B-D the same way." He instructed me to move down to E-minor, then up to F before returning to A-minor. It was hard to focus with him so close, especially when he smelled like rain again.

As I got the hang of the bass notes, he played a sparse melody in a higher octave, following my unpredictable rhythm perfectly. "You're a quick study," he said.

"Whatever. I keep hitting the wrong notes."

He touched my nose. "That's because you're thinking too hard. Close your eyes."

"Then I won't be able to see what I'm doing."

"That's the point," he whispered in my ear. "Sometimes the only way to connect is to let go."

I shut my eyes, trying to detach my brain from my hand. No easy feat. Justin played a few more notes. These were faster—more passionate. They gave me chills. I tapped my foot on the floor and pretended I was driving his melody. My fingers moved slowly at first, but I became less aware of everything as the music swam around me.

Justin took my free hand, his fingers sliding over mine and pressing them to the keys. My other hand twitched. I hit G-sharp instead of G.

He used my fingertips to play the notes. For a few moments I felt like a real piano player lost in my own creation. It was incredible. And I didn't want it to stop.

I leaned on him, letting his warmth draw me closer. His breath hit my cheek. My heart beat faster. I tilted my face up, and his lips met mine. Our hands slid off the keyboard and his fingers inched up my forearms. I had no idea what to do, or if I was even doing it right.

His mouth pressed into mine, parting my lips softly. My skin felt weird. Hot all over and sensitive to every movement.

I pulled back and opened my eyes. "I don't think I'm doing this right."

He smiled and ran his fingers through my hair. "The piano or the kiss?"

"Both."

"Do you want to stop?"

I looked at the faint freckle on his upper lip and the gold flecks in his eyes. "You're really beautiful," I said before shaking my head. "God, that probably sounded stupid."

He touched his nose to mine. "So are you."

His soft lips pressed into mine again, and I closed my eyes, kissing him back. His arm muscles tensed with my touch, and his breaths grew heavier. I was afraid the spit thing would gross me out, but I didn't mind it. It made him real. It made *this* real.

He pulled me closer and kissed my jaw, moving down my neck. His mouth found a spot behind my ear that sent tickles down my spine. The feeling was almost too intense to take.

And then the door upstairs swung open. "Andrea?" Grandma called. "Dinner is ready."

We pulled apart. I wiped my lips with the back of my hand, wondering if they'd look kissed somehow. Justin sat up straighter and put one hand on the keyboard.

Grandma's sharp eyes went from me to Justin when she reached the bottom step. "Where's Naomi?"

"She went home," I said.

"Oh." Her eyes rested on Justin again. "What are you two doing down here?"

"Justin was teaching me how to play piano."

"Don't you have homework to do?"

"I finished most of it at school."

"Well, come on, then. It's getting cold." She headed back up the steps, leaving the door open. "Juliana!"

I tucked my hair behind my ear and stared hard at my hands. They were still shaking. "Um, sorry. You should probably go, but . . ."

He moved closer to me again. "But?"

"I don't really want you to."

Grandma yelled for my mom again.

"What?" Mom asked. It sounded like they were moving into the kitchen.

"Andrea is down there alone. With that boy." Even my grandma's whispers carried.

"Oh, for Christ sake, Mom. So what?"

The corner of Justin's mouth curved up, but he covered it.

"Go ahead and laugh," I said. "My grandma is a freak."

"I'm sorry if I got you in trouble," he said.

Mom jogged down the stairs before I could answer. She grinned when she caught me smoothing my hair back. "Hey, Justin."

He smiled and waved at her.

"Sorry about my mom," she said. "She doesn't mean to be rude. She's just—"

"It's cool," he said, glancing at me. "I get it."

"You're welcome to stay for dinner."

He studied my face before answering. "Sure, okay. Thanks."

Mom winked at me before turning around and heading back upstairs. My face burned.

"My grandma's cooking is really bad. I mean, like mushy vegetables and stuffed pork chops bad."

Justin put his hand over mine, tangling our fingers together. "I grew up with a bad cook, remember? I can handle it."

I twirled my spoon in Grandma's version of vegetable stew. This included no salt, gravy like water, and a bitter aftertaste. She'd chosen twelve-grain bread as a side dish. It was untoasted and stale around the edges.

Grandma discussed the art of grocery store coupons with Mom, while Justin and I took turns kicking and dodging each other's feet. My stomach fluttered every time I caught his eye.

"I warned you," I said, motioning to his barely touched stew.

He put a finger to his mouth and shook his head.

"That's a nice car you have out there, Justin," Grandma said. "Are you going to pay your parents back for it?"

He swallowed a chunk of potato. "It was a birthday gift."

"How about some salt?" Mom asked, frowning at the stew.

"You're past forty now," Grandma said. "Menopause is right around the corner. Sodium is the last thing you need."

Justin used that moment to wipe his mouth, but his eyes crinkled at the corners.

"Your candor is always appreciated, Mother." She rolled her eyes and grabbed the salt from the cabinet.

Grandma nodded at Justin. "Who pays for your insurance?"

"I do."

"How old are you—sixteen?"

"Seventeen."

"Your rates must be sky high." She then launched into a lecture about the auto industry and insurance rates. Grandma loved to educate people about money, even though she'd always been a homemaker.

Justin smiled and nodded like he was interested the entire time. It was pretty impressive. Usually I left the room after about two minutes.

"Nobody cares," I said finally. Anything to stop her from squawking for a few seconds.

Grandma jabbed her finger at me. "You'll care when you start paying for it."

"She has a point," Justin said to me, knocking his foot into mine.

"Let's see. No license. Not exactly a pressing matter at the moment."

"It will be soon," he said.

"How's she doing?" Mom asked, salting her stew for the fourth time.

"Really well. We drove around downtown yesterday. Maybe we'll try the freeway this weekend."

I nearly choked on a bite of bread. "Do you have a death wish?"

Mom chuckled. "Just don't drive like Grandma and you'll be fine."

Justin crinkled his brow at me, and I laughed. "Grandma knows two speeds," I said. "Zero and eighty."

He raised his eyebrows at her, puckering his lips. "Nice."

Grandma shook her head. "I've never gotten a ticket." She snatched her bowl from the table and rinsed it in the sink.

Then Justin offered to do the dishes for some ungodly reason.

"Why are you being so nice to my grandma?" I asked, walking him to his car twenty minutes later. The cool wind painted my arms with goose bumps.

"I had about two bites of her stew—or whatever that was. I felt bad."

"She would've made me do the dishes anyway. It's not like you were saving her the trouble."

He leaned against the driver's door of his car. "Then you're welcome."

I glanced at the dim lights of Naomi's house. Her father's SUV wasn't in the driveway. "I hope Naomi's dad didn't let her down this time."

"Does he do that a lot?"

I told him about meeting her dad and what Naomi said afterward. "She really scared me last weekend."

Justin shoved his hands in his pockets and nodded. "You're a good friend. I wish I'd had someone like you back home."

"I don't know what to do."

He gave me a soft smile. "Just keep being you."

"That doesn't help much."

"Do you want me to talk to her?"

"What would you say?"

He shrugged. "I think I can relate to where her head is at

right now. And it doesn't seem like she has anyone to talk to about it. Look at the lyrics she wrote."

"She has me."

Justin shifted his weight. "Yeah, but you're so . . ."

I folded my arms across my stomach. "Clueless?"

"I was going to say levelheaded. Naomi's in a place that's hard to understand unless you've been there, and I think she knows that." He looked toward her driveway. "She may not even want to talk to me. But I'll try."

"When?"

"How about tomorrow? We'll tell her you have plans after school, and I'll ask her if she wants to hang out at Café Mars or something."

"Why can't I come?"

"It's better if I talk to her one-on-one—trust me. The members of my old band talked to me all at once, and it felt like a fucking intervention. Didn't go over real well." He looked down at his feet. "To say the least."

"Oh." The idea of Justin and Naomi going out alone bothered me. I felt left out of something important, but I wanted Naomi to feel better. "Isn't telling her about your past going to be hard?"

He exhaled, studying my face. "It was harder telling you."

I hugged myself tighter. What was that supposed to mean?

"Can you have your mom pick you up?"

My stomach tensed. "She has to work. It'll have to be Grandma."

"Hey, come here." He wrapped his arms around my waist and pulled me close. The copper hue of streetlights shone in his eyes. "I'd much rather have you there."

I looked away, unsure of where to put my hands. On his

shoulders seemed too much like dancing. And I definitely wasn't going to grab his butt.

He tilted my chin upward and ran his thumb along my cheek. I slowly met his stare again. He smiled and kissed me. My head spun and my knees shook, but somehow I managed to stay upright. His tongue brushed against mine, and I pushed back, wondering if that was what he wanted. The whole idea of mingling tongues baffled me. When he paused, I figured I'd done something wrong and pulled away.

"I'm sorry," I said.

"Why?" he whispered and tucked a lock of my hair behind my ear.

"I don't know how to do this, okay? Naomi is the only other person I've kissed. And it wasn't like this." I looked away again, wanting to smack myself. Now he knew everything. But at least he was almost as clueless in the romance department.

"It's different with every person."

"You've only kissed that one girl, right?"

His smile faded. "Does it matter?"

"Yes." Because I hated feeling like such a dork.

"I've kissed a few people."

"How many?"

He let go of my waist. "I didn't keep a tally, Drea."

"I thought you were more like me."

"We're a lot alike. We're both stubborn geeks with superb taste in music." He reached for me.

I backed away.

His head tilted back, like he was searching the stars for answers. Too bad it was cloudy. "I'm far from perfect, Drea. So if you want to walk away right now, I don't blame you. But I really like you. Everything about you."

I opened my mouth to speak, but every question I had blurred together in a mass of gibberish.

He leaned over and gave me a quick hug. "Just let me know what you decide."

It wasn't until after he drove off that I found the words. I stood frozen for a while, letting the drizzle melt into my cheeks, and they came to me. Simple, but more truthful than anything else I could say.

Thank you.

14

IT WAS OFFICIAL. Rummaging through dusty boxes at seven A.M. on a Saturday stunk.

Mom hummed "Bus Stop" and grinned like a kid discovering a secret attic. Don, the dentist, was picking her up at nine and whisking her off to the San Juan Islands for a romantic weekend.

"Do you realize we can get a hantavirus and die from breathing in mouse turds?" I asked her.

She rolled her eyes and unwrapped some figurines. "It's just dirt, Drea."

I adjusted the flimsy breathing mask I'd found in Grandma's closet. We sat in her freezing garage, placing various items on fold-out tables. Grandma would poke her head in every ten minutes or so to decide whether or not to sell them.

"Craigslist would be much easier. Who actually goes to garage sales anymore?"

Mom smiled. "People like Grandma. What's really bugging you today?"

I flipped through an ancient calendar and shrugged. Justin

had said about three words to me yesterday. I didn't get a single moment alone with him because we had a quiz in English, and Naomi spent lunch planning a move to New York City. Neither of them called me last night.

"Grandma said she had to pick you up from school yesterday. How come?"

"Justin took Naomi out so he could talk to her about stuff."

She wiped some dust off a green vase and frowned. "I thought Justin liked you."

I looked at the concern in her dark eyes, and an ache formed in my throat. I still wanted to tell her what Naomi did at the mall and about Scott. She might've known what to do, but I knew it would scare her. Maybe enough to not let me hang out with Naomi again.

She squatted next to me and gave me a hug, stroking my hair. "Talk to me, sweetie."

I breathed in the scent of her favorite shampoo. It always smelled a little like bubblegum. And that did it. I just started talking. About Naomi's situation and Justin's past. About how I felt sick every time I thought about last weekend.

Her eyes searched my face, and she gave me a weak smile. "I'm proud of you."

That wasn't what I expected to hear. "Why?"

"Because you knew what Naomi did was wrong and you had the guts to tell her that. You stuck by her and tried to help, even when you were scared."

"But I just let it happen."

"Yes, but now you know not to put yourself in that situation again. You can't stop Naomi from stealing or dating the wrong guy. It's not your job to be her mom." She ruffled my hair. "Just like it isn't your job to be mine."

"Do you think she'll stay away from Scott?"

Mom sighed and sat cross-legged on a throw rug. "I hope so. I know with me—I'm a hopeless romantic at heart. The idea of love blinds me. I see qualities that aren't there because I want them to be there. I want to trust their words because it hurts too much not to. I look at your grandma and I think, How can she live like this? But I also envy her. She's not afraid to be alone. I think Naomi and I need a little dose of that."

"You just made sense."

Mom laughed. "Well, that's pretty rare, huh? We should celebrate."

"Are you still going to let me hang out with Naomi?"

She sighed. "I'm not going to lie. I'll be watching you more closely—asking where you're going. No more sleepovers at Naomi's. I want you home by midnight on weekends. And I want to talk to her dad."

"No! She'll hate me."

"She's going to get herself into a lot of trouble. I can't sit back and do nothing in good conscience. Her dad needs to know what's going on."

"She promised me she would stop."

"And I have no doubt she means well, Drea. But we can't count on that. In the meantime, keep making music. Listen to her if she wants to talk. I think Justin will help look out for her too." She poked my arm. "Grandma likes him, by the way. And he must like you an awful lot to have listened to her go on the other night. Trust me, not many of my boyfriends were so patient with her."

"He's not my boyfriend." I turned my attention to another box, digging at the contents. "Does his past bother you?"

"I'd be lying if I said it didn't make me a little nervous. But

I think it's great that he's being honest about it. Does it bother *you*?"

"No. I like him—I mean, he's becoming a good friend."

She smirked. "He's quite the cutie."

I rolled my eyes. "Mom, please!" The thought of seeing him later today terrified me. I didn't want to make a fool of myself again.

I was filming Grandma lining up a row of angel figurines when Naomi showed up. Her big blue eyes appeared in the frame, looking red-rimmed and sleepy. But her lips stretched into a wide smile. She had no idea I'd ratted her out.

"Hey, gorgeous," she said, batting her eyelashes at the camera. The afternoon light pierced her blond roots, making her hair look thin.

"Hi." I panned to Grandma. The school camera weighed a ton, and using a tripod was the only way I could keep it steady.

Naomi walked behind me, peering at the little LCD screen. "You've got it zoomed in really far. I can practically see the dirt under her nails." She pressed a button, pushing the image of Grandma farther away. "There ya go."

I elbowed her arm. "I had it there for a reason, Naomi."

"Sorry. Damn." She huffed and sat on the grass. "So I guess you're mad after all."

"What do you mean?" I focused on Grandma's face. She watched the street, hands on her hips. Her eyes widened with each passing car.

"You said it was okay. I mean—*he* asked me, and we're just friends. It's not like it was like *that*, you know?"

Her words melded together in my head. All I could think about was what she'd do when my mom called her dad.

"Oh, what? You're going to ignore me now? You should've just said something, Drea."

Grandma turned then, her eyes piercing the frame. She instantly covered her face and spun around. "I told you to turn that off, Drea! You'll scare the customers away."

"What customers?"

"I'll throw it in the street. I'm not kidding," Grandma said.

"Then you can pay my teacher three thousand dollars to replace it."

Grandma crinkled her nose and stormed back into the garage, mumbling something about disrespect. "Get me if anyone shows up!" she called.

I clicked the camera off and knelt in front of Naomi. The grass was damp and cold.

"Do you want a blanket?" I asked.

She studied my face for a moment. "You aren't mad, then?"

"No—I just had a good shot and you messed it up. That's all."

"I was trying to help! But I guess I can't do *anything* right."

I looked away from her glare, hugging myself. "I don't know what you mean."

"Like, yesterday—you bit my head off because you dropped your lunch box. It wasn't my fault, Drea. I didn't knock it out of your hands."

The cutting sound of her voice made me want to get up and run, but I closed my eyes, trying to think of the right words.

"You could at least look at me," she said.

"I don't like seeing you so angry at me."

A few seconds of silence went by. Finally, she exhaled. "Sometimes it just seems like I annoy you. Like you don't want me around."

I opened my eyes. She was looking down, running her fingers through the grass. "I do want you around."

"Okay," she mumbled. We sat quietly for a minute before a smirk crossed her lips. "Justin told me about his juvie days last night. That's kinda hot, right?"

"Are you kidding?"

"No way. Justin in handcuffs? Awesome." She laughed.

Their talk didn't help as much as I'd hoped.

"Why is that funny?"

She leaned back on the palms of her hands. "Um—because it's Justin. That image is a little hard to picture."

"His mom died. Do you think that's funny and awesome too?"

Her mouth dropped open. "Of course not. But shit happens, people die. It's not a reason to stop living yourself."

I pulled up a chunk of grass and let it sift through my fingers. "Whatever."

"There you go again—acting all pissy."

My stomach tensed. "I just don't understand some of the things you say."

"It's called having a sense of humor, Drea."

I counted the loose blades of grass in my hand. "Okay."

"I should've been sixteen in the eighties," she continued. "I would've been the perfect punk chick."

"Why can't you be a punk chick now?"

"Because Sid is dead, duh."

I threw grass at her. "He died in 1979."

She rolled her eyes. "Semantics. Anyway, Justin had a conniption because I called Green Day old-school punk. So he gave me a CD with the Dead Milkmen, Sex Pistols, the Clash, and a bunch of others on it. Good stuff."

"Cool." I looked at her empty driveway across the street. "Is your dad home this weekend?"

"Nope, but his vacation starts next Saturday. He claims he's taking me car shopping."

My chest relaxed. At least I had a week to convince Mom not to call. "You never said how your dinner went Thursday."

"It was a dinner with Dad, not an all-night party. What exactly is there to talk about?"

"You seemed excited, that's all."

"What I really want to talk about is you and Justin. He's so gaga over you."

I let a smile slip.

"Ooh. You're blushing. Something's totally happened—fess up."

I buried my face in my knees.

"Oh my God. You hooked up with him!"

I put my hand against her mouth. "Shut up. My grandma will hear you."

She pulled back. "I wasn't talking that loud. Don't be so paranoid."

"We kissed," I whispered.

"What?" She leaned forward, her eyes widening.

I brought my mouth to her ear. "Kissed."

"Kissed what?"

"You know—with our mouths."

Her brows pinched together. "That's it?"

I ached to tell her the truth. That I'd never had a boyfriend before. I wanted to ask her all about her first time. What was normal, what wasn't. But she'd probably think that was funny too.

A slowing car caught my attention. Justin pulled up to the curb in front of us.

Naomi grinned, standing up. "Speaking of a certain ex-thug."

"Don't call him that."

She rolled her eyes and ran over to Justin's car.

I stayed back and watched them through the lens of the camera. The world looked so different this way. Naomi's smile seemed less real, and Justin looked almost shy. I zoomed in as he pulled out of their hug. He stared right into the camera, like he was trying to see inside my mind. Naomi glanced over at me and whispered something. He eyed the ground and shrugged.

I focused on Naomi's mouth as they walked toward me. It moved so quickly. Like she couldn't get the words out fast enough. Justin's lips curved up, not enough to be smiling. But enough to look unassuming. Pleasant.

"She can't seem to stop messing around with that thing," Naomi said.

Justin came within a few feet of me and stopped. "Hey."

I straightened, peering over the camera. "Hi."

Naomi's gaze bounced between us. "Hello, awkward." And then the wicked grin took over. "Drea tells me you two had quite the hot night." She punched his arm.

He shot me what could only be a confused look. "That's interesting."

"Don't," I said, hoping she'd drop it for once.

"Yeah, apparently you guys . . ." She put a hand over her mouth, pretending to giggle.

"What? I missed the joke, sorry," Justin said.

My heart thudded. "Naomi, please stop."

"Drea said you guys"—she nudged him and whispered—"kissed." Then she covered her mouth like it was the most shocking thing ever.

My cheeks burned, and I felt like I was going to throw up. I ran into the house, slamming the basement door behind me. Naomi must've known what a big deal that kiss was to me. And she didn't care. It was a joke to her. *I* was a joke.

I buried my face in the softness of my pillow, squeezing my eyes shut.

The basement door creaked open a couple minutes later.

"Give me five minutes, Grandma! Five lousy minutes."

But it wasn't her open-toed heels coming down the stairs. These steps were softer, more like tennis shoes. "Don't worry. Grandma and Naomi are holding down the fort," Justin said. "But I brought the camera down in case they decide to go Jerry Springer on each other."

"Thanks," I mumbled into my green pillow.

His footsteps echoed behind me and stopped as he set the camera down. He walked over to the side I was facing and leaned against the wall, peering down at me. I turned the other way.

"Do you want to talk about it?" he asked.

"Everything is a big joke to her, including me."

"She gets off on teasing people. But you aren't a joke to her, Drea. She went on and on last night about how talented you are."

"Why is she always trying to embarrass me?"

"Because she wants attention and doesn't know how to ask for it."

"You sound like Jackie."

"So be it. But it's true. Besides, she feels pretty bad. Your grandma asked where you were, and Naomi told her you didn't feel well. She got suckered into helping your grandma redo the table display."

I rolled over and met his gaze. "I told my mom what happened last weekend. She wants to call her dad."

"Did you tell her about me too?"

"I told her everything. I'm sorry. She still likes you."

He shifted his weight against the wall. "Don't be sorry. You guys are close. I tell my sister everything too."

"I need to convince her not to call Naomi's dad."

He shrugged. "I don't think you can."

"That doesn't help much."

"What can I say, Drea? I'm not very good at the comforting thing, especially when it comes to you."

"That's not true," I said.

"No? You seemed almost disgusted by me the other night."

I sat up. "And that's the problem, Justin. Sometimes I just don't know what to say or the right way to say it. By the time I figured out how to tell you what I was feeling, you had left. Don't assume my thoughts by the look on my face. Don't try and read between my words. At least ask me what I'm thinking or feeling first. It might take me some time, but I will answer you."

He folded his arms across his chest. "Okay, then, I'm asking. How do you feel about me?"

"It's hard to explain. You make me feel connected to the world in ways I've never felt connected before. Usually I hate it when people touch me, but with you—it's comforting. Not in the same way as my mom."

"God, I hope not." He gave me a strange look before holding up his hands. "Sorry, go on."

"It's a warm feeling, and my stomach kind of tickles. And . . . why are you smiling?"

He moved from the wall and sat on the bed. Close, but not close enough to touch me. "You're describing actual sensations."

"You asked me how I felt."

"I know, and it's the most real and honest answer I've ever heard. That's why I'm smiling."

"Oh." I ran my fingers along the threads of my purple comforter. "I wanted to say thank you the other night. For giving me a chance, for the driving lessons, for coming to get me and Naomi at two in the morning—and for saying you liked everything about me. Nobody has ever said that before."

"You don't need to thank me for liking you, Drea. It was a done deal when I saw you singing to yourself the first day of school."

I let my hair fall in my face, hoping it would cover up my dumb smile. "I thought you were laughing at me."

"No, I was wondering how to introduce myself to the beautiful musically inclined girl without sounding like an ass."

I peeked up at him. "I thought you were cute, but probably a jerk."

He smirked. "Yeah, I gathered that much—the jerk part, anyway. And you would've been right if you'd met me last year."

I moved closer to him, putting my hand over his. "But I didn't. So it doesn't matter."

He pulled away. "Drea, the stuff I told you about my past was just the highlights. I didn't get into all of it, because I didn't think it mattered. But I think it will matter to you—especially after your reaction the other night."

I moved back to the headboard, curling my knees under my chin. "Oh."

"I just know that the more time I spend with you, the more I like you. The more I want to be part of your life." He rolled his eyes. "And I need to shut up because I suck at this."

"I feel the same way," I said.

He sighed and laid back on the bed. "What did you mean by—you thought I was more like you?"

"I was hoping you were an inexperienced dork like me, because I have no idea what I'm doing."

"Nobody really knows what they're doing. We'd all like to think we do, though."

"So it doesn't bother you, about me?" I asked.

"No. I wouldn't have even known if you didn't tell me."

"You're lying."

"I'm not. When you kiss someone for the first time, it's usually awkward. It doesn't matter how many people you've kissed before."

"How many people have you kissed?"

His eyes lifted to mine. "I don't know the exact number."

"Yeah, you mentioned that."

"I slept with some of them too. But I don't remember much. There were times I woke up and couldn't remember what happened. That scares the shit out of me."

I grabbed my pillow and hugged it to my chest. "I don't know what to say."

"Yeah, I wouldn't know what to say to me, either." He settled on his back again, drumming his chest. "But I was tested right before I moved here. I'm clean."

"Isn't that a good thing?"

"I keep thinking about my mom. She was obsessed with

being healthy—ate right, exercised, didn't smoke. She wouldn't even touch alcohol. How's that for messed up?" He shook his head. "It just doesn't make sense."

"You made some mistakes, but you're a good person. That's what matters."

He covered his eyes with his arm, a smile crossing his lips. "Don't make me go over there and kiss you. Tell me how lame my T-shirt is or something."

"I like De/Vision. They're one of my favorite bands, actually."

"Who was I kidding? You're Drea. You can't help but drive me crazy." He dropped his arm and gazed up at me.

I hurled the pillow at his face, but it missed him entirely and hit my green acoustic instead.

He chuckled. "Nice aim. I'm about—what?—two or three feet from you."

"Shut up."

Justin sat up, shaking his head. "Let me show you how it's done, okay?"

He snatched the pillow off the floor and did a pitching motion with it. I covered my head, preparing for a blow. It didn't come.

"Oh, give me a break. You've got another pillow next to you. Use it," he said.

I grabbed it and jumped off the bed. He crept toward me, tossing the pillow in the air and catching it again. I charged at him and our pillow–sword fight began. Unfortunately, his height gave him the ability to bop me on top of the head. But I did have a lower center of gravity and better access to a more sensitive region. After he got me in the face, I ducked and flung my pillow at him like a Frisbee. Right where it counted.

He hunched over and winced. "Okay, that was a low blow. You don't play fair."

"How can I play fair when we didn't make any rules?"

"You need to have a reason to go for the balls, okay? Like what you did with Scott. That rocked. This didn't."

"Sorry, I didn't think it would hurt that much. The pillow being soft and everything."

He walked toward me, shaking his head. "Smart-ass."

I backed into the wall.

He picked up my pillow and smiled. "You might want to hold on to your *weapon* next time."

I squeezed my eyes shut as he raised the pillows, expecting to be hit from both sides. Instead, I heard the soft whisper of them hitting the floor when his lips touched mine. The kiss was gentle and a little salty. His hands ran down my back, and heat bled through the gauzy material of my black dress. I kissed him back the only way I knew how. My way.

I slipped my fingers underneath his T-shirt, enjoying the silky feeling of his skin. It gave him goose bumps, which made me smile because I had them too. He tilted his head to the side and moved closer to me, and I ended up licking his chin. We both laughed.

"Sorry," I said.

He cupped my face. "It happens."

His hands skimmed the curve of my hips. Stubble beneath his lower lip made my chin feel raw, but I didn't care. Every inch of me seemed to buzz, yet my mind probably couldn't string two words together. I buried my face in his neck, inhaling his scent. A mix of rain, salt, and trees—or bath soap and sweat, if I wanted to get technical.

His mouth hovered near my ear. "We shouldn't leave Naomi

up there any longer. They could be clawing each other's eyes out by now."

"They'll be okay," I said, pulling him closer.

He studied my face and traced the edge of my nose. "You think so?"

We leaned toward each other again, but the basement door swung open.

"Are you guys decent?" Naomi called, half laughing.

"Yes," Justin said before moving back and sitting on the bed.

I followed and sat against the headboard again, my lips still tingling.

"You guys have been down here a really long time. I was worried we'd have to call the fire department." She appeared at the foot of the stairs.

"Har, har," Justin said, rolling his eyes.

She stuck her tongue out at him and plopped in my computer chair. "Teaching an old person how to use eBay is like trying to teach a newborn how to read *Moby-Dick*."

Justin snickered. "I could've told you that."

"I'm not following," I said.

She spun the chair around in fast circles. "I just spent the last twenty minutes trying to convince your grandma to sell her crap online. She kind of lost it when she saw that people sell cars and houses on there. And the term FAQ is foreign to her. Anyway, you're off the hook. I just helped her put everything away. Only catch is she wants you to sell the stuff on eBay for her."

"That's what I wanted to do in the first place. She said no."

"What can I say, I have the magic grandma touch." She stopped spinning and looked at me. "So, are you still pissed at me?"

"No."

"I'm going to run around the corner to Subway. You guys want something?" Justin asked.

After we gave him our sandwich orders, he leaned in and gave me a quick kiss. "See you in a bit," he whispered.

I bit my lip and nodded, trying to hold back a smile. It was weird being mushy in front of Naomi.

She waited for him to leave before throwing herself on my bed. "Is he a good kisser?"

"I think so."

Naomi stretched her legs over the side and gazed at the ceiling. "I bet he is. The sensitive types usually are."

"I need to tell you something." I clutched the comforter between my hands.

She exhaled sharply. "Look, I'm sorry. It was just so cute how excited you looked. I haven't been that giddy over a kiss in a long time."

"That isn't it. I—"

Naomi sat up and crawled over to me. "Wait, don't tell me." She put a hand on each shoulder. "You and Justin are getting hitched in Vegas."

"No! Can you be serious for a minute?"

She let go of my shoulders and collapsed back on the bed. "I got you out of garage sale hell. It's Saturday. Your hot boyfriend is bringing us lunch. And you're still finding reason to be a downer."

"He's not my—"

"He's not your boyfriend, I know. You guys just smooch and hang out almost every day. And he talks about you like you're a goddess."

"He does?"

She looked up at me. "Uh-huh. He got *that look* in his eyes when he talked about you last night. Do you know what I mean?"

"Not really."

"And he talked about how smart and awesome you are. It was kind of sickening. I don't think a guy has ever called me smart. I usually get 'Hey, baby, yer hot.'"

I lay down next to her. "Because you date jerks."

"Guys like Justin aren't interested in girls like me. I've never been smart or arty enough. I'm not an endless source of music trivia, and I don't hate everything on the radio. Oh, well. Bad boys are more exciting anyway."

"Even when they call you a psycho bitch and hit you?"

"I said something really messed up about his family. Something I knew would hurt him."

"He hit you, Naomi."

"Can we talk about something else?"

I propped myself on my elbow and stared down at her. "Don't go back to him. You promised."

She sat up. "I'm not, okay? Just shut up about him already."

"Why are you acting like this?"

"Because you won't drop it!" She ran her hands through her messy hair. "You're just sitting there and judging me. It's so easy for you. You don't even know—"

Justin opened the door upstairs. "Food's here. Come up when you guys are ready."

Naomi hopped up and ran for the stairs. "Good, I'm starving!"

"Wait," I called after her. "We need to finish talking."

She spun around, a dark look in her eyes. "It's a nice day, Drea. Quit trying to ruin it."

After lunch we decided to walk around downtown Bellingham and film random things. Naomi gave us a guided tour around the pint-sized area. She interviewed various people we passed, asking them to list their favorite places. Most picked the bay, trails, or parks, and a few chose Railroad Avenue. But one person said jail and another said "wherever the pigeons hang out." Not everyone was sober. We left with plenty of interesting footage.

When we got back to my house, we looked at the music sites I had uploaded "Invisible" to. There were several comments—all of them very complimentary. People raved about Naomi's voice, saying she sounded like an angel.

Naomi smiled and covered her face. "I figured people would hate my voice."

"Why would you think that?" Justin asked. "You've got more raw talent than anyone I've ever met. You haven't even had any lessons, right?"

"Just years in my shower."

I scrolled down the comments, reading them over again. "This one says, 'Why isn't this song on the radio? Very catchy tune with great production and an incredible vocalist. Who is this girl, and how can I get her to sing on my tracks?'"

Naomi's ears turned red. "Wow."

"I've played this song sixteen times," I continued reading. "And that piano melody haunts me every time. Beautiful."

Justin smiled. "We've got our amazing producer to thank."

"I just polished it up and stuck it online," I said.

He stroked my hair. "You know you did a lot more than that. All of the programming you put into it. The drums are sweet. It sounds amazing."

"Naomi's live beat helped too."

Naomi announced she needed a bathroom break and ran up the stairs.

I stretched and moved closer to Justin. "Do you work tomorrow?"

"Yeah." He grabbed my hands and pulled me into his lap. "Did you tell her?"

I rested my head against his shoulder and told him what she said. "She won't let me bring up anything serious. How am I supposed to tell her that I'm a liar? Or that my mom is calling her dad because I opened my stupid mouth?"

"No offense, but you're a really bad liar. At least it wasn't a surprise for me when you admitted you never went skydiving."

I elbowed him.

"Be nice," he whispered.

I looked up at him. "What should I do?"

"I can't tell you that. You know Naomi better than I do." He stroked my cheek.

"That doesn't help."

"I know—I suck. I'm sorry."

Being so close to him relaxed me. I ran my fingers under his sleeve, trying to guess the shape of his tattoo.

Footsteps echoed from the stairs. I pulled back to see Naomi watching us. She wasn't smiling this time. "Maybe I should leave you two alone."

"No, we have to record 'Dawn,'" I said.

Naomi made her way down the stairs. "I'm in the mood to celebrate those killer reviews we got."

"How?" I asked.

"Let's take a trip." She moved in front of us and pulled a

baggy out of her jeans. A few shriveled brown pieces of something sat inside.

"What's that?" I asked.

" 'Shrooms," Justin muttered. "They make you hallucinate, basically."

"Why would anyone want to do that?" I whispered.

He shrugged. "Some people think it's fun."

Naomi raised her eyebrows. "Well?"

"I want to work on 'Dawn,' like we planned," I said.

"So, let's eat a couple first." She grinned. "It'll make practice more interesting."

"Why do we need to make it more interesting?" I asked.

She tilted her head back, rolling her eyes. "Ugh. Don't start with the dumb questions, Drea."

I clenched my fists. That was the second time she'd said that to me.

"It wasn't a dumb question," Justin said, his fingers tracing the back of my hand.

"Fine, whatever. I'll eat them by myself."

"Not during band practice," he said. "We agreed, remember?"

Naomi's eyes narrowed at him. "Oh my God—they're just 'shrooms!"

"It doesn't matter," he said softly.

She shook her head and shoved the baggy back into her pocket. "No offense, Justin. But maybe they let you out of rehab too early."

Justin's arms tensed around me. I sucked in my breath, expecting him to yell. I sure wanted to, but no words came out of my parted lips.

"Recovery takes a long time, Naomi," he said. "And being around people who are wasted doesn't help."

She looked at the ground, running her fingers through her hair again. "Maybe I should just go. I'm kind of beat anyway."

"I wasn't asking you to leave," Justin said.

"Yeah, I know, but . . ." She shrugged.

"Stay." My voice came out softer than I expected.

Naomi glanced up at me then. Something about the look in her eyes made my stomach hurt. "I'll see you later."

I watched her climb the stairs, torn between going after her and staying in Justin's arms. One route was unpredictable and draining, the other—warm and exciting. I chose Justin, but wished I hadn't let her go. Especially when she didn't answer her phone the rest of the weekend.

15

Friday, September 28

It's lunchtime, and I'm supposed to be finishing up my film review. Justin and I didn't get around to it last night. He's working on his right now. I like to watch him and guess what he's thinking about. Right now he's bobbing his head to whatever is playing on his iPod. His lips are moving a little bit, but there is no sound coming out. I wonder if he ever puts music lyrics into his homework. I've done that several times. He just peeked up at me and smiled. I love it when he does that.

Naomi is smoking with Roger. She's been spending a lot more time with him. Even riding home with him instead of us. She hasn't shown up for practice all week. Justin told her that she can't just keep blowing the band off, but she rolled her eyes and flipped him off.

She nods more and talks less. Her eyes look bruised underneath and red around the edges,

but wide open like she's afraid she'll blink and miss
something. I asked her if she was okay yesterday.
She said she was sick of me asking her that.

Mom keeps checking their driveway for her
dad's SUV. She asked me to get his cell number. I
told her I wouldn't do it. She asked me when he'd
be home. I told her I didn't know. I really don't
want the weekend to come.

Naomi was already in the locker room when I arrived. Her
eyes looked glassy and vacant today. Kari stood over her, mut-
tering something I couldn't make out. They both stared at me
for a moment before turning their attention back to each
other.

"I know it was you," Kari said before joining her friends
across the aisle.

Naomi chewed on her thumbnail, eyeing the floor.

"What happened?" I took out my gym clothes and shoved
my lunch box into the locker.

"Nothing important."

"Are we going to work on 'Dawn' tomorrow?"

She stood up and opened her locker. "That depends. Does
Justin want me to take a drug test first?"

"He's worried about you. We both are."

"I'm sorry that he couldn't handle his shit." She slammed
the metal door shut. "But it doesn't mean he gets to piss on
everyone's parade, you know? To be honest—I'm thinking of
quitting the band. I'm just not feeling it anymore."

I pulled my T-shirt over my head. It felt heavy and cold
against my skin. "You can't do that—"

"Cut the shit, Drea." She walked toward me until our faces

were inches apart. "When we first met, you looked at me like I was a pile of dog crap. And you haven't stopped judging me since. You and Justin are dying to get rid of me. Admit it."

"That's not true."

"Admit it!"

I backed away, avoiding her piercing eyes. They reminded me of a zombie's—lifeless. "I don't understand why you . . . why you're—"

She moved toward me until her breath hit my cheek. It smelled like curdled milk. "Yeah, that's right. Look away and play innocent, like always. Or better yet, run along and ask Prince Justin to save you. He's good at that, right?"

My eyes burned and my throat felt swollen. I couldn't breathe. "You're acting like Scott."

She flicked something off my shirt. "Better get to class. Wouldn't want Little Miss Perfect to be late." The edge in her voice made me shiver.

I spun around and ran to the gym, wishing I didn't have to look at her again. Being near her gave me this heavy feeling in my gut.

But she never showed up to PE.

When I entered the locker room forty minutes later, there was no sign of Naomi. But I could still feel her around me. On the cement walls. In the damp air. Heavy and unrelenting.

My lunch box seemed lighter when I pulled it out. I cracked it open to find my crayons and a few pennies. My iPod and roughly ten dollars in change were missing. Only one person knew my combination.

"Did Naomi take anything?" a voice asked.

I glanced up at Kari. She peered down at my lunch box, her thin eyebrows raised.

I nodded, letting the lid fall shut.

"Yeah, I forgot to lock up yesterday. She stole twenty bucks out of my jeans." Kari sat down next to me. "I heard you guys fighting."

I flicked the clasp on my box.

"That's how she gets back at people she's pissed at," Kari continued. "She steals from them."

Tears burned in my eyes. "I don't know what I did." I turned away, hoping she couldn't see them. "I thought we were friends."

"So did I," she said. "And the sad part is, I was this close to pounding her face in before class. But I couldn't do it. She's so pathetic. I fucking pity her."

All I could do was nod. The money didn't matter. Naomi took my music. The one thing I couldn't stand to be without. She knew that.

Kari said something else, but her words didn't register. She stood up, staring at me expectantly. "Right, well, see ya."

I sat in my sweaty gym clothes, unable to move. My teeth clenched together, and I gripped the sides of the bench. At that moment, I wanted to push Naomi to the ground and tell her what a disappointment she was. A selfish, stupid girl.

I threw my lunch box against the lockers, watching it explode open and fall to the floor. One of the pennies twirled for a few seconds. Almost like it was laughing at me. I crushed it with my foot and left the box where it fell. She might as well take it all. She obviously needed it a lot more than I did.

Justin asked where my lunch box was after film class. I didn't want to talk about it. He put his hand over mine when we got into his car.

"Will seeing my Bösendorfer cheer you up?" he asked.

I nodded. "Will your family be there?"

"My sister will be. She wants to meet you."

I stared out the window. Justin playing a real piano. It sounded like the perfect date, minus the whole meeting-strangers bit.

"Is Naomi coming to practice tomorrow?" he asked.

I shook my head and bit down on my tongue. Just hearing her name made me shrivel inside. We went up to Magnolia Street instead of Holly.

He looked over at me when we hit a red light. "What happened, Drea?"

I watched a group of skateboarders collide in a Quickie Mart parking lot. One of them had purple hair like Naomi. No matter where I looked, I couldn't get away from her. Or the sick feeling lurking in my stomach. So I told Justin, hoping he'd have some magical answer.

He didn't. We rode in silence until we pulled up in front of his house. It was a small, one-story deal on the south side of town. White paint. Black shutters. I guess it kind of fit him.

He gave me a long hug after we got out. We stood on his curb for a while, barely moving.

"What did I do wrong?" I asked.

He kissed the top of my head. "Speed makes people crazy. When I did it, I loved the world one minute and hated it the next. I had no control over what I did or said sometimes—at least it felt that way. Sometimes I wanted to tear everything apart." He backed away from me. "Naomi likes you, despite what she said. Chances are she won't even remember tomorrow. That's the fucked-up part."

"But I'll remember."

"Come on," he whispered, pulling me down a long driveway. It led to a white structure that I assumed was the garage. But he unlocked the side door and let me in first.

A shiny black piano was the first thing to greet me. It loomed in front of us in all its statuesque glory, itching to be played. The cement floor was covered with large rugs. The kind with kaleidoscopic patterns. Shelves of CDs and books framed the room, and a queen-sized bed with tousled blue sheets sat in the corner.

"Reminds me a little of my basement."

"Yeah. It was the garage, but my brother-in-law renovated it. It's not quite finished yet." He motioned to the floor. "They're renting it out to me."

I walked toward the piano and admired the pristine keys. "They didn't want to park in it?"

He brushed past me and sat on the bench. "They want to turn it into an art studio—eventually."

I scanned the black-and-white photographs lining the walls. They were images of odd things like bridge beams, rusty barns, alleyways, random body parts, and melted ice cream. "I didn't know you were into photography."

He looked around the room and shrugged. "I didn't go anywhere without a camera my freshman year. But I haven't taken any in a while."

"You should start up again. I like them." I bit my lip. It was weird being alone with him in his space. Yet somehow my problems stayed outside his door. I felt safe in here.

He smiled at me. "I'd like to. Have a seat anywhere. I'll play you something."

I had to decide between a black beanbag and the bed. The beanbag was closer and just my size.

234

He began playing as my body melted into the Styrofoam. The acoustics in the garage weren't half bad. It almost felt like we were in a mini concert hall. His notes inched through my skin and warmed me to the bone. He wasn't kidding. The difference between a *real* piano and my *crappy* midi was astronomical. I would've been embarrassed if I wasn't so taken in by the melody swirling around me. This song was white and silver with a touch of red for the harder notes.

I curled up on the bag, closing my eyes. The only thing missing was Naomi's voice. But I put the thought aside and got lost in my daydreams. Most of them involved kisses, nature hikes, and traveling to unknown destinations. Maybe in a clunky tour bus.

"Hey," he said after two songs. "Did I put you to sleep?"

I opened my eyes and nearly laughed at his pout. "No, you took me somewhere else."

He walked over and kneeled in front of me. "Want to tell me about it?"

I shook my head. "It's a secret."

He leaned over and kissed me. We'd made out almost every day, and I liked it more every time. Even the sore lips and the dehydration. But our clothes stayed on, and his hands avoided my chest area. Part of me really wanted to do more, and another part was terrified of it. What if I hated how it felt? What if he hated how I felt? I barely had boobs, compared to most girls.

Justin pulled back and sat on his heels. "We should go say hi to my sister."

I got up and attempted to smile. Obviously, I didn't do a good job because he touched my cheek and told me not to worry. His sister trusted his judgment.

The main house had pumpkin-colored walls and smelled like apples. Justin led me through the entranceway and into the kitchen. A woman took silverware out of the dishwasher and placed it in a drawer, and a dark-haired little girl frantically colored something at the kitchen table.

The woman looked up at me, smiling. She had Justin's eyes and high cheekbones, but honey-blond hair. I figured it was dyed due to the darker locks underneath.

"Drea, this is my sister, Nicci." He motioned to me. "Nicci, this is Drea—my girlfriend."

"Hi." He'd said *girlfriend*. It gave me a fluttery feeling, but a good one. At least I thought it was.

"It's really good to meet you. I've heard you are quite the talented producer," she said.

"Thank you. I mean, it's good to meet you too." I clenched my hands into balls. Why was I thanking her for hearing something?

"You guys sticking around for dinner?" Nicci asked.

Justin nudged me. "Don't worry. My sister is a decent cook."

"Decent? Oh, whatever, Mister I Blackened My Toast This Morning and Set Off the Smoke Alarm." She laughed, showing a set of dimples. She looked younger than I thought she'd be. No more than twenty-five.

"Hey"—he held his hands up—"someone changed the setting."

"Likely story." Nicci walked over to the little girl and peered over her shoulder.

"I'd like to stay," I said.

"I want you to meet someone else too." Justin took my hand, leading me toward the table. "This is my niece, Madison."

Madison drew spirals with a purple crayon. She hummed a

soft note with each circle. Justin sat on one side of her, and I took the other.

The phone rang, and Nicci rushed off to get it. Whoever it was made her frown and leave the kitchen. I turned my attention back to Justin's niece. She drew horizontal lines now. Her lips pursed together in deep concentration.

"How old is she?" I asked.

"Four," Justin answered. "She does the coloring thing a lot. I think we have a little artist in the making here."

"It calms her."

"How do you know?"

I smiled at him. "I just do."

Madison paused, her big brown eyes searching the table. She picked up an orange crayon and stuck it in my hand.

"Wow." Justin chuckled. "I was here a month before I got invited to color with her."

"I'm just special." I stuck my tongue out at him.

"Yeah, you are."

I reached for a blank piece of paper, but she slapped her hand on the pile.

"No," she said, pulling it out of my reach. She counted through five before handing one to me.

"She's got an order about them," Justin said. "Can't mess it up."

"What would you like me to draw, Madison?" I asked.

She'd gone back to spirals and humming.

"I drew her a pumpkin. She wasn't too into that," Justin said.

I mimicked her rhythm, starting at the corner and making my way down. Coloring always soothed me. The feel of a crayon against paper was satisfying in a way I couldn't explain to just anyone. But I bet Madison understood.

Nicci walked back into the kitchen. "Dad's on the phone."

His eyes widened at her. "He wants to talk to me?"

"He wants to say hi," she said.

Justin scrambled out of the chair and brushed his hand against my shoulder. "I'll be right back."

Nicci grinned at the crayon in my hand and sat down in his place. "She likes you."

"I have a bunch of coloring books at home. She can have some if she'd like," I told her.

"I think she'd really love that." She ruffled her daughter's hair. "Say thank you to Drea."

Madison repeated her words exactly but didn't let it stop her project.

"Did you like drawing too?" Nicci asked.

"I still do. It relaxes me." I kept my eyes on the paper. His sister seemed nice, but I felt as if I was under a microscope. What if she didn't like me?

"I use a punching bag to relax. We all have our methods." She laughed. It sounded almost nervous.

I nodded and attempted to smile. She asked me about San Francisco and if I liked Bellingham. Small talk wasn't where I made my best impressions, but I answered as best I could. I was tempted to ask her if she wanted to pick up a crayon and join us.

"I'm really glad you and Justin met. He was pretty down when he got here in June, but I see a little more of the kid brother I once knew every day."

I stopped scribbling. "You think that's because of me?"

She smiled. "Well, you're definitely helping. So thank you for that."

I handed my drawing to Madison. "He's helped me just as much."

She shuffled it in her pile, a little grin forming on her face.

"Hey, quit talking about me," Justin said, grabbing my shoulders.

"Oh, I wasn't saying anything bad. I—"

"I'm only messing with you," he whispered.

"How'd it go?" Nicci stood up.

He exhaled and massaged my shoulders. "A lot of awkward silence. But it was good to hear his voice, you know?"

She walked behind me. "He'll come around. I need to get started on dinner. We'll talk more later, okay?"

"Sure." He leaned into my ear again. "You want to go back to my room?"

I got up and followed him back to the garage. As soon as he shut the door, I gave him a hug. He looked like he needed it.

"What did your dad say?" I asked, sitting on his bed.

He stood in front of me, hands in his pockets. "He asked how I was. Told me a few friends called looking for me. That was about it. But it's the first time he's spoken to me since court. It's a step."

"Are you happy?"

He studied my face for a second. "Yeah, I am."

"You told your sister I was your girlfriend."

His eyelashes lowered to the floor. "Is that okay?"

"Only if that's what I am to you."

"I'd like that." He glanced up at me, his eyes filled with something I couldn't identify. Fear or uncertainty, maybe. At least that was what I felt.

"Me too."

A little smile played at his lips. "Guess it's settled, then."

I fell back on his bed. The sheets felt velvety against my hands. "Your bed smells like you."

"Imagine that."

"Come here." I wrapped my legs around his, pulling him closer. But he wasn't moving. I let him go.

Justin sat next to me. "I want to take things slow with you, Drea."

My body tensed at his words. I didn't feel ready for sex, but I didn't want to be treated differently either. "Why with *me*?"

He met my gaze then. "Because I didn't know the people I had sex with. Not like I know you."

I looked away and traced patterns against his sheets. "I don't understand."

"I'm not ready yet. Does that simplify things?"

"Yes." I glanced up at him. "Does that mean we can't mess around anymore?"

"No, it definitely doesn't mean that." He smiled and then kissed me.

We fell back onto his bed. His mouth grazed my neck, moving slowly to my earlobe. I wondered if the shivering would go away eventually. It hadn't yet. I moved my hands under his shirt, pulling it up.

"Can I see your tattoo?" I asked.

He smirked. "You're slick."

"What do you mean?"

"Finding a way to get my shirt off without having to ask." He pulled his shirt over his head and tossed it aside.

My cheeks burned. Considering the only shirtless guys I saw were on TV or the gag calendars Mom's friends gave her, seeing Justin was pretty exciting.

But I wasn't expecting silver bars through his nipples. "Whoa. Did that hurt?"

He propped himself up on his elbow. "For a couple seconds, yeah. Then the endorphins kicked in and I didn't feel much."

I poked at one of the bars, but tore my hand away for fear I'd hurt him. Just looking at them made me want to cover my own nipples and cringe. Maybe it was different for guys than girls. "Why did you get them?"

"Lydia, our singer, was friends with this guy who ran a tattoo and piercing shop. We weren't allowed to have visible piercings at school, so she thought nipple piercings would be *hot*." He rolled his eyes. "And I don't know—I've grown to like them."

My fingers ran across his biceps, tracing a tattooed band of black-and-white piano keys. His arms were muscular, but not what Mom referred to as "ripped." He was thin, but defined. Which I liked. I always thought the whole buff thing was overrated. Most of the guys in my mom's calendar had bigger boobs than me.

He rolled onto his stomach. A tattoo of a grand staff covered his upper back. A treble and bass clef. Rows of notes. Just like sheet music. Wings sprawled out behind it, stretching across his shoulder blades. They were mostly black but tinged with a little blue.

"It's the beginning of a song I wrote for my mom. Kind of my tribute to her," he said.

I ran my hands over the ink, admiring the etchings and shadows. "I love it," I said. "Maybe you can play it for me sometime."

He propped himself on his elbow again. "Do you have any?"

"What do *you* think?" I rolled my eyes.

"I was hoping for an excuse to get your shirt off."

I wrapped my arms around my chest, and my heart sped up. "The room is kind of light."

"That generally happens when the sun is out." He gave me a half smile.

"It's just I've never—um. A guy has never seen—"

"I know." He brought his face to mine. "It's okay. Really. I don't want you to be uncomfortable."

"I want to, but I—"

He cut me off with a kiss. My body relaxed with his touch, and whatever I had to say became unimportant. His fingers circled my breast, and his thumb brushed across my nipple. I sucked in my breath, tangling my tongue with his. My skin felt like it was on fire. I inched my T-shirt up, slowly at first.

He pulled back. "You sure?"

I swallowed hard and nodded. "Just don't laugh at my bra. It's kind of white and—"

He ran a finger along the curve of my upper lip. "I'm not up on the latest bra trends. You're safe."

I let him pull my shirt over my head and stiffened as his eyes skimmed my body.

He pressed his lips to my navel, working his way up until our mouths were inches apart. *"Sei bella."*

I stared back at him. He definitely made me *feel* beautiful. "I want to hear more about Italy."

His mouth tickled my ear. "You will."

I ran my hands down his smooth back, breathing him in. His hand inched up my thigh. My eyelashes fluttered and a pressure built inside of me. He hesitated.

"Don't stop," I whispered.

He kissed me harder, his fingers sliding over the edge of my underwear. My leg muscles tensed, and my heart felt like it

242

was palpitating. His touch moved higher until I was sure I'd pass out. An indescribable warmth blanketed my nerves.

Everything faded away, even the light streaming across his bed from the high windows. I had no idea being close to another human being could feel this amazing.

16

I WOKE UP SHIVERING the next morning. Raindrops pelted against the window, and the wind roared outside.

I hadn't wanted to get out of the car when Justin dropped me home, ten minutes before my midnight curfew. The night had been incredible. I already missed his soft lips and the way his hands felt on my skin. My boyfriend. I had a real boyfriend.

During dinner, Justin and his sister had told me about the concerts they went to in Italy and how easy Milan was to get lost in. They showed me pictures of dusky buildings, cobblestone walkways filled with people, and the most elaborate shopping mall I'd ever seen. I'd be going there someday.

I glanced at my cell phone. It read 11:00, but the muted light in the basement made it seem much earlier. The wind picked up again, sending branches against the house.

I buried my hands inside the sleeves of my thermal and sat in front of my computer. The server dinged with new e-mail.

From: Naomi Quinn
Subject: She waits for the dawn . . .

I stared at the name and subject until it became a blurry mess. Maybe she wanted to come to practice today after all. The knots in my stomach told me otherwise. I took a deep breath and opened the e-mail.

. . . to make her grand escape.

Hi Drea,

Where do I even begin? I guess I'll start with I'm sorry . . . for everything. In case you haven't noticed by now, I'm a horrible friend. More trouble than I'm worth. I know. You deserve better, and I think you have it with Justin. That boy is crazy about you. So much so it hurts to look at you guys. I've waited my entire life for someone to look at me the way you look at each other. To admire me for some reason, at least. But that's another story.

Your mom talked to my dad last night. She told him everything. He freaked and told me he was going to turn me in. He thinks I need rehab, which is hilarious. The guy pops Vicodin like it's candy.

Don't worry. I'm not mad at you. I've been looking for a reason to get out. That final straw. This did it. I'm at Scott's right now. He's packing up his shit, and we're heading south in a couple days. Maybe California. Maybe Vegas. Maybe the moon? I know you think he's scum, but he's my ticket out of here, and if you knew how he grew up, you'd understand his anger. I love him, Drea. I really do. People screw up. They make mistakes. I hope that you'll forgive me someday.

I left your iPod and money on your porch. Count it if you'd like. It's all there. I don't know why I took it. I don't know why I do a lot of things. Out of everyone here, I'm going to miss you the most. Especially your smile. You don't smile much, but when you do, your entire face glows. I've known you a month, but I feel closer to you than anyone else. Making music with you was awesome, and I'm sorry I can't keep doing it. It was the one thing I really looked forward to. But singers aren't hard to find. Did you know Roger sings? He's not bad either, LOL. No joke!

I have a couple favors to ask. Please keep my brother's drum kit and Lizzie safe. I obviously can't take either with me. And Dad sure as hell can't take care of Lizzie. I know she'd be happy with you. If you can't take her, then please find her a good home. I trust you.

Thank you for everything, Drea. You rock.

Until we meet again. (And we will!)

Naomi,
a.k.a. your pain-in-the-ass friend forever

I read her letter three times, hoping it wasn't real. Her dad wasn't supposed to be home last night. Saturday, she'd said. They were going to pick out a car Saturday. Acid crept into my throat. My friend was gone, and it was my fault. Mom didn't follow through on a lot of things—why this? Why now? I should've kept my mouth shut.

My cell phone rang, making me jump. Justin's name appeared in the tiny screen.

"Hello?"

"I got an e-mail from Naomi," he said, his voice somber.

I slumped in my chair, my eyes stinging. "It's my fault. I should've stayed home last night."

"You aren't why she's unhappy. Don't think that way." His windshield wipers squeaked in the background.

"I thought you had to work."

"I do, but I'm on lunch. I'm heading to Scott's."

"What are you going to do?"

He exhaled into the phone. "I'm going to try and talk to her."

"But Roger said Scott wants to pound you."

"If he wants to come at me in broad daylight, he can go for it. I'm not going inside."

"Take me with you."

"No, I don't want you around Scott."

"I don't care. She's my friend too."

"I'm going to try and get her home, okay?"

I nodded and realized he couldn't hear me. "Call me as soon as you leave." My throat was so tight it hurt to breathe.

"I will." His voice softened. "I promise."

I tried calling Naomi three times after Justin hung up. Her voice mail greeted me every time. Then I reread her letter.

I should've complimented her singing more. Told her how beautiful she was. She had more physical grace than anyone I'd ever known, especially when we jammed. A natural performer. Every movement seemed epic. I should've told her the truth about me.

Justin called ten minutes later. He said nobody answered, but the blinds were pulled up. The apartment looked vacant inside.

I ran upstairs, ready to confront Mom. A man's voice echoed from the kitchen when I opened the basement door. Mom answered him softly. I crept toward the entrance, but stayed behind the wall and listened.

"I used to build houses," the man said. "It was decent money. But then I fell and messed up my back. And the doc said no more construction or manual labor for me. Well, I don't have a degree, and the job market in this town is non-existent. What was I supposed to do?"

"I know," Mom said. "I'm always struggling to keep my head above water. It's not easy."

"I'm not a bad father." His voice shook. "I tried, you know? She's always been so self-sufficient. Her brother was always getting in trouble. Teachers called me about him all the time. But not Naomi. She had good grades. No problems."

I bit my lip to keep from shouting at him. He didn't try. He made her feel invisible.

Mom gave him one of her vague sympathetic answers. Her voice trembled a little, like it always did when she felt bad. "I got lucky with Drea," she continued. "I've made so many mistakes, dragging her across the country, living out of our pickup, one failed relationship after another. But she's so practical and levelheaded. It's not always about what you did or didn't do. I think Naomi just got involved with the wrong crowd."

"Do you know anything else about this Scott guy? I'd like to"—something banged against the table—"put his face through a goddamn wall," her dad said.

"What are you doing, Drea?" Grandma peeked out from her bedroom down the hall. "Don't eavesdrop on conversations."

"Drea?" Mom called. "You can come in here, sweetie. It's okay."

I rolled my eyes and walked into the kitchen. Naomi's dad sat at the head of the table, hunched over. His cheeks were sunken and his eyes red rimmed. He glanced up at me for a moment and nodded before staring at his hands.

I pressed my back against the wall, folding and unfolding my arms. Nothing felt comfortable. Nothing felt right.

Mom gave me a weak smile. "There was a bag for you on the porch this morning. It's on the counter." She studied my face. "Do you know what happened?"

"She's with Scott," I said. "I told you it wasn't a good idea."

Mom squinted at me. "Is she at his apartment?"

"No, Justin went over there. They're gone. She said they were heading south in a couple days."

Naomi's dad covered his face. "I don't know what the hell to do. I reported her as a runaway, but she's just one of the many. They said it's tougher once they've been missing for forty-eight hours."

"We'll help any way we can," Mom said.

"She wants me to take Lizzie," I said.

Her father looked up at me from under heavy lids. "The cat? Yeah, take her. I'll bring her over."

"Grandma won't allow it," Mom said.

"It's what Naomi wants!" I answered.

She rubbed her eyes, sighing. "Okay, fine. Just put her in the basement for now. We'll figure something out."

Naomi's father stood up suddenly, nearly knocking his mug over. "Thanks for the coffee. I should get back and see if the police called." He looked at me as he left the kitchen. "I'll bring the cat by in an hour or so."

Mom groaned into her hands after he shut the front door behind him. "This is such a mess."

"It would've been fine if you didn't open your big mouth," I said.

She looked up at me over the tips of her fingers. "Do you really believe that, Drea? Was Naomi *fine* before this?"

I focused on the tiled floor. "No."

"I'm sorry it turned out this way."

I stared back at her sad brown eyes and her crinkled brow. Despite her flaws, she loved me. And I knew it. "I wish her dad was more like you."

She walked over and wrapped her arms around me, kissing my forehead. "Why do you say that?"

"She doesn't think he loves her."

Mom's chest deflated against my ear. "I think he does. But some people don't show it as well as others."

I thought of Justin's dad and hugged her tighter.

The rain hadn't let up by lunch on Monday. Justin and I sat under the roof overhang of the gym, picking at our sandwiches. The fountain looked lonely across the quad. Its vacant surrounding wall gleamed back at us.

We were waiting for Kari. She'd gotten a letter too.

The weekend crawled by. No phone calls or e-mails from Naomi. We'd searched downtown, the parks, and Scott's apartment again but came up with nothing. Grandma threw such a fit about Lizzie that Justin offered to take her in. Apparently, she slept on his head.

"There's Roger," Justin said, standing up.

I followed his gaze and spotted Roger's lanky frame exiting the main building. If anyone knew where Scott was, he did. Justin ran after him, dodging puddles.

"Hey," Kari said from the other direction. She dropped her backpack in front of me and sat on top of it.

"Hi." I tossed my sandwich onto its plastic wrapper.

She scanned my face and looked over her shoulder at Justin

and Roger. They were standing close, talking. Neither looked angry, but Roger had his head down.

"Are you and Justin a couple now?" Kari asked.

"Yeah."

"Ah." She nodded slowly, eyeing the ground. "So, what did your letter say?"

"A lot. Nothing. Everything."

"Yeah, that was my reaction." She looked up at me, lacing her fingers together and twisting her hands. "She's done this to me since fifth grade. Pisses me off so much. And each time I'm sure I hate her. But then she says or does something that makes me crumble. Mostly, because I know she hates herself more than I ever could."

"Do you think it's because her dad ignores her?"

Kari shrugged. "They were closer when she was younger. He started drinking a lot after he lost his construction job. She didn't talk about it much. But Greg, her brother, was psycho. He chased us with a pocketknife once."

"She seems to miss him a lot."

"Yeah, I don't get it. He was nicer to her when they got older, but he just took off one day. She cried for weeks—and then dyed her hair purple and decided she was *over it.*"

"Hey," Justin said, sitting next to me. "Roger hasn't heard from Naomi since Friday. He claims he didn't even know what went down. But he says there's this abandoned house Scott deals out of sometimes. He's taking me there after school."

"I'm going too," I said.

"Me too," Kari chimed in.

"Not a good idea. Roger said that Scott's supplier got busted last week. And Scott's pretty sure he's next. It's why he's hiding out. You guys don't want to get caught up in that."

"I'm going, Justin. Whether you like it or not," I said.

"I already have a record. Let me take the risk."

"Exactly. That's why you're the last person who should be going."

"Wait"—Kari held her hand up—"you've got a record?"

Justin stuffed his untouched food into his bag. "What can I say? I wasn't always this charming."

She raised her eyebrows. "Wow, I totally had you pegged wrong."

He glanced over at me. "That happens a lot."

I stayed close behind Justin as we left film class. He was still trying to convince me not to go. But Roger and Kari stood in the parking lot waiting for us. We didn't have time to argue about it anymore.

We piled into the back of Roger's car. Kari rode shotgun. The two of them talked about their favorite metal bands.

"At least wait in the car while we check it out," Justin said in my ear.

"Quit treating me like I can't take care of myself. I was the one who protected you last time."

He laced his fingers with mine. "That's true. But Scott is twice your size. You could've gotten hurt."

"And you *did* get hurt. She needs me, Justin. You need me too."

He kissed my cheek and leaned toward Roger. "Where is this place?"

"It's off San Juan Road, where all those empty warehouses are." Roger made a left on Holly.

"You better not be dicking me around."

"I'm not! I care about her too, okay? She's my best friend."
He drummed the steering wheel.

That surprised me. I didn't think they were that close.

"But you didn't get a letter?" Kari asked him.

"I don't have a computer."

Roger made a right, and the bay glittered between rusty
buildings. Trash, sleeping bags, and the skeletons of cars littered
the gravel parking lots. A sour odor sifted through Roger's
cracked windows. It was strong enough to make me sick.

Two boarded-up houses sat at the end of the street. The
pointy rooftops and intricate pillars made me think of princesses
and frilly dresses. I bet someone cherished them a hundred years
ago. Now they were graffiti-covered ghosts, like everything else
around here.

Roger stopped in front of the pale green house. "I don't see
Scott's car here."

"Let's go in anyway," I answered, a shiver inching down
my back. "We need to be sure."

The four of us climbed out and walked toward an open
window. The boards had been torn off, and a filthy sheet hung
in their place.

Justin looked in all directions before peeking inside.
"Hello?" he called. "I think I see someone."

We followed him through the window. Bits of glass ripped
the hem of my skirt, but I didn't care.

Dim light revealed shredded floorboards and gouged walls.
It smelled like rotting wood and piss. I had to breathe through
my mouth to keep from gagging.

And then we saw it. A crumpled heap on the floor. Pale
skin. Strands of purple hair.

Justin ran over to her, Roger cussed under his breath, and a small cry escaped from Kari. But I froze. My fingertips and toes went numb.

Roger ripped the sheet from the window to let in more light. Kari joined Justin and covered her mouth. I walked toward them slowly. Justin pulled a small flashlight from his pocket. He touched Naomi's face, prying her eyes open and waving the light in them.

"Is she breathing?" Kari asked.

"Barely," Justin said. He pressed his fingers against the inside of her wrist.

I knelt next to Naomi, my limbs shaking. She was lying on her back, one knee bent at an odd angle. Saliva dripped down her chin, and her lips were tinged blue under the neon light. I grabbed her hand. It was hot and clammy.

Justin pulled out his cell phone and dialed three numbers.

Kari squatted next to me, hiccuplike sounds coming from her throat. "Naomi . . . ?" She touched her cheek. "She's fucking burning up."

Roger paced around us, talking fast. His words blurred together. I blocked them out, because they didn't make sense. Naomi wasn't going to die. She'd wake up and laugh at us. Tell us we were being ridiculous.

I squeezed her hand and brushed the damp hair off her forehead. "You can't give up."

"I just found my friend unconscious," Justin said into the phone. "She's burning up, her pulse is all over the place." He listened for a few seconds, his eyes wide and furious. "I think she overdosed on speed, but I don't know for sure. I just found her like this." More seconds passed. "I don't know!"

Kari cried into Naomi's chest, begging her to wake up. "Please be okay," she repeated over and over.

Their voices echoed around me. Too many words to process. I kept squeezing her hand, hoping she'd return the gesture. Nothing. I wiped the spit from her mouth with my sleeve and leaned toward her face. "You have to wake up so I can tell you what a dork I am. And you can laugh. You were the first person to give me a chance, and I'm sorry if I was mean to you at first. I thought you'd be like everyone else." I stroked her hair. "But you aren't like everyone else, Naomi. And someone will love you for who you are—I know they will. Because I love you."

Justin and Roger yelled back and forth, trying to figure out the address.

Kari's voice was muffled in her chest.

Justin checked her pulse again. "It's still erratic." He glanced at me and covered the phone. "They're on their way. But I have to stay on the phone until they get here."

A commotion erupted behind me. Someone yelled, and feet thudded against the floor. Roger and Scott wrestled each other near the window.

Justin tossed the phone at me and ran toward them. He pulled Scott off Roger and tried to force him to the ground. Scott was like a rabid animal, punching and shouting.

Everything in my stomach crept into my throat. I put the phone to my ear, trying to not throw up. "Hello?"

"Who is this?" the female voice asked.

"Drea."

"Okay, Drea. Can you tell me what's going on right now?"

"They're fighting. My friend needs help. We can't get her to wake up."

"I know. We have an ambulance on the way. I need you to stay calm for me, okay? It's the best way we can help your friend right now."

The guys moved toward us, shuffling feet and swinging arms.

"What the hell is going on?" Scott hollered.

The voice on the phone kept saying my name. "Drea, I need you to tell me what you see. Who is fighting?"

I rocked back and forth, still clutching Naomi's hand. "They won't stop. Please make them stop."

"Do they have weapons?"

"I don't know. I don't know."

Kari grabbed the phone from me and started talking about Scott. The guys moved closer. Scott was fighting them to get to Naomi. I braced myself over her, preparing for impact. There was a loud thud. The floor shook beneath my knees. I glanced over to see Scott's face a couple feet from mine. Justin and Roger pinned him to the ground, both struggling to keep him still.

"The cops are coming too," Kari said, covering the phone.

"What did she take?" Justin asked Scott.

His face contorted, and his lips trembled. "She did a line before I left, and I took the rest with me. That's it. She was fine."

Justin leaned toward Scott's ear, shoving his face harder into the floor. "What else did she have access to?"

"Nothing!" Scott's eyes watered. He'd stopped fighting them. "I took everything with me because she doesn't know when to stop sometimes. She was fine, man. She was fucking fine."

Kari grabbed the flashlight, illuminating the ground near Naomi's left hand. "Then what's on the floor next to her?" she asked. A baggy filled with white powder was spilled a foot away—as if Naomi had dropped it when she fell.

Scott squeezed his eyes shut. "She must've found my stash. It was under the floorboards."

Kari listened to Naomi's chest. "I don't hear anything," she said into the phone. Mascara streamed down her cheeks. "What are we supposed to do?"

I kept Naomi's limp hand in mine, telling her to get up. Telling her to fight.

More voices filled the room, and several people rushed at us. They were dressed in dark uniforms and carrying equipment. They yelled at me to move. I didn't want to. I couldn't let her go.

The room began to spin. Someone grabbed me from behind, prying my hand from Naomi's.

"No pulse," one of the paramedics said.

My head was against Justin's chest. Police officers stood in front of us. Two of them talked to Scott. He sat on the floor, bawling like a baby. His words were distorted. Nothing made sense.

I tried to pull away, reaching for Naomi. I could see her pale hands between the boots of the paramedics. "She needs me!"

Justin's breath hit my ear. He kept telling me to calm down—Naomi would fight this.

The paramedics scrambled, shouting things and passing equipment back and forth. One of them pushed on her chest. Justin tightened his grip on me.

Kari's cries came from somewhere behind us. Roger sat with his face against his knees, his back shaking. Every second crawled by.

They carried Naomi off in a stretcher and loaded her into an ambulance. We followed them outside, but the police wouldn't let us go. Sirens echoed down the street, taking her away.

The police asked for IDs and kept asking questions. Questions I couldn't answer. Justin told them we'd found her like this. Over and over. They acted like they didn't believe him.

Justin was led to a squad car and cuffed. All I could think about was Naomi. How lifeless her face looked.

A female police officer patted me down and shined a light in my eyes. She asked me if I'd smoked or ingested any illegal substances. I told her about my meds.

"What is your diagnosis?" she asked.

"Asperger's and ADHD."

She nodded and wrote something on a notepad. "What's your relationship with Scott Reynolds?"

I scanned the area for him. He was on the ground in cuffs. More paramedics were checking him out. "I don't have one. He's Naomi's boyfriend."

She asked more of the same questions.

"How many times do you have to ask me? I already told you, goddamnit!"

"You can answer them at the station, if you'd like. Your choice." Her voice was cold. Didn't she know that I needed to be with my friend?

"Just answer them, Drea!" Justin called to me. "It'll be okay."

I took a deep breath and finished answering her. They pushed Scott into the back of a squad car. Kari and Roger were nearby somewhere. I could hear their voices at least.

Mom appeared at some point. She leaned against her car door, her face crumpled, fingers hovering over her mouth. Grandma stayed inside the car.

They finally let me go, saying they'd call me with more

questions. I glanced over at Justin. He didn't have the cuffs on anymore. His sister was talking to him.

Mom hugged me tight. I tried to tell her what happened. She said she knew and she'd take me to the hospital.

Justin walked over to me and wrapped his arms around my waist. I rested my head against his chest, closing my eyes. His heart was still racing.

"Are they letting you go?" I asked.

"Yeah. Do you want me to ride with you to the hospital?"

I nodded, squeezing his hand.

"I'm going to go with them," he called to his sister.

Grandma glanced at us as we got into Mom's car. I expected her to start yelling, but she didn't say a word. Her mouth formed a straight line, and there was something different about her eyes. They were softer somehow.

Naomi's dad was a crumpled ball outside the hospital entrance. One look at his shaking hands, and I knew. Something was wrong. Very wrong.

Mom and Justin moved to either side of me as we approached him. Grandma trailed behind us, still silent.

"Tom?" Mom asked.

Naomi's father looked up at us with trembling lips. I'd never seen a grown man look so frightened. "She's gone. My little girl is gone."

Mom knelt down and put a hand on his back. He buried his face in her shoulder, his entire body shuddering.

Justin wrapped his arm around my waist and pulled me close.

"What do you mean?" I asked him. "She's inside. Isn't she?"

He pulled away from Mom and shook his head at me. "She had a heart attack in the ambulance. They couldn't"—he sucked in his breath—"they couldn't revive her."

I backed away from him, the world blurring around me. "No. Tell them to try again! She can't be. She can't." My breath came out in short bursts.

Strong arms pulled me close, but I shoved them away. Someone screamed. A high-pitched whirlwind in my ears that wouldn't let up. It was coming from my raw throat.

I collapsed on the cement, and Justin held me tight. His body shook against mine as he rocked me back and forth. Someone with a scratchy ring held my hand. Grandma.

Naomi couldn't be dead. Not the girl with the big blue eyes and the hearty laugh. Her voice was too strong. She was going places. They must've made a mistake. She deserved another chance.

I deserved another chance.

THE SUN BROKE THROUGH the clouds the day of Naomi's funeral. And the birds chirped. People mowed their lawns and walked their dogs. Like they didn't know the world had lost someone special.

Naomi made it into the local newspaper yesterday. TEEN'S DEATH BREAKS UP MAJOR DRUG RING, the headline read. Scott faced many charges, including manslaughter. Justin said he'd probably ratted everyone out within five minutes.

Naomi's official cause of death was a meth overdose. Justin said a dose that makes one person twitchy can kill another, depending on how their body reacts. Naomi probably didn't know she'd taken too much.

I scanned the comments on the newspaper's Web site. Some of the comments were nice, but others were cruel. None of these people knew Naomi, despite what they claimed.

> I know the Quinns. Believe me, she comes from a
> messed-up gene pool. This isn't surprising in the least.
> —R.L.

So Bellingham lost another junkie. How is this news-worthy?
—Anon

Look at it this way. That's one less shitty driver on the roads. Lord knows we got enough of them.
—Linda M.

What does driving have to do with anything, Linda? Naomi Quinn was the product of bad parenting. Nuff said.
—Anon

I typed my own comment. I wanted them to know that she was a person. Not just some name to trash.

Naomi Quinn befriended me a month ago when no one else would. No questions asked. She told me I was the coolest girl she'd ever met. She told me I was pretty. Things nobody ever said to me before. She had a singing voice that was full of life and passion. A voice that touched anyone privileged enough to hear it. No, she wasn't what you would call normal or perfect. But who is?

So keep making your ignorant comments. But just remember that Naomi was a real person. And our lives won't be the same without her.

Grandma made her way down the stairs. She hadn't said much to me the last few days. Justin and Mom hovered around me practically every minute, asking if I was okay.

"Are you ready to go?" she asked.

I slumped in my chair. My legs felt like tree trunks. "I'll never be ready."

Grandma walked over to my bed and sat down, her eyes combing my face. "I had a brother once. Did you know that?"

I shook my head.

"His name was Paul. He was drafted in World War Two— got shipped to Japan. I was only four years old when he hugged me good-bye, but I remember everything he was wearing that day. Everything he said. He gave me his guitar—a Martin—and made me promise I'd play it. Even if he didn't come back."

"And he didn't come back?"

She lowered her eyes to the floor. "No. He was a prisoner of war—almost made it out alive too. But his friend fell during the Bataan Death March. They'd make the soldiers walk for days without food or water and kill anyone who stopped. They caught Paul helping his friend up, and they killed him for it."

"What happened to his friend?"

"He survived to tell the story. But even at that age, I remember feeling cheated. Paul was only eighteen. He had his whole life ahead of him, and I never got the chance to know him. It's hard losing anyone, Andrea. And it's really hard when they go before their time. So in that sense, no, you'll never be ready. But it does get easier. You get to the point where you have no choice but to pick yourself up by the bootstraps and keep living."

I couldn't imagine that. Nothing felt real. I just wanted to wake up and see Naomi standing at the foot of my stairs again. Begging me to check out her drum set.

"Did you play his guitar?"

She smiled. "I did. Even did a little tour around the country with my sister. We dedicated every set to Paul."

"Do you still have it, the guitar?"

She nodded. "It's in my room, and you're welcome to play it anytime you want. But it can't leave this house. And it needs to be put back in my room whenever you're done. Right where you found it."

"Of course." I studied her face for a few moments. "Did you hate Naomi?"

Grandma frowned and exhaled softly. "No. She was a troubled girl who needed discipline, but I never hated her. We talked a little when she helped me with the garage sale. She was very smart. The kind of person who could do anything if she put her mind to it."

I looked at my hands. "People are saying horrible things about her online."

"People will always talk. But you have her memory inside you. They can't take that away from you."

But memories fade, I wanted to say. What happens then?

We went back to Justin's after the funeral. I didn't know what was worse—the muted sobs or the overpowering scent of roses. They weren't even yellow roses. I remembered the way Naomi's eyes lit up when she talked about the yellow tulips Scott gave her. Yellow was her favorite.

Kari tried to speak, but she choked up halfway through. Roger stood apart from the rest of us, unmoving. And Naomi's dad had this flat stare the entire time. He reminded me of a blank sheet of paper. Her mom was there too, with her hands over her face, crying.

I didn't know whether to laugh or cry. Naomi couldn't have been in that shiny box. It was too pristine for her. Too clean. She would've wanted frayed edges and bright colors. And laughter too. She would've hated the tears.

I fell back on Justin's bed and rolled onto my side. He pressed his body against mine and wrapped his arm around me.

"How're you doing?" he whispered.

"I don't know how I'm supposed to feel. I can't sit around with wads of Kleenex like everyone else. Naomi wouldn't want that—she'd probably tell me to laugh. But I can't do that, either. It's not normal. It's not right."

Justin stroked my arm, his breath warm against my ear. "Nothing feels right at first. And there isn't a *normal* way to deal with this. If you need to laugh, do it."

"If I'd been there Friday night, I could've talked to her."

"What would you have said?"

"I could've told her everything I liked about her. How she was the first person to give me a chance in a really long time, how much I wanted us to stay friends. That's why she got so mad at me and ran off with Scott. She thought I didn't want her around anymore."

Justin kissed my shoulder. "Naomi had one foot out the door before you even met her, Drea. Don't blame yourself. You were a good friend to her."

"Not good enough. I let her leave the day of the garage sale, Justin. And I knew something was wrong. Why didn't I go after her?" I punched the pillow underneath me. "I could've stopped this. I know it."

"I feel like I could've done more too. What? I have no idea. But I've been where she was. The more people tried to *help* me, the less I wanted it. With Naomi, I hoped that being there for her was enough. That our music was enough. But sometimes nothing is enough."

Lizzie hopped up on the bed and rubbed her face against mine. Her green eyes looked sad and lost—just like me.

"I don't understand why anyone would choose to need drugs. I've spent my entire life wishing I didn't need them. I feel like a guinea pig all the time." I ran my fingers through Lizzie's soft fur. "I want to know who I am without them."

Justin shifted against me. "I didn't want my life. I mean—I didn't want to die, but I wanted to be someone else. Someone who didn't care about coming home to an empty house. Someone who didn't feel alone all the time."

"I feel alone a lot."

He drew circles against my forearm. "But you aren't. I'm here for you, and so is your family. You've got Lizzie too."

The cat perked up at her name. Her entire body vibrated under my hand.

"I never told Naomi the truth."

"I think she picked up on more than you thought. And she cared about you. A lot. She told me to take care of you in her letter."

"What else did she say?"

He rolled off the bed and walked over to his computer desk. "Come over here and read it."

I followed and sat in front of his computer. My stomach tensed, and I closed my eyes. It seemed too soon.

"Read it, Drea. I think it will make you feel better."

My hand shook against the computer mouse. I opened my eyes, swallowing hard. My throat still felt scratchy. It began by telling him she was taking off with Scott, and that she was sorry.

I've been planning this escape for a long time. I kept hoping things would get better. They didn't.

We don't know each other that well, but I'm glad we got to talk that one night, especially about our dads. I hope yours comes around for you because he should be proud. You've got it together. I wish I had your strength, but I'm doing the only thing I know how to do. And that's to get the hell out of here. No way is anyone going to lock me up. I'm a free spirit who belongs on the road.

Take care of Drea for me. She's the most real chick I've ever met, and you're lucky to have her. But if you break her heart, well, let's just say I'll make a reappearance just to kick your ass. I know you won't though. You're a good guy.

I'll miss you guys and the music we made. You're an amazing pianist. Don't EVER stop!

Until next time,

Naomi

I didn't even realize I was crying until Justin brushed his fingers across my cheek. "I miss her."

"I know. I do too." He stroked my hair, his voice cracking.

We held each other as the sunlight faded into dusk. Lizzie cuddled next to our feet. I told him about the day I moved in. How Naomi slobbered in my didgeridoo. He laughed and told me it sounded like something she'd do.

Then he talked about Italy and said that his grandma wasn't much different from mine. But she's a better cook.

"I want to take you there in the summer," he said. "I have a couple musician friends there. We'll jam. It'll be cool."

The idea made me smile, but I still couldn't get Naomi out of my head. She would've really enjoyed a trip like that.

Going back to school was hard. A lot of people asked me about Naomi—they wanted every last detail. Kari eventually told them to *fuck off*.

Kari and Roger ate lunch with us nearly every day. Most of the time, we talked about music, or anything to fill the hole inside of us. I often looked at the fountain, expecting to see a flash of purple hair. And the locker room was so quiet without Naomi's incessant teasing. There was nobody to talk about Justin's butt or to insist that I lighten up. It was amazing how even the most annoying things about a person could be missed.

Roger offered to sing a couple tracks for us. But I wasn't ready. The mic still belonged to Naomi. People continued to post comments about her voice. One of my favorite indie musicians even wrote me on MySpace, asking if he could work with the vocalist. When I told him what happened, he said he was sorry. Her voice would've taken her far, he said. Then he asked me if he could remix "Invisible." He told me he'd dedicate it to her on his Web site. My heart hurt a little less that day.

It took a month for me to look at the videos we'd filmed of Naomi. Justin and I sat in front of my computer after we'd hooked up the camera. Neither one of us wanted to push play. But we had a project to complete. The world needed to see what we saw in her. A beautiful girl we'd never forget.

"I don't think I can do this," I said, looking at the still of her face. I hated the thought of hearing her voice and seeing her smile but not being able to hug her. I couldn't pause the tape and tell her not to leave. She'd be looking right at me, her eyes wide with some adventure in her head. And I'd see her on the floor of that house. Pale and crumpled.

"We have to try," he said, moving my hand out of the way. "For Naomi."

He pushed play and I held my breath.

Naomi walked down Railroad Avenue, her arms spread like she was planning on flying somewhere. She turned and faced us, her head tilting toward the sky. "I wish it would rain today."

I exhaled slowly. Hearing her voice again warmed me inside.

"Are you only happy when it rains?" Justin asked her, referencing the Garbage song.

Naomi looked at him then, a smile easing across her face. "Maybe." She spun around, approaching a grubby man with a guitar in his hand.

The guy's dark eyes widened when she put a hand on his shoulder. And I knew exactly how he felt. Because I felt the same way when she noticed me.

"What's your favorite thing to do in Bellingham?" she asked him.

"I'm a simple guy," he said. "I just like to sit here, sing my songs, and hope someone will give me enough change for one of those bagels they sell across the street."

She followed his gaze. "They're pretty good, huh?"

"Even one will make my entire week. They got this jalapeño cream cheese that zings. Gives me the runs, though." He let out a hoarse laugh.

Naomi dug into her pocket and handed him a few dollar

bills. "Here—get some for your friends too. And go easy on the jalapeño!"

He thanked her profusely, and she continued down the street. I hadn't noticed it when we were filming, but nearly every person stared at her as she passed. Most of them looked curious, even fascinated. She made a lot of people smile too. Everyone she approached—young or old. Maybe it was the purple hair or the fact that she was always humming a song under her breath. But people saw Naomi.

I wished she had watched this with us. Maybe she could've seen that she was only invisible to herself.

I saw the real Naomi when we began editing. Everything she never said was in her eyes. I didn't know how it happened. I was cutting a clip of her singing "Invisible." The camera zoomed in during these lines: *She knows her place in this world. She can tear down its walls and still nobody knows her name.* Her smile faded and her face tensed. She eyed the camera under lowered lashes, and her eyes glistened a little. Like she had a tremendous secret buried in her chest. Then she crinkled her brow, parting her lips for the next line. *Yeah, she knows her place. But she's not going down . . . without a fight.* She stared directly at the lens then. Right through me, demanding my attention. I froze the frame and copied it to the time line. The video needed to end here. With that look—the anger and the determination.

And the music video for "Invisible" was born.

18

Friday, December 14

My last entry of the semester. It almost feels too soon. You asked us to look at our first entry and write about what's changed and what's stayed the same since then. Well, a lot has happened since September 10.

History is still boring, and I still have no idea what to write half the time. But Naomi's words no longer fill the gaps in my mind. She was only in my life for a month, but I still miss her so much. I don't think I'll ever stop.

I've spent my entire life trying to define this little thing called "normal." Excuse my language, but what the hell is it? I'll tell you what it's not.

1. It's not smiling when you don't mean it.

Naomi wore that mask all the time, hoping someone would take it off and see how unhappy she really was. She didn't know how to be honest with the world. A lot of people don't. Not even me. I just thought I did because I didn't buy into the whole fake and plastic thing. I convinced myself that being lonely was better than reaching out to people. Because they'd end up hurting me. So, I told them to go away. But what I really wanted more than anything was a friend. Someone to take me as I am and love me anyway.

I only smile when I want to now. If people don't like it, that's tough. It's who I am. Love me or leave me. Sure, I'll say please and thank you. When I mean it. If the world calls this a disorder, let them. I call it me. Medication may clear my head some, it might help me be more patient and not freak out over things as much, but it doesn't change who I am. And it never will.

2. It's not little white lies. A lie is still just that. A LIE.

A lot of people think it's acceptable or even right to tell someone they look nice when they don't. To say you got stuck in traffic when you overslept. To pretend to like someone, even if you can't stand the sight of them. But most people don't think it's okay to lie about the BIG things, which are subjective anyway. Well, I think that's a really confusing way to live. If you like someone, you tell the truth because that, to me, is respect. If you hate someone, you tell them the truth because what do you have to lose?

3. It's not small talk.

If you don't care, don't ask me how I am.

Chances are, I don't care how you are, either. And it's not because I don't respect you or I think you're a loser. I just don't know you well enough to care yet. So, let's pass each other in silence and go on with our lives.

And there you have it. Three socially acceptable things I've decided not to accept.

Normal is an ideal. But it's not reality. Reality is brutal, it's beautiful, it's every shade between black and white, and it's magical. Yes, magical. Because every now and then, it turns nothing into something.

Roger told me that last bit. Actually, it's in his lyrics. He became the singer of M3 last week. Naomi wasn't kidding. He can really sing! Kari wants to be our new drummer, so she's been taking lessons. They'll never replace Naomi, but they bring something new to the band, and I'm glad they want to be part of it. Even if we don't always get along. Roger says stupid things sometimes, and Kari still thinks I'm kind of weird. But, like Justin says, we don't all have to be best friends to make great music together.

My mom and I are still living with Grandma, but Mom thinks we'll be able to move out by the spring. Grandma's meals are getting worse, and we still argue sometimes, mostly over my curfew. She doesn't think I should be at Justin's past eight! I think we've gotten a little closer, though. She lets me play her guitar and even said I could use her basement for band practice after we move out. But I still have to paint the walls back to white before I go.

And last, but not least, it took a lot of lessons from Justin and patience from me, but I did it! I got my license yesterday! I can't wait to drive by myself.

I'm pretty happy with my life right now, but I still think about Naomi every day. I'd sell my entire guitar collection for one more day with her. And my computer too. I'd dance with her in the rain and tell her how much she meant to me. I don't know if that could've saved her. But it would've put a smile on her face. A real one. I don't know if there is an afterlife, but if there is, I hope she knows her place in this world. It's inside everyone who knew her. Naomi Quinn was the kind of person nobody forgets.

"I guess you figured out how to write, after all." Justin smiled after reading my journal.

We sat on his bed, listening to the rain outside. I'd copied my last entry to hang on my wall. It would be there whenever I doubted myself, telling me to never go down without a fight.

"Every now and then, I have something worthwhile to say."

His lips inched toward mine. "Was that sarcasm?"

"No."

He smirked. "It should be. Because—"

I smacked his arm. "That cost you a kiss."

"Everything you say is worthwhile to me. Even when you

don't let me finish a sentence." He leaned in to kiss me, and I closed my eyes. But a pillow hit my face instead.

"Jerk." I grabbed another pillow and tickled him until he dropped his. "Rule number one: You might want to hold on to your weapon."

He squinted at me, shaking his head. "I think I've created a monster."

I held the pillow over my head, like I was going to bring it down on him. But I leaned in and kissed him instead.

"Sneaky," he said. "I'll be right back."

He rolled off the bed and turned on some music. "Bus Stop" by the Hollies. Our song. It was perfect with the hiss of the rain. The wind filtered in, making me shiver. I nuzzled under his flannel sheets.

Justin slid into the bed and kissed me without another word. This felt different. More intense. He peeled my shirt off and brushed his fingers across my bare stomach. We'd almost had sex a few times. At least it felt close. But he always stopped before it went too far. It was harder every time, though, for both of us.

I took his shirt off and enjoyed the feeling of his hot skin against mine.

His breath was ragged in my ear. "I love you," he said.

My heart beat faster. "What?"

He smiled. "You heard me."

"I . . ." Love. I knew it was a big deal for him to say it, but what did it really mean?

"It's okay if you aren't ready to say it. I just wanted you to know."

"I can top that. And be specific," I said. "I love who you

are. Because you accept me for who I am. You make me laugh, sometimes even at myself. And you make me happy."

He grinned wider. "I can work with that."

He brought his lips to mine, harder than before. Then he moved down, kissing places that made me shudder. Despite the cool wind blowing against my face, the room felt damp and hot.

I cupped his face. "Do you want to . . ."

"Yeah, I just need to . . ." His eyes traveled to the dresser next to us.

"Get something?" I bit my lip.

He rolled onto his back and opened the drawer, pulling out a condom. A short time later, he was kissing me again. His body melted into mine, and I felt dizzy. Like I was in a really good dream. It hurt some, but he was gentle and I saw those stars everyone talked about. For the first time, I felt connected to a rhythm that wasn't my own.

I rested my head against his chest afterward. His heart was loud and steady in my ear. My legs felt like Jell-O. I wondered if that was normal.

A bright light flashed across his pale blue walls, followed by a loud rumble. Thunder.

"I miss thunderstorms," Justin said softly. "It's kind of weird to have one in December, though. Isn't it?"

I thought of Naomi's face. The way she glowed as lightning streaked across the sky that one summer afternoon. "We should go outside and dance," I said.

His chest shook with laughter. "Yeah, right."

I lifted my head and looked into his eyes. Another flash illuminated the outline of his face. "I'm serious."

"I think I'd rather cuddle in a warm and dry bed."

I kissed his cheek. "Suit yourself." Finding my clothes was quite the scavenger hunt in the dark, but I managed to get everything on in record time.

Justin sat up. The shadows of raindrops moved against his chest. "You're really going out there?"

"There are certain moments in life you can't miss. This is one of them." I stopped by Justin's bookshelf to give Lizzie a kiss on the head. It had become her favorite perch. "Wish me luck."

I opened the door and ran into the freezing rain. Mist hovered around the rooftops, and the sky had a pink glow. The air was filled with a magic I couldn't explain. But every nerve in my body buzzed with anticipation.

A bolt carved a jagged path above me, silencing the world for a few seconds. And then a roar pierced my ears.

Justin ran outside. He covered his head and squinted down at me. "So, this is your idea of fun?"

I grinned at his rumpled T-shirt. "Your shirt is on backward."

He shook his head, pulling me close. Another flash illuminated his eyes. "We should go inside."

I rolled my eyes at him. He didn't get it. "It's a present from Naomi." I grabbed his hands and swayed my hips. Grace was something I'd never have, but I could still enjoy looking like a dork. "Dance with me."

He wrapped his arms around my waist and pressed his lips against my ear. "I can't dance."

"Neither can I."

We moved together in our own clumsy way. Our slick hands made any kind of grip difficult. The thunder faded into the distance, and the rain lightened some. Justin touched his forehead to mine, a half smile on his face.

"Have you ever kissed someone in the rain?" I asked.

"No. Am I missing out?"

I ran my hands through his wet hair, pulling him close. "Definitely."

Wind echoed through the clouds, resembling laughter every now and then. I imagined Naomi looking down at us, a wide grin across her face. She wouldn't have let me miss this moment for the world.

Author's Note

I'd like to start off by saying that this book is not about defining Asperger's syndrome (AS) or Attention Deficit Hyperactivity Disorder (ADHD). It's about one girl's story and experience— which I hope everyone (whether on the autistic spectrum or not) can relate to. Each individual has a unique personality and set of challenges, and this is an ongoing theme in *Harmonic Feedback*, both with Drea and the people in her life.

Drea's story was inspired by my own experiences living with ADHD and by my younger brother who is on the autistic spectrum. Both of us experienced difficulties with socialization as children and as teens. I recall teachers calling me "socially immature" and feeling like I was on the outside looking in. My brother experienced this to a larger degree, both academically and socially, but he has made amazing strides. He is now a twenty-one-year-old college student living on his own and, like many of us, battling a tough job market.

I've learned a lot from my brother and from others in my life who have been diagnosed with AS or an autistic spectrum disorder (ASD). They are among the most self-aware people I know, because most have been trying to compensate for their differences since childhood. Some display very mild symptoms. In fact, you probably wouldn't know they'd been diagnosed with anything if they didn't mention it. This describes Drea. She attends mainstream classes and exhibits only very mild symptoms, but she still has every-day frustrations and challenges, including questioning whether anything is "wrong" with her at all.

For more information, please check out a couple of my favorite Web sites:

Wrong Planet (Asperger and Autism Community): www.wrongplanet.net;

Dr. Tony Attwood, author of several books on Asperger's syndrome: www.tonyattwood.com.au.

You can also find clinical information on Asperger's syndrome, other autistic spectrum disorders, and ADHD at the following Web sites:

ADHD: www.cdc.gov/ncbddd/ADHD/index.html;

Autism Information Center: www.cdc.gov/ncbddd/autism.